REXAR (SPECIAL FORCES: OPERATION ALPHA)

NEMESIS INC. BRAVO TEAM
BOOK ONE

BELLA STONE

Editing: Rebecca Hodgkins
Proof Reading: Julie Deaton & Allyson Mingo
Cover Design: Golden Czermak

Dear Readers,

Welcome to the Special Forces: Operation Alpha Fan-Fiction world!

If you are new to this amazing world, in a nutshell the author wrote a story using one or more of my characters in it. Sometimes that character has a major role in the story, and other times they are only mentioned briefly. This is perfectly legal and allowable because they are going through Aces Press to publish the story.

This book is entirely the work of the author who wrote it. While I might have assisted with brainstorming and other ideas about which of my characters to use, I didn't have any part in the process or writing or editing the story.

I'm proud and excited that so many authors loved my characters enough that they wanted to write them into their own story. Thank you for supporting them, and me!

READ ON!
Xoxo
Susan Stoker

ACKNOWLEDGMENTS

Thank you to my Sailor for always having my back. You have owned my heart for almost three decades, and you will always be my hero—even when you make me insane, and I find pens and other crap from your pockets in the dryer. You and our amazing kiddos, Potterhead and Pottermonkey—you make this crazy life worth it.

Thank you, the family of my heart, who not only claimed me as theirs, (in public I might add...) who read this story as it was written, answering all my military questions, and helping ensure my information is as factual as possible. Any mistakes I have made are mine. Thank you for the middle of the night conversations and virtual smacks upside the head that were needed to keep me on track.

Thank you to my Operators. All y'all put up with my crazy, without a second thought. You laugh at my silly memes, and you love the stories and characters in my head as much as I do. I am forever grateful to have y'all in my life. #Lovelikeanoperator

I'd also like to take this opportunity to thank the god who discovered that Coffee is an amazing way keeping my eyelids propped open when the characters in my head are yelling out their stories at 3 AM... Without the aid of the coffee gods, these stories would never be written.

#Neverforgotten
For the 31 heroes of Extortion 17.

Brothers don't always have the same mother.
Until we meet again to feast in the halls of Valhalla.

Special Warfare Operator
Chief Petty Officer (SEAL)
Kevin A. Houston

FOREWORD

I have been a Susan Stoker fan since I first read Beyond Reality when it first came out. When Protecting Caroline hit my kindle, I became a huge fan, and I landed firmly on the Stalker Posse. It's been a dream and an honor to be allowed to borrow The SEALs of Protection Heroes and to write them into my world. Susan, thank so you very much for allowing me to play in your sandbox. Being allowed to borrow your characters is a dream come true. I can never thank you enough for the opportunity you so graciously gave me. I really hope I did Wolf, Caroline, and the rest of the SEALs of Protection family, the justice they deserve.

Sometimes a story grabs you and won't let go. This was one of those stories for me. I couldn't wait to get on the computer to write. I needed to know what happened next, and I was so mad with myself that I wasn't writing it fast enough. I wanted to see Rexar get blindsided. I needed to see Lily remember what it's like to feel safe and loved, and I craved knowing how their son loved having a daddy like all the other kids he knew. I hope you all feel how much I loved writing this story.

I'd also like to say a huge thank you to our fellow Stalker, Becky Coleman who beta read for me as I went along. Thank you for listening to my ramblings and reading Rexar before the editor got it. I'm so happy you enjoyed it and grateful to you for picking up what I missed. The road of life isn't always smooth, and it rarely offers us plain sailing, but you and your mini sidekick have got this.

Thank you also to Allyson & Becca y'all are crazy for taking on my disorganized chaos. I appreciate everything to do to keep me in line and on track.

One of the biggest thank yous has to go to Riley and Olivia, both of these ladies sprinted with me, cheered me on, and reminded me to practice what I preach and follow my dreams. Both of you are my tribe, there will never be a time that you call, and I won't drop everything and come running. Thank you both for sprinting through long nights and too many days to count. This story is what it is, because I have you two as my sprinting sisters. I love you both.

Operators thank you for asking for this story. For telling me how much you wanted Rexar to have his happy ever after. Each and every one of you are why my fingers keep scribbling. I couldn't do the job I do without all of you on my six. #LoveLikeAnOperator.

Stalkers and Operators, magic happens when you trust your gut and follow your dreams.

XO
Bella

PROLOGUE

Lily Mitchell sat on the toilet seat and stared at the little blue line on the test. How was this possible? They'd been using protection, both the pill and condoms. She'd only taken the test because of stupid Google. When she'd plugged all her symptoms into the search engine, she'd been sure it was going to tell her she was overworked or something.

"Shit." She wrapped her arms around her waist and rocked back and forth in an effort to calm her racing mind. Rexar was going to freak.

Her husband was on a mission; he'd been gone six weeks and she had no idea when she'd even hear from him, never mind when he'd be back. Oh, God, she couldn't do this on her own.

"Pregnant? How the shit can I be pregnant? Never mind him freaking, I'm going to beat him, chop his dick off, and shove it up his ass." They'd agreed no children until he transitioned out of the Navy. They would wait until he wasn't rapid deploying with his SEAL Team at twenty-four hours' notice for heavens knew how long multiple times a year. She was meant to finish school; they were meant to buy a house. They were not ready for a baby.

Her mind raced. There were a million and one things she needed to do before Rexar got home. She had to go to the doctor, get this confirmed. Maybe it was a false positive.

"That's got to be it. The test is wrong. It has to be." There was only one way to find out.

She raced down the hall to find her phone. She'd call the doctor's office right now and make an appointment. She dug into her purse, looking for her cell.

"Come on, where are you?" She shook the bag to mix up the contents, and finally her fingers wrapped around what felt like her phone.

* * *

REXAR MITCHELL'S eyes popped open. He'd been expecting hospital lights, maybe the inside of a medevac helo, or someone leaning over him to check that he was breathing. The last thing he remembered was the truck ahead of him going over the IED and its front lifting, sending it flipping toward him. The dark which didn't disappear no matter how many times he blinked sent a shaft of fear skittering down his spine. Shit, was he blind? Maybe he was dead? Was this what dead felt like? He inhaled sharply and groaned. If death meant pain and agony, then he had a complaint letter to write to anyone who'd listen. He didn't see 'pain of a thousand needles stabbing in under his skin guaranteed' on that contract he'd signed.

"Ow."

Shut up, idiot. Don't let the devil or the archangels or whoever is waiting know you're awake. He strained his ears, listening for sounds of breathing or of anyone moving. For any sign he wasn't alone in this hellhole of darkness. Nothing, he heard nothing, not that he could hear much over the pounding in his head.

He tried to move his hands up to his eyes. Maybe if he rubbed them, he could get the blackness to retreat. He struggled to focus, and it took him longer than it should have to realize he was chained in place. Okay, he was going to take a WAG at this shit and assume he wasn't dead just yet. Had he been captured? *Fucking fabulous.* Trust him to be the only SEAL to make fucking history and be a POW. Noble Bauer, his commander, would have a freaking cow. Although he'd gladly take the yelling and stomping from his pissed-off commander should he decide to show up any time—like right now—right now would be fucking awesome.

He shifted his hands, testing the strength of his restraints, but just his luck they didn't even give a fraction of an inch. The fucking asswipes, tying him with freaking chains was an asshole move if he ever saw one. He tried to move his feet, but all that achieved was the clinking of the chains holding him in place and sending whatever he was sitting on rocking.

Fuck! Lily was going to kill him. He hadn't even responded to her message. He'd read it just as he'd dropped his phone into the holding box in the war-room before they'd headed out beyond the wire. He was going to be a father; failing to escape was not an option. Not now. Not ever.

Routine job my left nut.

Their convoy was only supposed to be guarding the supply train… Hah, not really, but that's what the orders said. Running into an IED, while not abnormal in this shithole part of the world, wasn't exactly a surprise, but it still freaking sucked.

I'm coming home baby girl; you keep on waiting for me.

"Argh," He tugged against chains. If he twisted in just the right way, maybe he could get a smidge of extra room. He didn't need much. He'd break every damn finger if he had to; for freedom it would be worth it. He moved a fraction and hissed when a sharp piece of the chain bit into the flesh on his wrists. He knew his wrists and ankles were swollen; the throbbing with every beat of his heart confirmed it.

How long was I out?

Shit, where were the guys?

He refused to believe they were gone. He'd feel it. He'd know it, right? Hell, he was almost closer to them than he was to his wife. He'd know if they were gone. Which meant they had to be okay. His team was out there looking for him. His job was to keep his ass alive until they found him.

Sometimes you just knew it was going to be a bad day at the office and everything was gonna suck.

"Easy day." He mouthed the two words. Hopefully, he hadn't given them sound, because if there was someone else in this godforsaken place then they knew he was awake. His messed-up brain didn't recognize that his movements and testing of the chains would have given it away anyway.

Whatever it was he was sitting on lifted into the air and back again. Reality slammed into him. He was in a vehicle. This wasn't some room, that wasn't the feeling of blood pumping in his veins, it was motion—the motion of a vehicle moving at speed. Well, double fuck it, now he had to escape, and he had until this vehicle got to wherever it was it was going. If he failed, he was done for.

* * *

HE JERKED AWAKE. There used to be a time when he could wake up and give no indication he'd moved from the land of dreams to the one of wakefulness. After way too many years in the hellhole that was Section 209 of Evin Prison in Iran, he learned to come up fighting. No pretense, no fucking around, come up swinging, punching, and kicking as hard as he could.

He wasn't sure how long he'd been here. He'd tried to keep a record of the days by scratching lines into the wall. But he figured he'd missed more than a few. Especially on the days when he'd been passed out after a visit to the torture rooms. His belly growled loudly, but he ignored it. Every now and again, the dumbfuck grumbled and complained about the lack of food. But no more, he would no longer eat the slop which passed as food.

Maggots and MREs in the fucking sweltering heat of a jungle would be pretty damn awesome right about now.

He cocked his head to one side when the noise which had pulled him out of his unconsciousness sounded again. Were the prisoners rioting in one of the blocks? It wouldn't be the first time. The guards would just shoot them down without a second thought.

"Should have run the bell, bud." He made his lips form the words through cracked lips. Reminding himself of shoulda, woulda, couldas was the only excitement he had for himself these days.

He shuffled closer to the wall, avoiding the damp spot. How the heck anything in this freaking place managed to remain damp was beyond him. Either way, based on the smell he was guessing it wasn't water. He turned his back to the door. If the prisoners were rioting and got down here to solitary confinement, he'd take the bullet gladly. At least he'd be out of this hellhole.

After seeing the photo of Lily and the baby, which the Iranians had used in an attempt to break him, he'd known his road had come to an end. Drax, his twin wasn't coming. His team were dead as the fuckers who beat him daily said. It was time he pulled on his big boy panties and came to terms with that shit. He should have known avoiding an op named

Operation Twisted Sister had been a bad idea. Working for the CIA was a gamble at the best of times, but their fucked-up idea of a simple undercover job was a hell of a lot more twisted than any of them had realized. Had Drax even found his clues? Had he believed in the flag-draped coffin?

He remembered laughing at his stupidity as he'd planted a clue in the lockbox in Zurich. God, he was an idiot. He should have called Drax instead of planting the note in the caves in Slovenia. If he tried hard enough, he could remember every freaking word on that note:

Hey Shortass,
You'd probably piss yourself laughing or kick my ass if I told you I
have a bad feeling about this next one. Going UC is not my jam,
brother, that's your game. But something stinks, and that smell tells
me I might need backup they haven't planned for. So, you're up.
If I don't come back, or they don't let you see me if I'm in a bag,
look for me in Section 209. If I'm not in 209 or you do see my body,
look after my girl.
Your big brother.
Rexar

ALMOST AN INCH TALLER made him the big brother. That was his story, and he was sticking to it, even if there was nobody here to hear it.

* * *

DRAX

THIS WAS IT. Drax watched Noble's hand move to the door in slow motion. Every inch took an hour. Logically, he knew it was unlikely his twin would be in the first door. There was no more than a fifty percent chance that he was even on their side of the corridor. Hell, all he had was his guts telling him that Rexar was actually here. He could feel their twin connection sparking. It was so freaking faint, but still there, and still stronger than when he'd believed Rexar was dead.

Noble pulled back the bolt and pushed the door open. Gagging, they crossed the room to the pitiful shape on the floor. Naked, with no mattress, no blanket, chained to the wall and covered in feces, Drax already knew by the regret he could see on Noble's face that they would not be cutting this woman free. He hardened his soul and swallowed down the bile burning the back of his sore throat as they turned away, relocking the door behind them. He wasn't sure if the woman had even known they had been there.

On and on, door after door. By the time they were halfway down, Drax was busy shoving every feeling and emotion he had into a mental box in his brain, shoring up the defenses around it. These poor bastards suffered. He had no idea if they deserved the missing fingers and toes. Or the burns and scars most of them carried. But still no Rexar.

Keep going. Keep looking.

Following Noble through the next door, Drax mentally added reinforcements to his 'keep me sane' box and resigned himself to finding another poor fucker who had been savagely brutalized.

"Rexar."

Noble's breathed-out word was followed by a click on his comms unit, *we have reached Checkpoint White Mountain.* Another series of clicks told him *package located.* That was the one that snapped Drax back to attention. That bag of bones? Rexar? *No fucking way.*

Drax's feet were moving. He shouldered Noble aside. He needed to see. Tears dripped from his eyes, but Drax didn't even notice. *Please be alive, Jesus, Rex, please be alive.* His fingers trembled as his hand reached out to touch the face that was almost unrecognizable under the scars and bruises. The instant his fingers touched Rexar's skin, static electricity gave them both a jolt.

Rexar tried to move. Without opening his eyes he wrenched his body away, his legs kicking out, but the lack of muscles made the kick he gave feeble at best.

"Rexar." Drax slipped into the language they had spoken most as children. "Sono io, fratello mio, andiamo a casa." *It's me, brother, let's go home.*

"Piccolo?" *Shortass?* Sadness filled the scratchy voice that responded with the nickname Rexar had called Drax for years.

"Si." *Yes.* Drax didn't want to hurt Rexar but cupped his face anyway. Above them, he could feel more than see Noble working on the chains holding Rexar to the wall.

"Cosa ti ha trattenuto tanto…" *What took you so long?*

The sadness and pain in Rexar's question nearly snapped what remained of Drax's heart in two. He wasn't sure if Rexar was aware this wasn't a dream or a nightmare yet. But he would.

"Non sapevo fossi vivo." *I didn't know you were alive.*

As soon as Noble freed Rexar's hands, they flopped down next to him. Drax wanted to rail at the injustice. How the hell had he survived? Nope, that didn't matter right now.

"We gotta move," Noble whispered.

Drax knew he was right, knew they had to go. No matter how much he wanted to give Rexar a second to adjust. To realize he was there. They needed to move.

"Questofara male." *This is gonna hurt,* he warned his brother, before hoisting him across his shoulders in a fireman's carry. Noble helped him adjust Rexar's arm across his chest, enabling Drax to grip both his arm and legs with one hand while allowing him access to his guns with the other.

They didn't know how hurt Rexar was, or if there was internal damage. But even an idiot could see being carried was going to hurt a lot. Resting across both of Drax's shoulders would at least mean less jarring than having his body dangling over one shoulder. Right now, Drax would take every tiny bit of advantage they could get.

"Got him?" Noble asked.

"Yes, Sir." In his ear, Drax heard the one-click signal. *We are passing Checkpoint White Mountain. We got him, he's alive, and we are coming out.*

Zenko took point position to lead them back up the stairs. Shaun followed right on his six. Weapons at ready position, they carefully checked every twist and turn before leading the team onward.

Drax gritted his teeth, resisting the urge to adjust the weight of his twin on his shoulders. Moving him would hurt Rexar. Nope, not going to happen on his watch. Behind Drax, one of Noble's massive hands covered Rexar's head, making sure it didn't bang off the walls as Drax moved forward. Drax saw Zenko's fist flying upward almost too late to stop; only Noble's steadying hand on his waist kept him vertical. The sounds of fighting around the corner had him turning Rexar against the wall. Holding his arm and leg with just one hand, Drax grabbed his M16 from where it crossed his chest, secured by a battle sling, and aimed it at the corner from where the sounds of hand-to-hand fighting came.

"Fucker," Zenko swore. "Awesome, stabbing me pisses me off, dickwad." A loud crack echoed all around.

"Fire in the hole," Shaun whispered from where he watched the action, making sure a second tango didn't blindside his guy.

"Shit." Noble stood in front of Drax and Rexar, protecting them with his own body should anyone make it past Zenko and around the corner. He looked over his shoulder. "Sax hit the damn timer, that's our countdown. We have five minutes to get to the gates."

"They might think it's a guard executing a prisoner," Reese advised. "Shit like that happens here all the time."

"Maybe." Noble moved from his position next to Shaun. "We know better than to expect a clockwork op."

"Guess again," Drax muttered. "This is more snatch and grab style." They all had multiple experiences with the precarious, risky operations that entailed snatching a high-value target. The possibility of a goatfuck or clusterfuck on one of those ops was over-the-top high. On those ops, they were most often operating in a hostile environment with no backup. They knew that the US government would be fast to disavow their actions if they were caught. The goatfuck factor that pissed off Drax the most was if you were caught and the locals did get their hands on you, the odds were that you'd end up being dragged behind a car or truck for a few hours while they cut off significant pieces of your anatomy joint by joint.

Here at Evin Prison...yeah, getting caught wouldn't be pretty either.

"Rexar?" Noble didn't give the order to move yet. "You hear me, kid?"

"Yeah, Boss, I hear you." Rexar's voice spoke of too long spent in an arid region. He mumbled more than spoke but clear enough that both Noble and Drax could understand his words.

"We've gotta move fast," Noble told him. Which means Shortass needs to run. You up for it?"

"I'm not dreaming?"

Damn, for hearing the wonder and awe as realization sunk into his twin that this was not a dream, not a figment of his imagination, Drax could even let the fact that his boss appeared to be adopting the nickname Rexar had always used for him slide.

Who are you kidding? If you kick up a fuss they are all going to be calling you Shortass by the end of the week. Drax had been mostly broken for a long time, but not broken in his body as his brother was; for him, it was his soul that had suffered. Maybe now they could both start to heal. They just had to get out of here first.

"Boss, y'all are a bunch of choirboys compared to what they been dishing out," Rexar muttered. "Bring it." Thank fuck his mind didn't appear to be as broken as the rest of him.

"Time to pop smoke. Move out." Noble gave the order. As a single unit, they made their way through the workshop. Carefully checking that their way remained clear, Zenko and Shaun led them down corridor three B. Prisoners yelled and rattled the doors as they passed. The racket alerting the next cell and the next. *Shit.* They were lighting up the path Red Squadron was taking.

Fuckers, shut up! Drax knew his thoughts were unreasonable. A lot of these people were only in here because they had supported the previous government or were in the wrong place at the wrong time.

As they approached the exit to the indentation where Shaun had taken out the sniper, Zenko held up his closed fist.

"Sitrep," Noble whispered as loudly as he dared.

"I hear voices," Zenko responded with hand signals. "Tangos. Lots of them."

Noble immediately turned to Saxon. "Blow it," he signaled. Saxon nodded once in response and pulled the remote device he had programmed to the charges, turning the dial two clicks to release it from the lock—a fail-safe in case he fell on the box while fighting or moving—and depressed the button.

To Drax, it felt as if the nation held its breath, the world on pause until a whoosh followed by a boom announced their intentions by blowing the gates clean off their hinges. Now all they had to do was make it out of the gates and disappear into the streets of Tehran.

Piece of cake.

Zenko rummaged in the pockets of his armor, pulled out some earbuds and his earpiece, secured it into the webbing attached to his vest, and stuffed an earbud into his left ear to hopefully give his eardrums some protection for the shot he was sure Shaun was going to take.

"Ready?" he mouthed over his shoulder at Shaun. He smiled at his guy when Shaun aimed the muzzle of his rifle just over Zenko's shoulder. Zenko pulled his foot back and kicked the door hard, just where the lock met the frame, splintering it. The door slammed outward; in the timeframe it took for the door to rebound off the wall, three things happened simultaneously: Zenko shot two tangos, Shaun two more, forcing the others backward, and an old, battered truck drove straight through the door. The driver had one hand out the window, firing a Sig while the other hand steered the wheel. The passenger picked off tangos, laying down cover fire for Drax and Rexar's race to the vehicle as soon as it skidded to a stop in a handbrake turn with its nose almost facing out of the gates.

How the hell they made it down the football stadium-length space to the truck without a bullet hitting them, Drax would never freaking know. *Thank fuck, no rear door!* Turning his back, he deposited Rexar in the rear of the truck. Turning with his M16 already in firing position, he started picking off guards, giving his team some breathing room to make it to the truck.

"Gimme a damn gun!" Rexar yelled behind him. Drax didn't even think twice. His brother was a SEAL. He had survived captivity in hell on Earth for years; yeah, he had earned the right to have a fucking gun. Without looking, Drax pulled his handgun free from its holster on his thigh and held it out. It was immediately snatched.

"Got it?"

"Fuck yeah." Rexar's answer was immediately followed by the distinctive sound of the Heckler and Kock VP9 pistol joining the firefight. "Assholes!" Rexar screamed in Italian. "You didn't fucking break me."

"They are ours." Drax spotted Zenko and Shaun making their way to the truck and warned Rexar, sticking to the Italian he seemed to find easier to speak in.

"I recognize Marks."

Drax should have known he would, Rexar had no doubt worked with Zenko in Teams.

"Good to see you're not pushing up daisies as rumors suggested, brother." Zenko dove around the side of the truck and scrambled aboard, taking care to keep low and avoid making himself a target. He moved out of the way to make room for Shaun.

"Hurry your slow coach ass up!" the driver yelled, while still laying down cover fire.

"Is that freaking Rock?" Shaun frowned at the front of the truck. "Oh, shit, Allie is gonna be pissed." He jerked his thumb toward the front of the truck. "That's Grif, too."

"She's got a bird, Max, and the other dude from the safe house and is waiting at a parking lot about a klick that way," Grif told them.

One by one, Red Squadron made their way to the truck, some with blood and other wounds marking the strength of the defense the prison guards had put up.

Finally, Noble jumped past Drax, pulling him onboard after him. Slapping his hand on the bulkhead, he yelled, "Go! Go! Go!"

Rock took Noble at his word and gunned the engine. Grif sprayed bullets in an arc, sending prison guards diving for cover from the deadly projectiles, giving them time to speed through the gates and hopefully disappear into the night.

Zenko pulled the earbud out and replaced it with the comms device. "TOC, Ambra One. We have passed Safety."

"Ambra One, TOC," Max responded. "Sled is on its way, target location, Nome."

Hell, Drax even managed to crack a smile at Max calling their extraction helo a freaking sled.

Within minutes they made it to the top of the multi-story parking lot where they loaded onto the bird. It was surreal. It wasn't happening, right? Rexar was alive, and they had done the impossible, broken into and out of a prison everyone said was more secure than Alcatraz. He managed a smile for Noah and Max, both sitting strapped into flight seats on the Bell UH-1N Twin Huey. How the hell had Rock managed to get them an Iranian military helicopter was anyone's guess. But right now, he didn't give a shit if it was from Santa Claus or the Easter Bunny, it was their ticket out of this country.

"Someone pinch me." Drax jumped and immediately rubbed his ass. "Not my ass, fucker."

"You didn't say where, dumbass." Noble hugged Drax hard. They watched Grif working on Rexar, inserting an IV and giving him fluids. "I can't fucking believe it."

"You ladies strap your asses in and quit gossiping." Allie's voice came over the radio. "It's gonna get bumpy until we are outta Irani airspace."

"Shut up and fly, Allie!" Noble yelled at his cousin. "Who let you near the damn helo in the first place?"

"I did!" Rock yelled back. He didn't bother using the comms system; his voice was loud enough to be heard over the power of the rotors. "We were bored."

"Idiots," Noble grumbled. "Freaking pregnant and

allowing her to operate in freaking Iran. I am gonna kick his ass."

Grif got the bag of fluids and painkillers working. "We left her at home with Lexi," he told Noble. "She followed us anyway." He shrugged. "Rock tied her to the seat of the helo, so she didn't try to drive the damn truck."

"Sucks to be Rock then. She sounds like one hell of a woman... you should keep her," he told Grif.

Rexar pulled the oxygen mask off his face. "I don't need fucking oxygen. I need to touch my brother, need to know I'm not fucking dreaming."

"We plan on it." Grif injected painkillers and antibiotics into the drip. "If she doesn't give us a damn heart attack first."

The second Grif nodded at him and moved, Drax filled the space next to Rexar. They were no longer identical—the scars and wounds would see to that. Making eye contact, he tried to show how fucking sorry he was that he hadn't gone to Zurich sooner.

"Did you find them?" Rexar asked.

"Huh?" Drax was confused for a second. *Oh, maybe he meant the asshole behind Rexar's undercover role going to shit.* "No, we don't know for sure who the fuck—"

"No," Rexar cut him off before he finished. "My woman and kid."

"Your what now?" The memory of opening the box in Zurich slammed into him. *The fucking wedding ring. Oh, fucking shitballs.* Not only had he screwed up by not knowing Rex was still alive, but he'd also left the family he hadn't known existed to survive alone. "No." He cleared his throat. "I didn't know about them until just now."

"We'll find them," Noble promised. "We won't stop until we do."

CHAPTER ONE

Nemesis Inc. Headquarters, Montana

Rexar Mitchell slammed a glove-covered fist into the bag, hard. Once again, his dreams had been filled with torture, pain, death, and tears. Worse than the dreams of Iranian torture, was a dream that he was with Lily and that she'd never betrayed him. Their child slept in the next room while they made sweet, sweet love. He woke up from those soaked in cum and pissed as hell that he still wanted and craved the one woman he should hate... but found he couldn't.

He'd given up trying to sleep in the dark a long time ago, but even a nightlight or a TV wasn't enough to chase back the memories tonight. He grabbed the bag with both hands, hanging on to it. Using its solid anchoring to the overhead metal beam to keep himself from going to his knees, he watched the second hand on the clock as it slowly moved toward its target.

Tick, tock, tick tock, tick tock.

Normally the repetitive noise would drive him batshit, especially when it ticked. He'd be looking for a bomb to disarm, or an exfil route to get his ass clear of the blast zone. Tonight, he stared at that clock. Finally, it hit zero three hundred, marking one year since his darkest hour, the hour he'd considered 'call time' on ringing the bell of life. Four years in Iran's Evin prison, hidden away in the torture chambers of Section 209, he'd finally given up.

Then like the ghosts which had haunted his dreams, his twin brother had appeared out of the dark. Armed to the teeth, rage and grief pouring off him like water off a shaking dog. Just like when they were kids, Drax had saved his ass when he needed it most.

"Fuck you, assholes, I won." They'd tried to break him, had been determined to break him. He'd screamed, he'd bled, and he wasn't ashamed to admit he'd cried like a goddamned baby, but break was the one thing he hadn't done.

"Yes, you did, bro."

He spun around at the sound of a voice; his hand had palmed the cold steel recon tanto SK-5 he kept strapped to his lower back. He drew his arm back, searching the shadows for the man attached to the voice.

"If you throw that at me, I'm telling Momma."

"You came." He lowered the knife and replaced it in its scabbard.

"You call, I come." The figure of a man stepped into the open doorway, "A deal is a deal, one twin calls, the other comes."

"Yeah." He gripped the straps on his gloves with his teeth, ripping the Velcro open, first on one, and then the other. He tossed the gloves aside as he crossed the room. "I remember." He came to a stop in front of his brother and offered his hand.

Drax stared at it for so long, Rexar thought he was going to refuse it. He huffed a silent breath when Drax gripped his forearm up to the elbow and dragged him into a massive bear hug.

"I know you hate being touched," Drax muttered, "but we are two halves of one, so you will deal to thank me for saving your ugly ass."

"Yeah." He counted off the seconds in his head. How soon was it acceptable to step back, he wasn't sure. But when the feeling of ants marching along his skin became unbearable, he pulled free. He hated the hurt look on his twin's face, but there was exactly jack shit he could do about it right this second. He wasn't even going to try. When all you knew was pain for four years straight, people touching you was going to be an issue.

"I brought booze." Drax held up a bottle of Maker's Mark.

"It's open." He'd started drinking without him. That hadn't been part of any deal they'd had before.

"Yup, I was bored watching you watch the damn clock."

"One year." He flexed his fingers in a Gimme gesture and took the bottle when Drax offered it to him. He popped the cork and took a swig, letting the burning whiskey send fire into his belly. He took another sip before handing it back. "It's exactly one year since..." His voice trailed off. He didn't need to remind Drax. He no doubt remembered every second of that mission with vivid memory.

"C'mon, let's find somewhere we can drink this." Drax shook the bottle and turned toward the door, "I'm assuming Nemesis has a safe place on this ranch of his."

"You think it's a ranch, that's cute."

"Ha, I know what it is." Drax followed him into the changing rooms, "You're showering first?"

"Hell no, I'm just grabbing mammoth-style clothes so I don't freeze to death in the snow as we go to the fire pit." He kicked off his sneakers and swapped them for his combat boots. "How'd you get in here?"

19

Normally people didn't make it into the depths of the Nemesis Inc. complex. His boss, Dalton "Nemesis" Knight had been his sidekick in Teams. When Nem had needed him at his six, Rexar had been more than happy to oblige him. Somehow, he'd never made it back to their family bar, The Corner Pyrate, in the Carolinas. Slinging beer and dealing with drunk assholes was not something he enjoyed. Working for Nemesis's paramilitary organization was more his style. When Nem had offered him second in command of Bravo Team, he'd come pretty close to biting his hand off to accept.

"Nem brought me down. He's in the war room with Noble, Zenko, and Mike."

They'd all come? Seriously?

Drax obviously saw the look on his face and snorted. "I may be your twin, but they are your brothers, too. Brothers don't always have the same mother, remember?"

"I'm telling Momma you said that. She'll kick your butt all the way from the bar to Bragg and back again."

"She's worried about you."

He lifted one shoulder; he knew his mom was worried about him. Hell, she'd buried him, she'd spent four years grieving him, and now that he'd come back from the dead, she was wary about letting him out of her sight. "You bring more of that booze?"

"Yup, a whole damn crate," Drax confirmed. "I figured with y'all living out here in the sticks of the Crazy Mountains, if I was flying in then I'd better bring enough booze."

"Y'all mean that you brought Zenko Marks and you're covering your ass in case he pulls some prank shit and fucks up my boss's—um—ranch, you wanted to be covered with payment in advance.

"Pretty much."

"I can hear you two fuckers." Zenko stuck his head around the war room door and gave them the bird.

"You were supposed to." He couldn't have stopped the smirk he threw Zenko's way if he tried. "Nem?" He raised his voice so his boss would hear him, "We'll be at the firepit."

"I'm gonna need some cold weather gear," Drax muttered. "Our island in Italy doesn't get much snow, so I'm not acclimatized."

"We were just in Finland, dumbass," Zenko reminded him, "If you didn't figure out the cold shit there, you're never gonna."

"Hah, I thought that might have been you." He'd seen on the news about some extra help the Finnish government had received for an attempted invasion a couple of weeks ago. "We've got gear in storage near the front desk." He led Drax down the hall. "I'm not risking Momma's wrath or Noah's if you go home with a cold."

"Yeah, my Noah is kinda fussy about the sneezing stuff lately." Drax placed his back to the side of the elevator. The corners of his lips curved up at the mention of his partner.

Rexar was happy for him, but he couldn't help the twinge of devastation and envy, that his brother now had something he'd lost... a person to own the other half of his soul. He placed his hand on the scanner to activate it and hit the button for the main floor on the elevator. Most of the working parts of Nemesis Inc were buried in the ground here on the ranch in the middle of the Crazy Mountains. It had taken him some time to be able to not freak the fuck out at being buried into the ground again, but with free access to weapons, he'd been able to convince his brain to deal.

The doors swished open onto the main floor. Rexar waved at the security guards and led Drax to the storage cupboard. He grabbed the spare set of gear he kept there for himself and handed it to his brother. He already knew it would fit; they'd been sharing clothes since they were in diapers.

"Let's go."

Ten minutes later, he dropped an armful of firewood next to the massive fire pit. "You haven't lit it?"

"With this damn wind I can't get the flame to catch," Drax muttered. He cupped his hand around the lighter and flicked it again. "Damn it."

"Give it here." Rexar dug into his pocket and pulled out his secret sauce for lighting fires in the wind. He ripped off the paper and unzipped his coat. He took the lighter, turned his back to the wind, and flicked it, holding it to the cotton wool of the tampon. Within seconds the flame took, and he managed to get the burning tampon into the fire pit without it going out.

"Only fucking you would use a tampon to light the damn fire."

"Hah. You're only pissed because you didn't think of it first."

"I keep tampons for plugging bullet holes, not lighting fires."

"But you'll use them for the fire from now on."

"Damn straight." Drax caught the back of one of the chairs and dumped the snow off it, then planted his butt.

Rexar mirrored him unconsciously. He lounged back in his chair with one foot out in front of him.

"Pass me the bottle," he ordered Drax. "I need something to warm my cold dead heart."

"Here." Drax handed over the bottle then reached for another for himself from the crate next to his chair.

"Did you find her?"

He coughed and spluttered as the whiskey went down the wrong pipe. Of everything he'd expected Drax to ask him, that was not it.

"No."

"Did you look?"

"I looked."

"Did you call him?"

"If Trev can't find her, I don't think Tex can."

"There ain't nobody better than Tex and you know it, bro." Drax reached into his pocket and held something out to him. "That's his number. Call him."

"When I find her, I'm gonna kill her."

"I know." Drax glanced over his shoulder to check if any of the guys had come up from the war room yet. "Does Nem know that?"

"Hell fucking no. Since he found Lina again, he's gone all softhearted and there ain't no way he'd sanction it."

"Are you sure it was her?"

"Yes." The word was clipped, and he was irritated that Drax even asked. He'd had four years to figure it out. "She was the only one who knew where I was going. The only one who knew I'd be dark and where I'd be undercover."

"Except for your handlers on that CIA-sanctioned mission," Drax pointed out.

"She has my child. If you think I'm leaving my kid to be raised by a traitor you're fucked in the head." Rexar was done figuring out if what he planned was kosher or not. He didn't give a fuck if it was on the right side of the law or not. "Hell, maybe I'll just drop her off as a gift for the Iranians and let them deal with her."

"Bro, I get you're mad as fuck, but..."

He lowered the bottle from his mouth. "What do you know?"

"Call him." He nodded to the paper Rexar still held in his hand. "Tex will help you."

"D, spit it out..."

"Call. Him."

"I'll think on it."

A slight sound behind him warned him they had incoming, but he recognized the footfall so convinced himself to stay in place. Stabbing his boss for coming up behind him in the dark was not a good idea if he wanted to stay gainfully employed.

"Think on what?" Dalton pulled up another chair and settled himself into it. Noble and Zenko sat on the opposite side of the fire.

"Nothin'"

"My ass." Dalton took the bottle he offered him and took a swig before passing it on to Noble. "Where's Mike?"

Rexar blew out a silent breath of relief when Nemesis changed the subject and let it go. Thank fuck; he didn't think he could face that interrogation tonight without screaming like he had in the past.

"He said he was grabbing some dogs for the fire off someone called Kacey?" Zenko replied.

"Yeah, Kacey is our kitchen guru," Dalton told them, "If there's anything you want food-wise, let him know and if it's possible he'll do it."

"Big pizzas, Chicago style," Zenko muttered. "Italy may be the home of pizza, but I'd shoot someone important without a second thought for a deep-dish pizza."

Rexar reached for the bottle of Maker's Mark, sipping as he listened to the surviving members of his Platoon shoot the shit, sitting on chairs around a fire pit, in the snow. Just like his twin, Noble, Zenko, and Red Squadron had crawled into the depths of hell that was Section 209 to save his ass, and they'd all come here for him tonight. To ensure he didn't have to deal with the memories and nightmares alone. This was what family was all about... his family... he just needed his child for it to be complete.

CHAPTER TWO

Riverton, California

Lily Yelverton glanced in the rearview mirror as she steered her minivan around a construction zone sign on the street. How the heck was it December already? Today she was braving the mall for the Santa shopping. Since she'd moved to California six months ago, she'd setting aside some of her cash and shopping sales. Christmas wasn't easy to manage at the best of times, for any single parent. But when you worked a low-paying, cash-in-hand job, it was almost impossible. But she was determined that RJ would have a good Christmas this year.

This year they were not running. They would have a tree —a small one—but still a tree. Decorations and enough food that they'd have leftovers for the month of January. She would make it happen. If she'd had the resources, she'd have bought a passport for her son on the black market and taken him to Europe. Coming back to the United States just before he'd been born had been a stupid move. She should have kept running in Europe. She could admit that to herself now. But in her defense, giving birth in a foreign country where she didn't speak the language hadn't been high on her list of priorities that year. Not with the overwhelming grief from losing Rexar sucking every tiny scrap of energy she'd had.

She eyed the idiot driving right on her bumper. "Seriously, dude, if you're in that much of a hurry, go around me." She hit the hazard lights and pulled her old minivan as close to the sidewalk as she could, giving the asshole enough room to overtake her. But the fucker just followed her lead and kept right on her bumper.

Every internal warning system she had kicked into life. Was this it? The day she made her kid an orphan? They didn't need Christmas… but she shook off the instinct which warned her it was time to run again.

"This is nothing—some kids acting like assholes—nothing more. Fuck." Thankfully, RJ wasn't in the car to hear her swearing. They'd only had a conversation a couple of days ago, that swearing was for adults, not for almost-four-year-old boys.

She kept the car moving. There was no way she was pulling over unless it was for a cop. Even then it was iffy, and she'd be more likely to drive toward a police station than stop in the middle of the street and hope like hell whoever it was got the hint. Because if it came right down to having to go into the police station—that wasn't something she was quite willing to do. Keeping off the radar of law enforcement and all government agencies was vital to her freedom and her son staying out of the system.

The jacked-up truck behind her stuck right on her butt like a burr on a horse. "Dude, if you get any closer, you'll be sitting on my lap." She made a snap decision and continued on toward the mall. If she'd had RJ in the truck with her, there was no way she'd have even considered what she was about to do. Thankfully, her son had a playdate with one of the neighbor's kids.

She scowled at the truck behind her, "I do not have time to deal with the likes of you today. Can you do me a favor and go bother someone else?" She hoped if there were other people around, these two men would lose their bravado. She made the turn into the mall parking lot, and just like she knew he would, her tail followed. Picking a parking spot was ridiculously easy for once, and she'd never been more grateful for it. She purposely parked in a spot which had three free spaces across the divide. Leaving the engine running, she sat in her seat, her eyes glued to the rearview mirror as the truck came to a stop behind her minivan. The passenger mimicked holding a weapon in his hands and pulled an imaginary trigger.

"Shit." Every instinct she'd learned over her years in the CIA came roaring into life, kicking her butt, warning her this wasn't just some asshole who'd grabbed an opportunity to be the big man. A bully wanting to flex his muscles against someone he saw as weaker than himself. She should have paid attention sooner. Getting comfortable in a place had been stupid. She knew better. Her hand dipped into the side pocket of the door, her fingers searching for the concealed Glock she kept there. Her just-in-case security blanket, kept in case she somehow messed up and tripped someone's radar and needed to fight her way free. When the CIA burned you, everyone was a threat… or the possibility of being a cleaner sent to take care of the problem—you.

In the rearview mirror she could see the closest man's mouth moving, clearly talking. It could be to the driver, it could be directed to her, she didn't have the brainpower to concentrate enough to read his lips right now. If they were going to make a move, she had to be ready. She slowly depressed the clutch and put the minivan into gear. If they got out, she was going straight over the divider and out of the parking spot on the opposite side.

As if someone upstairs had been paying attention to her thoughts, a car pulled into the spot she had the nose of her minivan pointed at, effectively trapping her in place.

"Shit." *Now what?* With the truck behind her and the car in front of her, she wasn't going anywhere without causing damage and a scene. Wrecking her minivan wasn't an option. "Why with all the free spaces do people park directly in front of another car? Jeez."

She watched three women get out of the car, chattering and talking as they grabbed purses, and slammed their doors shut. Inspiration struck and she switched off her engine, almost jerking the minivan forward as she forgot to take it out of gear before lifting her foot off the clutch.

She grabbed her weapon, stuffed it into her purse, and jumped out of her van.

"Hello, ladies."

"Hi, isn't it a beautiful day for shopping?" The driver paused and smiled at her over her shoulder.

"Alabama, let's go, we have shopping to do."

"Coming, Caroline."

Lily kept waiting for a bullet in the back, but she hit the locks on the minivan and walked just behind the three women as if she were part of their group and it had been her intention to wait for them all along.

She glanced over her shoulder to check on the truck and spotted it pulling into a parking spot a couple of spaces down from her. Two Hispanic men got out and hurried after her and the women she'd attached herself to.

Of course, you didn't freaking leave. Why on earth would things go my way for once? These women may never know that they'd helped her. She didn't want to put a target on their backs. But she had. Now that she'd drawn attention to them, she had to play the cards she'd dealt for them all. Hopefully, she'd be able to lead the men away from the women and lose them in the mall.

Walking behind these women, listening to them chatter and talk about their men, and the stores they needed to hit, made her heart ache. When was the last time she'd been part of a group like this? She didn't think she ever had been.

Someday, sister, someday you can stop running, and might be able to have friends...

But she knew that was probably never going to happen. Pipe dreams didn't come true. If they did, Rexar would be here, right on her six as he'd called it. Protecting her—not that she'd admit to needing protection very often—helping her raise RJ, living the life he shouldn't be missing.

She shook off all thoughts of her dead husband. She didn't have time to go down memory lane today. She needed her wits about her. She could not under any circumstances fall into the trap of despair which constantly haunted her.

"Fiona, do you want to grab an iced coffee before we start shopping?" The woman who'd been called Alabama asked.

"Sure."

"Caroline?"

"If Fee wants one, let's get one that's almost a dessert."

The way Caroline and Alabama were taking care of Fiona, she was going to guess that the woman was going through something and needed a little pampering.

I'm not jealous that she has that. Not in the slightest.

But she kind of was. She stole another covert look over her shoulder. It took her a hot minute to see them, but there they were looking in the window of a clothing store. Unless those two had wives or honeys at home, that red dress was not going to suit either of them.

She allowed the women to get a couple of steps ahead before she called after them, "Have a nice day, ladies."

"Have fun," Alabama waved over her shoulder, "Nice to meet you."

She couldn't have asked for a better response if she'd given them a script on what to say. Hopefully the two men had heard it, and maybe if one or the other possessed at least one braincell they would understand that she didn't actually know these women.

"Get a move on, Lil. Lose the dudes and get back to what was important." Muttering softly to herself, she briefly considered going after the women and warning them of the possible danger she'd put them in. But how the heck did you walk up to what were essentially strangers and tell them you'd been so stupid as to put them in danger? But then walking away would make her a bitch. "Shit." She'd just have to wander around the mall and see if the men followed her. If they split up and one went after the women, she'd circle back and lure them away if she could.

She deliberately walked down the center aisle of the mall, leaving herself out in the open when all she wanted to do was find an escape route. She kept an eye on the two men, using the glass in various store windows to track their movements, and heaved a sigh of relief when they followed her and didn't take the left-hand route after the three women.

Her intention in coming here today had been to buy all the toys and decorations on her list. There was no freaking way she was letting these two men know she had a child. Instead, she hit up every single store and tried on jeans, tops, boots, shoes, jewelry. She didn't buy anything, not a single thing. When they still trailed after her as she came to the lingerie shop, she hoped they'd finally gotten bored with following her around, but she already knew it was a futile hope. She paused inside the door of the store, using the mirror on one of the displays to check the assholes' progress.

If they came in here, she was going to ask the manager if she could slip out the back to avoid them.

Watching her flip through bras and sexy underwear, combined with the lack of other men in the store would hopefully deter them. But somehow, she didn't think so.

Familiar voices chattering at the back of the store drew her attention. She wandered in that direction, taking her away from the door where the men had been watching her, and immediately regretted it when she spotted Caroline, Alabama, and Fiona.

"Oh no."

"What do you think of these, Fee?" Caroline held up two nighties, "Do you think the black or the red will suit me best?"

"Girl, either or, and Wolf will swallow his tongue."

"I think I'll get it." Caroline turned back to the display, "I just need to find my size."

Lily's eyes widened when Fiona suddenly stopped smiling. The expression on her face turned to one of pure terror. Lily whipped around, bending her knees, widening her feet, her hand dipping into her purse for her weapon. She heard a whimper behind her and Caroline's voice, although she couldn't make out the words.

Alabama rushed past her. Lily hadn't been expecting a shove from behind so she was pushed to one side as Fiona barreled past her to grab her arm, pulling her back. By the time Alabama was directly in front of the men who'd been following her since before she'd entered the mall, Fiona was yelling about how they couldn't have them and to take her instead.

What on earth is going on? Does she know these men?

The men took a couple of steps back from Fiona and Alabama. They flicked their gazes toward where she'd stepped out of the way. She couldn't hear what Alabama said to the men, but they turned and hurried away from the store.

Caroline and Alabama wrapped themselves around Fiona, obviously trying to calm her down. Fiona collapsed to the floor, and both the other women followed her down. As much as Lily wanted to hear what was being said, she recognized a flashback when she saw one, and she didn't dare intrude in case she made things worse than she already had by leading those men here. This was her fault. All her fault. Why the heck had she come here today? It was so unfair this woman, Fiona, had to deal with her nightmares just because Lily had been running from hers.

When Alabama rooted around in her purse and came up with a bunch of keys, Lily knew she was probably going to get their car. She couldn't allow her to go back there on her own, in case the men were waiting for her. She put the underwear she still held in one hand back on the shelf and followed Alabama out the door all the way back to the parking lot before she called out to her.

"Alabama?"

"Yes?" The other woman glanced at her as they crossed the parking lot.

"Is your sister alright?" She wasn't sure why she used sister instead of friend. She just knew it fit.

"She will be. I'm sorry I don't have time to talk. I need to get the car and get around to the back entrance, stat."

Stat?

That was a strange word for a civilian to use. She didn't think they were military themselves. At least they didn't move like they were. Wives, though. That they were military wives was more than a possibility considering the proximity to Coronado Naval Base. Fuck, had she just put these MILSOs, into the crosshairs of a tango?

"I totally understand. Do you want me to follow your car around the back and make sure the men have left?"

They reached their cars, and she could already see the truck was gone. She scanned the look looking for the massive spotlights which had lined the roof over the front window but didn't see it.

Alabama ripped open the driver's door and jumped in. "Thank you, but it's okay, I promise."

She slammed the door, started the engine, and reversed her car out of the parking spot. She took off with her wheels spinning, in a manner which would have done a street racer proud.

Lily stared after Alabama for a hot minute before she shook herself and got her head back in the game. She checked over her minivan as fast as she possibly could, then jumped in and started the engine. By the time she made it to the exit, she paused to allow the vehicle she recognized as Alabama's car to go first as it came from a side street at the back of the mall. She returned Alabama's wave of acknowledgement and eased into traffic. Now she just had to figure out how to grab RJ and get out of here before anyone found their house.

"Easy day. The only easy day was yesterday." She mouthed the words Rexar had said too many times to count and switched off the radio to concentrate better. It was time to run—again.

CHAPTER THREE

Nemesis Inc. Headquarters, Montana

Glancing at the treadmill, Rexar ignored the ache in his thighs as he pressed a button to increase the incline. He was never going to recover if he didn't push harder. He'd only run eight miles and already he was breathing hard. Over the front of the machine, he kept his focus on the computer screen. The blinking mouse was his focal point. He still hadn't decided what to do with the long stream of hash numbers that proceeded the mouse. To hit enter or not, that was the question. Doing so would open up a can of worms he wasn't sure he was ready to deal with yet. No doing so meant he missed another day, another week, another minute with his son.

"Bite the bullet, man, when did you become such a pussy?"

For the record, he did not need an answer to that question. He knew exactly when that had happened. The treadmill beeped, warning him that the session was coming to an end. His pace adjusted automatically to the machine as it slowed. Once it stopped, Rexar refused to bend over in an effort to breathe easier. Nope, the sawing pain in his lungs as air was sucked in and blown out—that reminded him he was alive. Everything and anything that reminded him the tangos had lost was a good thing.

Grabbing the towel from the arm of the treadmill, he wiped the sweat from his brow and walked across the room. God damnit, decisions had never been so freaking difficult before. When the hell had he gone from a Navy SEAL who flew by the seat of his pants and made shit up on the fly to the broken, scared man staring back at him in the mirror? Oh yeah, since he'd been held and tortured in Section 209, of Evin Prison, Iran's infamous black site, for almost five years. Until his twin Drax had rescued him just over a year ago.

"Push the damn button." Rexar blew out a breath, grabbed the mouse with his left hand, and clicked search. God, he hoped doing this gave him the result he wanted—needed. The can of worms could just stay shut, thank you very much.

Within seconds the phone on the desk next to his laptop rang.

Yes! He grabbed the phone and hit answer.

"Who the fuck are you?"

The man's voice laced with a slight Texas drawl made his eyes slam closed. Was that relief? Possibly, but knowing it didn't stop the lone tear that managed to escape through his squeezed shut eyelids.

"You have five seconds before I call people you do not want to deal with," The man warned. "Who the fuck are you and why are you searching for me?"

"Shut your pie hole, Keegan." Rexar pulled back the office chair and sat into it. There was no way he was keeping himself vertical when his knees were shaking like they had when he'd gotten to the ground after losing his first para-chute during a helo drop into some hellhole country he wasn't going to name. "I need your help."

He winced as the sound that could only be a shattering coffee mug filtered through the phone. Shit, maybe he should have sent an email. If he managed to give John "Tex" Keegan a heart attack, there were a hell of a lot of people and government agencies who would lose their shit in epic style.

"You're dead."

"Nope." Rexar popped the end of the word. "Not for lack of people trying though, but no, I'm very much alive." If alive was scared as fuck, with a metric ton of PTSD along with a side dose of nightly flashbacks.

"I'll call you back in twenty minutes," Tex told him. "Be there to answer my call."

"You—" Rexar scowled at the phone as the line went dead before he could agree, or to ask Tex to swear on his Trident that he would call back. Scrubbing a hand over his face, he refused to consider the idea that Tex would refuse his request. Nope, Tex was a team guy. Solid, dependable, and he had a skillset Rexar needed badly. He could find anyone, anywhere, and Rexar had someone to find. Two someones— his woman and kid. His ultimate goal, vengeance. There was no way the woman who betrayed him was going to raise his kid. That was never going to freaking happen on his watch. His wife was going to jail, and his kid was coming home. Hell, he didn't even know if he had a son or a daughter, and he didn't care. He'd love either one just as much as the other.

He chewed on the side of his thumb, watching the clock counting down the seconds. Tex could do some amazing shit on the computer. Many of the SEAL teams relied on him to get them information faster than going up the chain of command. The government relied on Tex Keegan more than they would probably ever want to admit, and Rexar knew for a fact there were several top-secret military groups out there who also relied on him. But most importantly, he trusted him. Trusted Tex would have his back, as only a fellow SEAL could.

As long as Rexar hadn't fucking killed him by calling like a ghost in the dark.

Virginia

TEX'S HANDS came down on the keyboard hard.

Tex: Njhaouiunjg;ljaoihuygdlmpoohb

He'd just accidentally sent CC_CopyCat a jumbled-up mix of words. There had never been a time in his life when he'd sent someone, anyone, something like that. He didn't have a cat to sit on the keyboard to butt-type.

CC_CopyCat: Tex? What happened? Is this some new code you are challenging me to break?

Tex: I just talked to a dead man.

He wasn't meant to say that online and he knew it.

CC_CopyCat: Um you just what now?

Yeah, Tex understood her confusion. Normally, he pretty much made sense all the time. It was a rare occasion where he didn't. This apparently was going to be one of those unicorn days.

CC_CopyCat: I'm not sure I understand.

He got out of the chair and grabbed a broom and pan from where they stood in the corner of the room and got to work cleaning the mess that used to be his favorite mug. He needed a minute to figure out how to tell her what had happened. His computer dinged again.

CC_CopyCat: Explain. If you can.

Tex: Five years ago, I worked for a company.

CC_CopyCat: Go on.

He wondered if she could tell he was choosing his words carefully. If so, did she understand it?

CC_CopyCat: I don't need the detail-details.

She reminded him when he didn't respond straight away.

He didn't blame her. She was probably sitting where the weather was crappy trying to figure out why he was telling her all this shit.

CC_CopyCat: You don't have to answer if you don't want to or if it's not possible.

She was astute. He was still guessing she wasn't an undercover cop looking to catch the bad guys who lurked in chat rooms looking for unsuspecting victims.

CC_CopyCat: Are you still there?

Tex: Yes, just thinking.

CC_CopyCat: Take your time.

If this was a woman, she was pushing every single one of his buttons. Every. Single. One.

Tex: We had a man who didn't make it home.

That was another thing he knew he shouldn't be telling CC_CopyCat. He should be on the phone calling Wolf, or even better Bauer or Knight. One of those two men would know for sure what the hell was happening.

CC_CopyCat: I'm so sorry.

Tex: Thank you.

CC_CopyCat: Are you allowed to tell me what happened?

Tex: No.

CC_CopyCat: Are you going to do it anyway?

Tex: Maybe, but if I do, there won't be detail-details as you called it.

CC_CopyCat: I'm good with that, talk it out. Make it make sense.

Tex: unless they allow phone calls from Valhalla there is zero chance of it all making sense.

He snorted even though he knew she couldn't hear him and leaned over the desk peering at the screen. Then smacked himself on the forehead when that word, Valhalla, jumped off the screen at him. Shit, he was already too comfortable with CC_CopyCat. He should cut ties. He should do it now. But he enjoyed talking to her. She was funny and smart, and she made his days just a tiny bit brighter. If he ever found out she wasn't a woman like he suspected, he was going to be one disappointed SEAL.

CC_CopyCat: Okay, go on.

He emptied the dustpan into the trash and grabbed another mug from the shelf at the side of the room, then filled it with coffee before taking his seat at his desk again. It took him so long to decide how to continue that he was almost at the point of backing out and not telling CC_CopyCat anything more than he already had.

Tex pulled up a second laptop which was ring-fenced off from the one he used for gaming. His fingers flew over the keyboard. He logged into a database and pulled up a photo of the man who'd called him. He was dressed in a Navy uniform, with a Trident displayed proudly on his chest. He had his arm slung over the shoulder of an identical man, but this one wore the Blue Cord of the Army's special forces unit. He stared at it for long heartbeats and tugged the other keyboard closer again.

Tex: Something went wrong, and he didn't come home alive.

CC_CopyCat: "Was he a close friend?"

Tex: We both worked for the same business and had crossed paths a few times.

CC_CopyCat: We can change to talking about the weather again if you'd prefer.

She was either reading his mind or maybe she figured if

she made small talk, she'd give him time to get his thoughts together.

Tex: No. It's okay. I do need to make a phone call in a couple of minutes though.

CC_CopyCat: No problem, do what you need to do.

CC_CopyCat: I do have one question though.

Tex: Go ahead.

CC_CopyCat: If he died, how is it that he called you?"

Tex: I have that exact same question.

He glanced at his watch. He was down to ten minutes before he had to call the number back.

Tex: I need to go, CC.

CC_CopyCat: If you need to talk later, ping me.

Tex: Will do. Thank you, CC.

Tex's fingers still hovered over the keyboard on his work computer. It wasn't often he didn't know how to proceed. Maybe he *should* call Wolf or any of the girls. He loved his girls and usually chattered with them. But this was work and he found he was totally lost for words.

What he wouldn't give to have someone here to offer some moral support or something. Maybe his CopyCat girl would have cupped his face with her hand and dropped a soft kiss on his lips and offered to stay while he checked this out.

"Phone call." He hit up his list of contacts and dialed an international number and waited for the funky ringtone to start. If he got no answer here, then he'd call Wolf and get his thoughts.

He tapped through the screens. "Well damn it, scratch that." The information on his screen told him Wolf and the guys had rapid deployed last night. "You're going solo, Keegan, you can figure this shit out."

Faster than he'd ever managed before, he pulled up a

different screen and checked the phone locator signals, triangulated them against cell towers, and verified the location. A shopping mall in Riverton. Good, the girls were shopping. That would keep them occupied and hopefully out of trouble for a couple of minutes while he figured out the shitshow which had landed on his desk via a phone call from a dead man.

CHAPTER FOUR

Riverton, California

Lily took the long way home, driving into neighborhoods and through side-streets. If a vehicle followed her for too long, she diverted from her course and tried again. Every evasive move both Rexar and the CIA had taught her, she utilized.

Her phone dinged from its holder on the dashboard and she glanced at the number of the incoming call. She hit *answer*.

"Marion, I'm so sorry. I'm on my way, traffic is terrible."

"I thought it might be."

She struggled to keep her voice normal as she spoke to the other mother. "Is RJ okay?"

"He's fine, playing with Thomas in the bouncy house." Marion said, "We are going to have some really tired boys tonight."

"I can't thank you enough for having him today."

"You are welcome." Marion replied, "Take your time coming back, I just wanted to make sure you were okay."

"Thank you so much." When was the last time someone checked on her welfare? She couldn't remember. "I'm not far, I promise. Do you need me to pick you anything up at the store?"

"Girl, if I try to fit another bite of anything in my mouth today, it won't be Thomas up with a belly ache tonight."

"I feel that in my soul."

"See you in a few!" She took another turn which would add five minutes to her drive. But she figured it was better to be safe than sorry at this point.

"Bye."

Even though Marion had hung up on her end, Lily hit *end* on the call on her side. She felt much better now that she'd spoken to her friend. But she dreaded what was to come later when RJ realized they were going to have to move again tonight.

"At least he had today."

But reminding herself that her little boy had been able to have a normal play date for once in his short life was little consolation for the trauma she would cause him. She'd freaking known better than to stay in one place for too long. Had known it. Had ignored it. Now RJ would pay the price.

"Damn it. Just freaking damn it."

Lily pulled her minivan into Marion's driveway less than ten minutes later and had to sit for a couple of seconds after she'd switched off the engine. She reached deep down inside herself for the strength she'd found to pick the shattered pieces of her life up off the floor when Rexar had died five years ago. If ever there was a time she needed that strength, it was today.

She peeled her fingers off the steering wheel and held her hands out in front of her. Hands were not supposed to shake like that. They really shouldn't. She shook them out, hoping to send the blood flowing back into her fingers. She'd almost cut off the circulation completely by gripping the wheel so tightly on the drive here.

"Come on, Lil, get a grip."

Movement through the window warned her that her time was up. She slapped the everything-is-fine-Momma's-got-this expression she used for RJ onto her face. It took more effort than it did with her son, mind you, but by the time she stepped out of the car to greet Marion, she hoped she mostly looked like there was nothing wrong in her world.

"Are you okay?"

Well, there went that hope. Marion was more astute than she'd thought. Which she knew was unfair as she only knew her from their walks in the subdivision.

"Traffic." She lifted one shoulder. "It's crazy today. Everyone and their grandmother is out, and none of them have remembered the rules of the road or what a turn signal is for."

"I told you to go early for just that reason." Marion nodded sagely. "Riverton, two weeks before Christmas loses its fricking mind. Come on through, the kids are in the back yard."

"Thank you so much..."

Marion waved her off and led her into the kitchen. "Don't worry about it, he's no trouble at all." She opened the fridge. "Would you like some sun tea or water before we brave the back yard?"

"I'd love some water please, sparkling if you have it. If not, natural is perfectly good, too."

"I have sparkling." Marion handed her a bottle. "If you want a glass they're over the sink." She refilled her own glass from the jug of tea and replaced it in the fridge.

"It's fine like this." She unscrewed the top and took a sip. "Oh, that's good, thank you."

Marion pushed a plate of cookies across the island

toward her. "Help yourself. I managed to save these from the hordes earlier."

"Did they eat like they hadn't seen food in a month?"

"Oh yeah." Marion sat on one of the bar stools across from her. "They ate like they'd never seen food at all, never mind in the last month."

"I hope RJ was polite about it at least."

"He absolutely was. Said his pleases and thank yous and all that."

Sitting here chit-chatting with another mother as their children played in the bounce house out back did a lot to settle her nerves. Being able to hear RJ's squeals of laughter through the open patio door did the rest. She smiled at Marion. She could do this, the friendly mother thing. Later tonight she'd pack herself and RJ up and disappear into the night. In time Marion and her son would forget about the little dark-haired boy who'd lived down the street. RJ would take longer to forget, but there wasn't much she could do about that now.

* * *

LILY SCANNED THE LIVING ROOM, looking for anything which might indicate she'd been living here. She gripped the edge of the couch and pulled it away from the wall, making sure the curtain didn't come away from the window with it. She grabbed a runaway Lego block and stuffed it into her pocket.

She double checked each and every piece of furniture, gathering a stray sock and a couple of more pieces of Lego, before going into the kitchen. She meticulously went through each cupboard. Ensured every cup, plate, knife, fork, and glass, along with all the cooking utensils were in the dishwasher. She blew out her breath and grabbed the spray bottle and cleaning stuff she'd purchased earlier on her way home from Marion's.

"You won't get done if you don't get started." She got to work wiping down each and every surface in this part of the house. She'd already done the bathroom and the bedrooms; all that remained after finishing in here was RJ's room, and she couldn't do that until she had him in the car.

Lily pressed her hands into the small of her back, twisting from one side to the other, trying to ease the stiffness which came from scrubbing the house from top to bottom. Keeping her hands on her body served a dual purpose; it meant her glove-covered fingers couldn't touch anything. The possibility of getting a fingerprint through the latex was minuscule but she wasn't about to take the chance that she'd be part of the tiny percent. Latex was thin enough that sometimes fingerprints transferred.

"Come on, move every second counts."

She blew out a silent breath and pushed open RJ's bedroom door farther with her elbow, taking care not to hit it too hard so it didn't bang off the wall and wake him. Despite the urgency creeping into her soul, she took a heartbeat to watch her son sleeping peacefully, curled around the bear which had arrived in the mail a couple of days after she'd emailed Rexar to let him know she was pregnant. She hated doing this to him again. But after the incident yesterday at the mall, what other choice did she have?

You could go to Drax.

No, she couldn't. Drax, Rexar's twin, could never know she existed. She wasn't even sure if Rexar had told him about her. Even if he had, her brother-in-law had never come looking for her. Plus, he lived and worked out of Europe these days; there was nothing he could do for her and his nephew.

Lily put the special tennis shoes on his feet and scooped

RJ out of the bed, ignoring her protesting back, and tucked the blanket around him.

"Momma?"

"Shh, baby, go back to sleep." She pressed his head into her shoulder. Feeling his breath against her neck drove a metaphorical iron rod up along her spine, giving her the strength she needed not only to carry him, but to do what needed to be done.

"Are we leaving?"

The sadness in his little voice ripped her heart right out of her chest. "Yes, baby."

"I no wanna go."

"Me neither, baby, me neither." She managed to depress the door handle with her elbow and got close enough to her minivan that the automatic lock opened it for her. She slid back the door and settled him into his car seat. "I promise this won't be forever," she whispered softly, tucking the blankets in around him.

He watched her with those big sad eyes of his, and she had to steel her resolve to ensure she didn't just carry him back into the house and say to hell with it, bring it on, assholes. If it had just been herself, she might have considered doing just that. But there was no chance in hell that she'd put RJ in danger.

Lily made quick work of wiping down RJ's room, the hallway, and the front door, before returning to the car.

She made sure to hit the locks on the car before she stripped off the gloves and dropped the cleaning supplies into the footwell of the passenger seat. She swallowed hard as she adjusted the rearview mirror to give her a view of her sleeping son. By the time he woke up tomorrow, they'd be in a different place, with different faces. She opened the garage door. As she reversed out of her driveway and turned the nose of the minivan north, she considered if she should change their names again. Going back to her real first name had been a stupid move. That had to be what tipped off the people who chased her… it had to be.

Lily waited until she was ten miles down the highway, before she tossed her already broken down phone out the window and watched it disappear under the tires of an eighteen-wheeler in the next lane. The song on the radio changed. Recognizing the intro, she scowled at the dash just as the first strains of 'Hit the Road Jack' filled her ears.

"How freaking appropriate."

CHAPTER FIVE

Nemesis Inc. Headquarters, Montana

Rexar paced across the room and back again. His eyes never left the phone, even if it meant he had to turn his head and watch it over his shoulder.

"What is it momma says? A watched kettle never boils."

Nineteen minutes had passed. Tex must have been able to confirm it was him in that time frame. Someone as good as he was with computers and shit didn't take long to verify something the DOD was fully aware of. Although if he had to hazard a guess, there was an irate commander in Italy getting an earful right about now. Fuck, he hoped so. He knew Noble Bauer would have his six.

At the twenty-minute mark on the nose, the phone rang. Even though he'd been expecting it, Rexar jumped a freaking foot into the air. He pressed answer, once again not speaking but waiting for the person on the other end of the line to do so first.

"Rexar?"

"I'm here, Tex."

"What the actual fuck, man?"

It didn't take a genius to hear the fury in his friend's voice. "I know."

"You should have called me."

"I know, I'm sorry." It hurt to admit he was sorry about anything. But he'd always done it before when he was in the wrong, and this time he'd suck it up and admit it. "I…"

"Can it." He heard Tex's annoyed huff. "I fucking…wait… how secure is this line?"

"I'm not sure," he admitted. "Our tech guy pretty much shut down all external communication last week. I haven't had an update since." Fuck, *that* should have been what he'd led with.

"Shit. Okay. Go find a throwaway cell. If you are where your commander says you are then the man who took over team lead from him will have one you can use. Email the number to this address."

"Copy that."

"Rex?"

"Yeah?"

"Don't fucking try to set that phone up by yourself, have your tech guy do it…feel me?"

"Yes, sir, I do."

Trust Keegan to remember his ineptness with mobile phones. Give him a computer or a laptop and he could hold his own, but a phone with his fingers… yeah, that was asking for trouble. Especially now that said fingers were twisted and damaged from the years of torture. He didn't think his thumbnail would ever grow back.

"And Rex?"

He waited for Tex to continue.

"It's fucking awesome to hear your voice."

He guessed that was as close as Tex was going to get to

saying he was happy he hadn't died. In the background he heard a song blaring.

"What the?" Tex muttered in his ear. "I gotta go, I need to take this."

"Thanks, Tex."

"Don't thank me yet. You haven't told me what you're looking for and I haven't decided if I'll help you or not. Because, not gonna lie, man, I'm pissed." Tex's voice trailed off. Before he hung up, Rexar heard him ask someone else, "What's wrong?"

Rexar replaced the landline phone on the hook and slowly sank back into the chair. Now that he'd taken the first step, he wasn't sure how he felt about it. While she was out there—while his *child* was out there—he had a reason to sulk, to push himself harder because he needed to be ready to move as soon as he'd found her. Putting that task in Tex Keegan's hands was as good as saying 'Job. Done.'

Except it isn't. You didn't tell Tex anything yet.

He pushed aside the snarky voice inside his head. The one who told him day in and day out that he was broken, a washed-up damaged SEAL with nowhere to be but the bottom of a bottle. He didn't need to listen to that dumbass in his head today.

A loud police-style knock at the door told him who was there without him even opening it. Here in the Bravo Team house, there were only six of them. Himself, of course. Kentucky Smith, Bravo Team's leader. Draven Kilkenny, Bravo's resident shit stirrer. Tate Sullivan, their infiltration and reconnaissance expert. Caleb Hunt, Bravo's muscle man. His brother Kasey ran the kitchens and kept them all well fed and ready to deploy at a moment's notice. The sixth and final member of their team was Bryan Boyer, aka BB. Rexar was pretty sure it was after the gun rather than his initials, but with BB, there was no way to be sure.

"Rexar, move your ass," Caleb yelled through the door. "If you're sleeping, you're gonna miss the lasagna you asked Kase to make tonight.

"Coming." He glanced at himself in the mirror and made sure none of the emotions rioting inside him showed on his face. For once looking in the mirror wasn't about penance and remembering why he wore the scars found there. Caleb would give him shit, and he didn't have the patience to deal with that tonight. When he was done with dinner, he could go ask Trev for a burner phone.

Dalton was anal about the teams bonding. He firmly believed they should eat together. Along with living, breathing, working, and playing together. He could even hear those exact words in Dalton's voice in his head, along with, "The family who eats together, stays together." Knight was a hard-nosed asshole, but he'd been one hell of a commander when Noble had moved further up the chain of command to TOC.

Rexar secured a weapon at the small of his back and yanked open the door. Ignoring Caleb, he scanned the corridor, looking for the four-legged menace which was Dalton and his wife Lina's malamute puppy. If Buddha took off with another one of his belts, he'd never live it down.

"Where are the others?" he asked.

"Waiting in the truck."

"Awesome." He stuffed some gum into his mouth and chewed it really fast, then pulled the door closed behind him. After locking it and hanging the keys on a carabiner on his belt, he took the gum out of his mouth and smooshed it into the doorframe at the top, then tugged the gum across and stuck it to the top of the door.

"You know we all know you do that, right?" Caleb yelled from near the front door.

"Yup, but you all know it makes me feel better so you aren't going to give me shit about it."

"Damn straight, bro."

This right here was why he liked working with these guys. Bravo *got* him. They understood his quirks and they liked and trusted him anyway.

He followed Caleb to the pickup and jumped into the open bed. Caleb planted himself next to him. Rexar reached out to grab a fistful of Caleb's coat when Kentucky spun the wheels and the truck fishtailed around a corner on the ranch road.

"Thanks."

"No worries."

Thankfully it only took them eight minutes to drive from Bravo house to Alpha house, where the mess—aka the dining room—was located. Through the windows he could see the room was almost full. Meaning most of the teams and the ranch hands were onsite.

They jumped out of the back of the truck and waited for the others before entering Alpha house as a team.

Rexar fell into step behind everyone. His call sign might be Bravo Two—and he took his role of second in command seriously—however, his preferred position when they moved was behind the team, sweeping from left to right, ensuring nobody came up on their sixes. Even here on their home turf, a location he knew was a safe zone, his instinct had him at the back of the team, making sure no man was left behind. Even for dinner.

He paused just inside the dining room door. The chatter and noise from the other teams and the ranch hands washed over him in a tsunami wave which was almost too much for him to handle.

But then he caught a whiff of it...lasagna.

Two days ago, he'd given Kasey his Nonna's recipe, and from the smells...holy shit, the memories were slamming into him faster and harder than the noise had a couple of seconds before. For once it took effort to remain behind Tate. He cocked his head to one side. This was Nonna's Lasagna; maybe he could give him a nudge or two.

"Rexar, that you?"

He turned toward the voice. "Yup?"

Braddock Keane, a former Recon Marine he'd known from back in the day, stood up from his chair. Judging from the team he was sitting with, he was clearly assigned to Charlie team, Nemesis Inc.'s Global Rescue Division.

"Hey man, I heard you were dead."

"Aria didn't tell you that was all rumors and lies, huh?"

"No, man, she didn't." Braddock scowled in the direction of the Alpha Team sniper. "My little cousin is gonna get her butt kicked when I tell our mommas."

"Don't worry about it, dude. I'm sure she has her reasons." He didn't want to go down that particular memory lane this week. He had bigger fish to fry.

"Rexar, it wasn't your fault." Braddock offered his hand.

"Sure." He shrugged off the sympathy he could hear in Braddock's voice. "I'm gonna go grab some lasagna before those hounds eat it all." He gave Braddock a chin lift and walked away. Braddock's cousin Aria, aka Snow, hated him. She had since that fateful day on a rooftop in Afghanistan when her spotter had been faster to sacrifice himself before Rexar made the jump across from the next building. That woman was going to be pissed with him for the rest of her life for slamming her into the rooftop and not allowing her to die with her spotter.

He grabbed a tray and waited behind Tate for the line to move forward.

"You're not loading up on food?"

"Nah, man, I'm just having lasagna."

"These bread things are awesome." Tate stuffed one into

his mouth and wolfed it down. "Seriously awesome. You should try them."

Bruschetta *was* awesome, he just had to be in the mood for it. After Drax had visited and they'd heard their conversations in Italian about growing up in Italy for six months every year, both Kasey and Willow Cormack—Alpha Team's 2IC's wife—had begged him for some recipes. His momma had been thrilled when he'd called her to fulfill their request. He refused to feel guilty for not calling her more often. Momma wanted him to come home, to work behind the bar in the Corner Pyrate, near Fort Bragg, but he just couldn't do it. Neither he nor his twin had been bred to be barmen—they had war in their souls.

By the time he made it to the main course section of the hot counter, there was only one piece of lasagna left.

"Crap." That was never going to be enough. "All y'all are fuckers. That's not enough to feed a budgie, never mind me."

"I got you, bro." Kasey walked out of the kitchen carrying another tray of magical cheesy goodness. "Your momma said to make a couple of extra trays too in case you want to raid the fridge."

"Thanks, man, but she's mixing me up with Drax. He's the one who raids the fridge."

"What about me? Do I get to raid the fridge?"

"Hell no, Caleb. If you come in my kitchen, I'm shooting your ass and blaming Mitchell." Kasey replaced the empty tray over the steam-filled bain-marie with the full one, then scooped two huge portions onto a plate before passing it to Rexar. "Last time you tried to make grilled cheese in my kitchen, you used three frying pans and set off the smoke alarms. Cook that shit in your own damn suite."

"If you set off the smoke alarms," Kentucky reached over and smacked Caleb on the head, "I'm gonna shoot you myself, and Bossman won't even object."

"Thanks, Kase." Now that he had his lasagna and didn't need to pick up dessert, he circled around the rest of the team. He'd spotted Trev at the Alpha Team table when he'd come in and decided now was as good a time as any to ask for a phone. Instead of heading to Bravo's table, he headed for Trev.

"Hey, man, I know you're busy and shit, but can I grab a burner from you after dinner?"

"Sure."

"What you need a burner phone for?" Dalton leaned around Lina and pinned him with a stare.

"Tex." He figured he didn't need to say much more than the man's name.

"That will do it," Trev muttered. "Come on down to the war room after dinner and I'll set you up with one."

"Can you set it up with email, too?"

"Hah, Keegan is still a wary bastard." Trev snorted. "Sure. No worries."

"Thanks." He left them to their dinner. By the time he was finished with his, and maybe indulged in seconds for once, he'd be able to email Tex the number.

CHAPTER SIX

California

The last person Lily expected to see getting out of a car in front of the room she'd taken at a high-end hotel on the outskirts of San Francisco for the night was Fiona, the woman she'd practically driven into a PTSD episode yesterday with her carelessness. She peered out the window, craning her neck to watch as Fiona scurried across the parking lot in sweats and an oversized T-shirt.

Is someone following her?

Fiona disappeared through the hotel door, but Lily kept watching the lot. Four different vehicles arrived after Fiona. The first with a family, the next contained a couple who were all hot and heavy making their way to the door. She was going to guess those two were not meant to be together at a hotel tonight. She turned back to watch the blue sedan as the doors opened; someone else's affair wasn't any of her business. Her breath caught in her throat when the first man out of the sedan was Hispanic, and she knew that was racist as all get-out, but she didn't know how else to think of him. When she got a look at his face, she realized this wasn't either of the men who'd followed her at the mall yesterday. When he was joined by a woman and toddler, she was one hundred percent sure of it.

I should go down to the lobby and see if Fiona is okay, bring her up here... No, that's a stupid idea. With RJ sleeping on the bed, she couldn't afford to take a chance that this was a setup of some sort.

When a bunch of college students spilled out of the fourth vehicle, Lily determined that whatever Fiona was running from hadn't followed her here. Muffled voices in the hallway outside her room pulled her attention from the window and she hurried across the room to peer through the peephole. Her eyes widened when she recognized the color of Fiona's T-shirt. She could make out the profile of the other woman as she pushed a keycard into the slot for the room just past hers.

"I should go out there..."

No, you shouldn't.

If she recognizes you then she may run again.

Fiona disappeared from view, and for a high-end hotel Lily was surprised to hear the door slam shut in the next room.

You could offer her one of those hotel room locks for extra security.

No, she shouldn't... again she didn't want to spook her into running more if she needed rest. She recognized a fellow person who was freaked out of her wits. No matter how much she wanted to move in the morning, her butt was staying here until Fiona left.

"If Fiona is here, where are Caroline and Alabama?"

She reached for the laptop she'd bought at a secondhand store just off the highway on her way here, and placed it on the table which she'd set up as a mini office space. She glanced at the phone next to where she'd placed her laptop. If she'd had a number for the other two women, she'd have called them and let them know where Fiona was. She connected the laptop to a VPN, and then bounced it around the globe a couple of times before pulling up a Tor Browser and searching for the Riverton Police Department's website.

Pausing to glance over her shoulder at RJ and make sure he was still sleeping, she clicked on the link and navigated to the page for missing persons. She clicked on every single link and checked the photos, breathing out a sigh of relief when none of them were Fiona.

"Who are you, and who are you running from?"

"Momma, I need to potty."

"Hi, baby." She closed the laptop and helped RJ off the bed.

"I can do it." He swatted at her hands.

"I know you can, bud, but Momma needs to feel needed right now."

"M'kay." He gave her a swift hug and as soon as his feet hit the floor, he took off running toward the bathroom.

The corners of her lips curved upward when she heard him peeing. "Don't forget to shake."

"I won't, Momma," RJ called. "Shake, shake like a little lamb's tail."

When you were female with a boy child, potty training required using your imagination on how to get them to tinkle in the pot. "Don't forget to wash your hands."

"I's doing it."

She leaned back on her chair until she could see him standing on the folding stool she'd brought in from the car for just this purpose. "Good job, buddy."

RJ came running out of the bathroom and skidded to a

stop in front of her and threw himself into her lap. "G'night, Momma."

She took a moment to bury her nose in his shampoo-scented hair, hugging him close. When she faltered and considered holding up a big sign over her head saying 'Here I am, come and get me' RJ was the reason she kept going. Another day, another foot in front of the other. Another mile between her and the ghosts which haunted her.

He wriggled to get free. She put him back on his feet and got out of the chair to tuck him into bed again.

"Are you thirsty?"

He shook his head and tugged his teddy bear into his arms, his fingers stroking over the almost bare patch on its cheek. "No."

"Okay." She tucked the blankets in snuggly around him. "Goodnight, bud." She pressed a kiss to his cheek. "I'll be right here in that chair working until I climb into bed next to you." She reassured him she wasn't going anywhere, just as she always did. But RJ's eyes were already drooping. Oh, to be four again, and not have a care in the world. There were some days she'd bribe the pope for the possibility of having that option.

Lily took an extra couple of minutes to snuggle with her boy. When he snored softly in her ear, she knew that was her cue to get back to work. She brushed his bangs back out of his eyes; it was almost time for a haircut again. She'd meant to get it done next week and had even booked the appointment with a barber Marion had recommended to her back in Riverton.

Wishes and dreams are not for the likes of you. Have you not learned that already?

She went to the door and cocked her head near the wall dividing her room from Fiona's but could hear nothing. Either Fiona was also sleeping, or she was keeping the TV so low she couldn't hear it. Lily hoped the other woman was alright. She considered calling down to the front desk to ask if anyone had seen her, but decided it was better not to draw attention to either of them.

She took a fast shower and changed into fresh sweats and a clean T-shirt, allowing the pounding water to wash away the aches of the past day, before going back to the desk and her computer. Another search of Riverton PD's website didn't show any new missing person reports.

"Damn, who are you, Fiona, and why are you running?"

Was she a domestic violence survivor, trying to escape her man's clutches? If so then she'd give her what funds she could and drive her as far as she needed to go. But how did she let Fiona know that without freaking her out? She'd have to think about it. Lily chewed on the corner of her nail before she wrenched it from her mouth. She'd worked too freaking hard to stop chewing her nails to let a quandary set her off again.

Lily double checked that her VPNs and security systems were in place and pulled up another search engine. It had been too long since she'd checked her mail, but even she didn't expect the three thousand odd messages.

"Holy shit."

Resigning herself to be doing this all night, she filtered by unread and selected them. Scrolling down the page she deleted the first fifty without thought and then repeated the action for the next three bunches of fifty. Her mouse hovered over the trash can icon when one of the email addresses caught her eye.

"Who's hideandseek2019?" She unticked the box next to that email and trashed the others after a quick scan of the rest.

She didn't have to download the email from the server as

the preview box worked. Now she only had one email selected.

Email address: hideandseek2019@hidemyass.com
Subject: *%*%*
Run, run, as fast as you can...
Peek-a-boo we can see you.
Your cub looks like he'd fetch a pretty price.

"SHIT." She copied the email address and ran a search through the CIA databases she wasn't meant to still have access to. It was in her opinion worth the risk. Any threat to RJ was one she'd take seriously. Whoever this asshole was had called him a cub. He was right in a way, but hide and seek freaking two zero nineteen had neglected to take her cub's momma bear into account.

"If you come after my boy, I'll put you in the ground. Period."

She scowled at the screen when her database gave her exactly nothing. It didn't matter, she had at least six more to search. She'd find him eventually. If she couldn't then maybe Aria, the only person she'd stayed in contact with before, could. Until then, her job was to stay at least five steps ahead of whoever this was. Tomorrow morning the burner cell she'd ordered off Amazon should be here. Once it arrived, if she hadn't found anything, she would swallow her pride and call Aria.

She wasn't sure how many hours later it was, when the faint sound of a phone ringing jerked her attention away from the screen. She jumped out of her chair and rushed to the door to listen at Fiona's wall. Sometime during the night as she'd listened at the wall to her crying in her sleep, the wall had become Fiona's wall.

"Answer the phone, honey," she whispered softly. Not that Fiona could hear her, but as if her metal encouragement through the wall had an effect, the phone finally stopped ringing, and she could make out the murmuring of Fiona's voice. Lily reassured herself that the other woman was okay. That was one shining good point in this messed up week.

CHAPTER SEVEN

Nemesis Inc. Headquarters, Montana

Rexar scanned his hand on the security system on the front door of Nemesis Inc.'s HQ and went through the procedure of divesting himself of his weapons for the scanner. After a threat against Lina, Dalton had upped security here. It fucking sucked, even if he understood it. Getting into HQ was now similar to going through airport security. In his humble opinion, Lina, who'd been an assassin named Mamba for a terrorist organization determined to take over the world, didn't need much security. She could take care of herself.

But then when your family ran Knight Oil and were richer than sin, he supposed money was no object when it came to creating a secure bolt hole. Nemesis Inc. also had bases in the Middle East. He'd been to that one, a containerized unit set up within one of the US military's compounds. After too many deployments to count, that one felt like home.

There was a penthouse suite owned by Dalton's brother

67

in Dubai, but that one was way too fancy for his taste. He'd been terrified he'd break something if he touched it with his gun-oil-stained fingers. Yeah, it was better if Dalton kept him running the Ops which didn't involve dressing up in monkey suits and going to expensive places.

He nodded to the security guys and weaponed up again before heading to the elevator which would take him down into the working underground center which was the war room.

"Hey, Trev?" He knocked on the frame of the open door.

"Come on in."

"What the hell happened here?"

Trev knelt on the floor surrounded by the guts of computers, hard drives, and a hell of a lot of other stuff he didn't recognize.

"The fucking Organization happened." Trev climbed to his feet, "First I need to verify we don't have some alien hardware, which found its way in here, and then I have to start the software."

"You had to strip it all down?"

"You break down weapons and put them back together if there's something whacked with your gear, right?" Trev pulled a phone from a box on the corner of one desk.

"Yeah."

"This..." Trev waved his arm, taking in the whole room, "is my weapon and I've got an extra fucking trigger."

"Shit. That sucks."

"Pretty much," Trev agreed. "I built it from scratch so it's a custom build, which means only I can find that fucker." He pointed to the notebooks on the floor where he'd been sitting, "Those are my blueprints."

"Could anyone have gotten their hands on those plans?"

"Not unless they could get down here and into my quarters on the other side of the security door at the end of this corridor."

"A mole?"

"I hope not."

It wasn't a denial and that concerned him.

"Email is here." Trev turned on the phone. "Messages here, phone calls here. Swipe green to answer, red to refuse a call."

"Thanks." He appreciated Trev taking the time to go through the smartphone with him. He'd had his previous Nokia for nearly ten years, before his stint in Section 209, and some of this new technology didn't work easily for him. "Can you send an email to Tex Keegan with the number if I give you the address?"

"Sure, hit me. It's a throwaway account, that okay?"

"I assume so." He rattled off the email address Tex had given him earlier.

"That's a throwaway email, too." Trev snorted.

"Tell him to give me a bit to get back to my house."

"How about I set it up and you only have to hit send?"

That might work, but this was too important to mess up. "I—um—"

"Operators." Trev's fingers moved at speed over the tiny keyboard on the phone's screen. "There. I told him you're tech-phobic, who I am, and to call you on this number in twenty."

"Perfect. Thanks, Trev, appreciate it."

"I'm sorry I couldn't find her for you."

"I know." He wasn't mad at Trev. He was shit hot on comput-ers, but apparently his wife was better at hiding than he'd ever suspected. That shit was gonna change. "Thanks, dude." He picked up a black box and turned it over in his hand, until Trev plucked it off him and slapped the phone into his hand.

"Don't touch that, and you're welcome." Trev pointed to the door, "Please leave before you break shit."

"I feel so fucking loved."

"Asshole."

* * *

REXAR STARED at the mile counter on the treadmill as it climbed higher and higher. *Tick, toc, tick tock, tick tock.* The fucking clock in his head needed to come out. The ticking was making him batshit.

Tex had to be working a job. He couldn't remember a time before when the man hadn't called when he said he would.

"Come on. Can you hurry it up?"

Muttering and bitching to himself helped—or rather it made dealing with the slow snail crawl of the passage of time easier. He'd learned while in captivity talking to himself was the only way to stay mostly sane.

Ring. Ring. Ring.

He jumped off the still-moving treadmill and shot across the room to where he'd placed the phone. After keeping it in his hand—and he'd kept lighting up the screen, nearly causing him to faceplant on his chin—he'd decided it was better to leave it where he couldn't break it before Tex called him back. He swiped *answer* on the phone and waited.

"Mitchell, I don't have time for fucking around." Tex sounded exhausted.

"Sorry. If you're stuck in a mission, this can wait." He was a dick to put a team in danger because of his personal shit. "It's waited five years; another few days won't matter."

"No," Tex replied. "It's a personal thing, not work-related."

Thank fuck.

"Anything I can help with?"

"Not right now," Tex said. "A friend's woman is in trouble. I'm helping her out while he's at work."

"Okay." He hated the awkward silence, where only their breathing could be heard.

"Are you going to tell me what happened?"

"Did you talk to Bauer?"

"I did." Tex's swallow was audible. "If I'd known, I'd..."

"You didn't." There was no way he was going to allow Tex to blame himself, "You didn't betray me, and you didn't know I was alive. So don't do that to yourself, dealing with Drax and his guilt is hard enough."

"I'll bet," Tex muttered. "Talk to me. What do you need?"

"To find someone."

"Who?"

"The reason I was in fucking Iran and the reason I fucking stayed there until Drax found me."

"Who is he?"

"She."

"Go on."

"My wife." He could hear choking over the phone and figured it was better to wait a second or two for Tex to clear his throat, before adding on, "and my child."

It wasn't often John Keegan was caught by surprise. Doing it twice in the space of thirty seconds flat should come with an award or something, right?

"First, you have a wife and kid?"

"I'm assuming I have a kid," Rexar interrupted. "Lily was pregnant when I went on that last mission."

"It's not in your records."

"It was new. I hadn't filed the paperwork."

"Stupid."

"Don't I know it." It was standard procedure; he should have freaking updated his next of kin. He hadn't done it. He was a dumbass.

71

"Who is she?" Tex asked.

Thankfully, besides a huff of annoyance, Tex didn't appear to be going to grill him for being stupid. Rexar already knew he was. He'd paid the price for it. "How do you know *she* was someone important?"

"Because there is no fucking way you married someone and didn't file the paperwork," Tex shot back, "unless she had the potential to affect your security clearance. I didn't come down in the last shower, Mitchell," he warned. "Give me everything, or I'm out."

Of course his brain was working on overdrive today. But wasn't that what he needed? Tex on a whirlwind, doing his thing.

"She was working for the DOD, based out of Vincenza. I met her there when we laid over on our way to somewhere." He didn't need to give the location. No doubt if it became important Tex could find the information for himself. "I took her home to Zurich to meet Drax, but he wasn't there."

"I'd forgotten you guys had that bolt hole."

"We still do. If you ever need it, it's yours."

"Noted. Thank you."

"Anyway, I got the buzzer for wheels up in twenty-four." He was freaking still kicking himself for what had happened next. "I must have lost my damn mind or something, because I pulled some strings and married her, then went out." He paused and swallowed hard. "I didn't come back."

Over the phone he could hear something tapping in the background. Tex was probably taking notes on one of his computers. "So how do you know she was pregnant?"

"Email, before I went dark."

"You responded to it, didn't you?"

"And sent a teddy bear."

"Fucking idiot," Tex muttered. "Giving her an IP address and a country based off a postage stamp. You've got more balls than sense, Mitchell. Send me everything you have on her. I'll look."

"Thank you." Relief slammed into him. He hadn't known how much he'd needed Tex to agree... until he did.

"Mitchell?" The determination was clear in Tex's voice. "You do nothing until I say so."

"Now you sound like Dalton." And that made him sound like a child who'd been told he needed permission to have ice cream from the freezer.

"That asshole is still kicking around, huh?"

"Yeah."

"Good, stick with him. He'll make sure you don't fuck up," Tex advised.

"Why do I feel like everyone is expecting me to fuck up?" Up until that last trip, he hadn't fucked up that he was aware of. He'd worked his ass off to make sure he didn't put anyone else in danger.

"I've met your brother; it's a family trait."

Okay, he couldn't argue with that. It was a trait of Drax's to be a little dramatic.

"Dude, I have a check-in to meet. I'll see what I find," Tex promised.

"That's all I can ask."

"I'll be in touch."

Before he could say anything else, the line went dead. Rexar tapped the desk twice with his knuckles. Now he just had to hurry up and wait.

Hurry up and wait sucked.

CHAPTER EIGHT

California

"I'm sorry, Joe, I'm going to need at least another day." Lily hated changing stuff around. She should be miles out of California by now. Four days stuck in a hotel room with a four-year-old wasn't the most exciting experience on the planet. But she refused to leave until she knew Fiona was okay.

Every four hours the phone in the room next door rang like clockwork. The routine told her Fiona had someone watching out for her. But she, herself, needed more. If Fiona didn't come out of that room in the next twenty-four hours she was going to knock and see if she was okay. The only thing which had stopped her so far was the regular delivery of room service and those phone calls every four hours.

"I have the perfect vehicle for you, Ms. Jones, but I can only hold it so long," Joe said. "My boss is startin' to ask questions like why I'm not showing it to customers."

"I paid you a deposit."

"I know, I haven't spent it," Joe reassured her. "I need to move it off the lot."

"Then I'll send you the balance and you take it home tonight." She could do that. It was outside her comfort zone, but she could make it work. "I'll pick it up from your house."

"I can't do that, ma'am," Joe replied. "My boss would never go for that."

Well fudge-buckets.

"Can you deliver it to my hotel, and pick up my trade-in?" That would keep her off the radar of any of the street cameras. It would also mean she wouldn't have to take RJ out in public. While she was almost certain the threat in her email was a hoax…She would never take a chance with RJ's life.

"I'll see what I can do," Joe replied. "Can I call you back on this number in a couple of hours?"

"Of course. I'll be waiting for your call."

"The boss is at lunch. When he comes back, I'll talk to him."

"Thank you, Joe, I appreciate it." She hit *end* on the call. RJ thankfully was distracted by cartoons. It probably wasn't her best momma move to have him in front of the idiot box, but he'd been a trooper these past few days. She glanced at her watch. It was almost time for the phone to ring next door again. "You doing okay, buddy?"

"Yeah, Momma. Tom is chasing Jerry wif the skillet."

"I see that." She ruffled his hair as she passed him on the way to the room door. As expected, the phone rang again, but this time she heard a yelp from Fiona.

"That's it, I'm going over there." She turned to RJ. "You stay right here. Don't move from that chair, okay?"

"Yes, Momma." He didn't even turn around to look at her, the cartoon cat and mouse holding his full attention.

She reached up to the top shelf of the closet where she'd stashed her handgun out of RJ's reach and pushed it into the waistband of her jeans at the back, then pulled her sweater down to cover it. Not that she thought she'd need a weapon, but she also wasn't willing to take the chance that she would need it and not have it.

She peered out into the corridor. "Who are you?" she kept her voice low so it didn't reach RJ over the sound of the cartoons. She could just about make out the sleeve of a man standing outside Fiona's door. She threw open her door and was just about to ask the dude if he had the right room, but before she could say anything, Fiona's door opened.

"Hunter." Fiona flew into his arms.

Oh thank heavens. This Hunter was someone Fiona not only knew but was apparently thrilled to see.

"You came," Fiona said.

"I came. I'll always come for you."

OMG he is so freaking sweet with her.

She was going to ignore the pang of nostalgia aching in her heart. What Fiona and her Hunter had, wasn't for her anymore. Been there, tried that, and ended up with a baby, and a flag-covered coffin at a funeral she hadn't even been invited to, because her husband hadn't submitted their marriage documents to the Navy.

She turned her head to scan the corridor, her eyes widening when she spotted a short pregnant lady in jeans who was watching the reunion. The door closed behind Fiona and Hunter, and Lily raised one eyebrow in query at the woman.

"I'm with him."

Her hand was already reaching for the Glock, "Excuse me?"

"I mean, I'm a doctor. I'm here to help her."

She didn't understand. "You aren't married to him?"

"Oh, no." The woman rubbed her belly. "Definitely not. But who are you?"

"Just someone who saw she needed some help." There was

no freaking way she was telling this woman anything. Just because someone was female and pregnant didn't mean they weren't dangerous.

"Thank you for keeping an eye on her." The woman's phone dinged. "That's my cue, I've gotta get."

Lily nodded and pulled back into the room, shutting the door behind her. She still wasn't quite ready to just trust that these people had Fiona's best interests at heart though, so she pressed her ear to the wall between the closet and the door and pushed her finger into the other ear to block out the sounds of Tom and Jerry. After listening intently for at least five minutes all she could make out was the murmuring of voices.

She heard a door open and close, and frowned. Going back to the peephole, she could see people passing her room and opened the door a fraction. When she didn't see anything, she leaned out to stare down the corridor toward the elevator.

Hunter carried Fiona in his arms. He turned around and placed his back against the wall of the elevator, his chin touching the top of Fiona's head. The doctor hit the button to close the door and spotted her watching them. She stepped close to Hunter and spoke to him. Hunter pinned Lily with a nod and dipped his chin in silent acknowledgement and mouthed, "Thank you."

She went to the window and watched Hunter place Fiona into a car and follow her in, along with the doctor. Within minutes they had left the parking lot.

I hope I did the right thing letting them take you.

"Hey, bud, what do you say we go and find some burgers for dinner and then go get our new car?"

"Yay. McDonald's?"

"If you like." She sent a swift message to Joe, informing

him of the change of plan, and went about packing their stuff.

"Where are we going next?" RJ asked.

"I don't know, baby." She paused with one of his tiny sweaters in her hands and thought about it for a second. Kids were unpredictable. "Where do you want to go?"

"Home."

"Where is home?"

"Riverton. I can play with Thomas every day." RJ bounced out of his chair. "Can we, Momma?"

"I don't know, baby. Do you remember the rule?"

"Never go back, never look back." He scuffed the toe of his sneaker against the carpet. "I like Riverton."

"Me, too." She continued folding their clothes and putting them into the backpacks. "How about we think about it over a Big Mac?"

"Yeah."

She could already tell he didn't believe her, by the way his shoulders drooped, and he went to grab his bear from the bed.

Sometimes running from a threat you couldn't see sucked donkey balls. Today was one of those days. At some point she was going to need to pick a town and make a stand. She just didn't want RJ in the crosshairs when she did so. And she had exactly zero clue about how to make that stand and keep him safe. Maybe it was time to reach out to some of her old contacts and see if they could help her out.

You have one favor you haven't called in yet.

She shook off the reminder that last favor was her final line of defense. She couldn't—no, not wouldn't—she absolutely couldn't use that unless it came down to RJ living or dying.

CHAPTER NINE

Nemesis Inc. Headquarters, Montana

Rexar sat cross-legged on the floor of his cage at HQ. He pulled back the slide and visually checked there wasn't a round in the chamber of his Glock, then pushed the take-down latch downward. He needed to do something with his hands, to keep them moving. His knuckles were already bruised to shit from spending so much time at the punching bag.

"Why're you hiding in here?" Kentucky stuck his head around the side of the locker in his cage next door.

"Probably the same thing you are." He held up the Glock. "Cleaning weapons."

"Want to talk about it?"

"Not particularly." He removed the recoil bar with the captivated spring. "Why, you upgrading to shrink?"

"Nope. I just wondered..."

"Wondered what?" If it didn't involve getting off his butt to retrieve it, he'd have considered throwing the barrel at

Kentucky. But he figured that wouldn't do him much good as the fucker would probably keep it. Plus, he would be pissed with himself if he damaged it.

"If you want to come down to California with the rest of us for a couple of days?"

"Why?"

"I want to..." Kentucky scrubbed his hand over his shaved head. "I want to see how Becky's doing and maybe meet up with some of the guys from Teams."

"Ah." He thought about it for a couple of minutes. Tex had worked with a lot of people out of Cali; maybe he'd moved there after he'd retired. Although he didn't think so. "Um, we aren't on rotation next week?"

"Yeah, that's why I'm going this weekend," Kentucky explained. "Draven is going home to see his grandfather, and Tate has a date in town on Saturday night."

The others are goin' with you?"

"Thinkin' on it."

"I'm not sure I want to be the third wheel on your date with Becky." He remembered the terrified woman who'd been rescued with Cormack's Willy. *Willow*, he reminded himself. She wasn't the kid he'd watched growing up anymore. She was Jeep's wife. But if she ever stopped calling him Uncle Rex, he was introducing Jeep to his fists. She'd been theirs first. Eli's daughter, his and Dalton's goddaughter.

With the weapon laid out on the tarp in front of him, he went through the motions of cleaning it. "Driving or flying?"

"Flying. We don't have time for a two-day drive."

Dayum, he'd been just about ready to say yes. But, flying. "Man, I'm not sure... civilian flight, confined spaces, it's not really my jam these days."

"You fly on planes all the time with us."

He understood Kentucky's confusion. He flew on planes all the time. "But with assault weapons, handguns, and as many knives as I can strap onto my body."

"Ah."

"What the fuck does, 'ah,' mean?"

"I didn't think."

"Didn't think what?" Another side effect of his time in Iran was attempting to read between the lines on everything. Orders, work, those were so ingrained in his psyche he understood them, and he didn't have trouble with them. Dealing with people on a one-to-one level... that was a bigger issue than he cared to admit. Especially when he couldn't fall back on the habits of a lifetime and rely on Drax to translate for him.

"Mike's coming with us." Kentucky changed the subject and sweetened the deal as he did so.

"I thought he was going back to Isolde della Magdalena to see Castiel and Red Squadron." But maybe he'd heard him wrong. These days his attention span for anything aside from routines and orders wasn't anything to write home about.

"He's gonna fly out of San Diego." Kentucky stuffed some of his gear into his locker and slammed the door shut. "It's easier to go to Italy from there than Billings."

"True." He still didn't feel like Kentucky was giving him all the information. He knew this fucker way too well after working with him so closely for the last few months, and something was way off. The way the bunch of angry wasps took flight in his stomach warned him he was missing something.

"Spill it, Ken. What aren't you telling me?"

"Nothing."

"Lies."

"Watch your tone."

"Now you're sounding like the boss." Careful not to disturb the weapon pieces on the blanket in front of him, he got to his feet and crossed the cage to the wire. "Spit it out."

Kentucky squeezed both his eyes and fists closed, a sure-fire indicator he was praying for patience. "What makes you think there's more?"

"Because you've never worked so damn hard to get anyone to go on a weekend bar crawl, swarming with slags and bar flies, since I've been here."

"The boss thinks Mike is spiraling."

"My ass, there's no harder motherfucker than Mike."

"Truth, but that hardness he learned from the Taliban's whips and chains has also made him..." Kentucky trailed off as if he were searching for the right words, "...it makes him vulnerable."

"I dare you to say that to his face." Something still didn't fit. "Why are you saying this to me?"

"Because you both are good buds." Kentucky eyed him as if he expected to get punched for what was to come next. "You both dealt with the shit of being the POWs nobody will ever admit to, and you both lost years of your lives because you fucking *were* left behind when you shouldn't have been."

Suddenly the art of reading between the lines, which he'd perfected with his twin, came roaring into life. "So essentially you and the boss both think Mike and I are spiraling and all y'all are hoping by taking us back to Coronado, that being in a familiar place will snap our brains back into shape?" Well, wasn't that a kick in the balls he hadn't known he needed? He supposed it was sort of true in a way. Except he wasn't spiraling, and he didn't think Mike was either. "So..." he had to choose his words carefully here. Getting punched in the mouth for being a disrespectful dick wasn't something on his shit-to-do list today. "So, what you're saying is you think we need an intervention?"

That sounded reasonable... right?

"What I'm saying is, we think you need to get your asses off this ranch and around people who aren't operators."

"Soo, that's why you're taking us down to Coronado. To get away from Operators?" He could do factitious with the best of them if he had to. "San Diego is crawling with Spec Ops. Kinda defeats the purpose to bring us there, doncha think?"

"Maybe, but it's that or send you home to your momma and let Mike figure out how to get his shit together enough to fly across the Atlantic without being arrested by the time the bird gets its wheels on the ground."

"That how you persuaded Mike to go?" He quirked up one eyebrow in Kentucky's direction. The Mike he knew would have punched the fucker for even suggesting he needed to gather his collective shit and stuff it in a suitcase for the trip to Italy.

"Hell no, I don't have a death wish." Ken crossed his cage and sat heavily enough onto the bench against the opposite wire wall to make the wooden seat creak under his weight as if it were deciding that today was the day it had enough of two hundred-plus pounds of muscle abusing its purpose. "I was kinda hoping you'd talk him into it."

"I call bullshit, bro. You just said a minute ago that he was going."

"Oh, he's coming to California," Kentucky clarified. "I need you to get him to agree to see the shrink before he gets on that plane."

"Why aren't you doing it?"

"Because like I said he's kinda hard for me to understand," Kentucky muttered. "I haven't walked in his shoes lately...."

"And I have?"

"Pretty much."

"Dude, he's pretty easy to deal with, you only need

three sentences with him." He couldn't help himself. The shit that was going to come out of his mouth confirmed once again that coming here to Montana had been the right decision. He ticked the sentences off on his fingers. "Jesus, help me. Are you for real..." He glanced at Kentucky to see that he was watching. when his commander nodded for him to go on, he did. "And most important, what the fuck?"

"Sounds about right."

He understood that they'd both been in similar positions, but still it burned his biscuits like an overheated oven that the job fell to him. "The boss can give him an order, Mike follows orders."

"Mike doesn't work for us."

True, but he had worked for Noble, or at least under his command in Teams. "Then have Noble give him the order."

"He doesn't work for Noble either," Kentucky reminded him. "The DOD revoked his security clearance, remember?"

"Yeah, mine too," Rexar muttered. "Didn't stop Dalton from hiring me."

"Bauer didn't threaten to cut Dalton's balls off if he hired you."

Whoa that pony and back the fuck up... what now?

"So why did he do that for Mike?" He was guessing he knew that answer, but he wanted Kentucky to admit it.

Ken scrubbed his hand over his head, from front to back a couple of times, "Because Noble likes to keep his Operators happy, and Castiel..."

Yup, that confirmed it. He didn't need him to finish that sentence and interrupted him. "And Castiel wants Mike back in Italy."

"Pretty much sums it up, I think."

"Fuck," He went back to his place on the floor. His hands worked from muscle memory as he went through the motions of cleaning the Glock. "What do you want from me?"

"We'll get him to California," Kentucky said. "You get him to agree to see the shrink."

Fabulous, how the hell am I supposed to do that?

It probably wouldn't hurt to try, but man, he knew from experience that the last thing Mike probably wanted to do was talk about it.

"No promises." He pointed a trigger toward Kentucky. He'd suck it up and fly freaking commercial to help Mike. "I won't force him, if he doesn't want to go."

Kentucky pulled out a whet stone and went about sharpening a knife. "No point if he doesn't want to. Seeing the shrink never fucking works if the one visiting doesn't agree to it in the first place."

"Truth."

Silence settled between them as they worked. "When do you want to go?"

"Later today."

"Okay."

Kentucky's brows drew together. "I kinda thought you'd put up more of a fight."

"It's not me who's going to visit the shrink."

"Maybe you should, too."

Yeah, he'd seen that one coming a mile off. He sucked the instinct to refuse to go deep down inside him.

"Fuck off," he snarled. "If you want my help, you'll drop that shit right now."

"Roger that."

He raised both eyebrows, and probably looked like a freaking cartoon idiot, but didn't care; Kentucky could deal. "I'm serious Ken, the second anyone starts taking about me going... I'm outta there, even if I have to hire a fucking truck and drive all the way back myself."

He was going to take Kentucky's shrug as agreement. Now he just had to figure out how to tell Mike he was visiting the shrink... maybe he could just hogtie him and drop him off at the front door... that might be simpler.

CHAPTER TEN

California

Lily double checked the car one last time, making sure she had everything. Joe, bless his heart, didn't mention the leather driving gloves she wore. Although she was sure if she'd taken out her disinfectant spray and a cloth, it may have raised more than his eyebrows as the gloves did. His suspicions would be sky high then for sure.

"I think that's everything." She smiled at the older man. When she'd saved his butt from going to jail five years ago, she hadn't known theirs would become a business friendship.

"I think so too, missy." Joe scratched the side of his head with a pen before he handed her the clipboard, "Sign here and here."

"I think you just want my autograph."

"Yeah, I'm going to upload this on that eBay site and be a millionaire before dawn." Joe grinned at her. "You're a famous rockstar in disguise."

"No." She shook her head, a soft smile on her lips. She

quite enjoyed the guessing game they had going on. Every time she bought a vehicle from him or through one of his contacts across the country, he took a guess at what she was running from. "You said that one last time."

"I did, huh?"

"Yes, you did." She scrawled an illegible signature across the two spots on the change of ownership document. "Seeing as you already used that one, have another guess."

"I'm running out of options here," Joe muttered. "You're an informant for the cops, and the Mob are after you."

"No, not the Mob."

"But you are running."

Dang it, he would pick up on that wouldn't he? Joe was more astute than he let on. But being a used car salesman, she supposed that was necessary for his job.

"Not from anything I've done." She resisted the urge to squeeze her eyes shut. Doing so would let him know she'd screwed up and given him more than she wanted to.

"Missy, if you need some help, you call me, and I'll come fetch you and the boy."

"That's very sweet of you, Joe." She trailed off as she didn't know what else to say.

"I'm serious, Missy. Anytime, day or night, if you call my number I'll come running." He took the clipboard back, "I have some people who might be able to help."

"No." She winced internally at her sharpness, and softened her tone. "No. I promise, we'll be okay." It was time to find a new place to source her vehicles. She didn't want to risk putting Joe and his family in danger. "We're thinking of going down to Mexico to ride out the rest of the winter."

"Baja is nice this time of year."

"Yes, it is." She sat in her new-to-her-once-again car and placed the key into the ignition, turning it over. It may be an older model, but it also didn't have GPS. Being untraceable was important right now. With this car registered to Joe's wife, as long as she didn't get pulled over, she was relatively safe.

"Thanks again, Joe. Look after yourself."

"That's sounding an awful lot like a goodbye, Missy. Careful or you'll make me mist up." He closed her into the car.

Once again, he confirmed how astute he was.

She hit the button on the electric window. "It's a see you later. I don't like goodbyes." She'd figured out real fast what happened the last time she'd used the word 'goodbye' when she wasn't going to see someone who mattered for a long time. Goodbyes were tempting fate. She'd never do that again. Ever.

"Me either." Joe tapped his hand on the roof. "You and the little man drive safe now."

"Thank you. See ya." She adjusted the mirrors and reversed until she was facing the street. "Whatcha say we go and get that Big Mac, RJ?"

"Can I get a toy too?"

"You sure can."

"Yay."

Four hours later she lay on the bed, curled around RJ, and gently took the book which had come in place of a toy in the Happy Meal she'd bought him, along with his Big Mac. Who knew McDonald's gave fairytale books in place of toys? Whichever employee had come up with that brainwave... they deserved a raise.

She carefully extracted the book from his hands and closed it one-handed. "Night, baby." She kept her voice low enough not to wake him and crawled off the bed.

Please be empty, please be empty.

She hit the power button on her laptop and fired it up. Going through the motions of bouncing her IP address across the globe was second nature at this point. She drummed her nails lightly on the small worktable. Delays, even one for less than a minute, drove her nuts.

"Finally." She pulled up a TOR browser, just to add another layer of security, and navigated to her email account. "You better be empty."

She went to grab a bottle of juice out of the to-go bag and returned to the computer in time for the program to open... and scowled at the little red dot on her notifications.

"I will find you, fucker." But she knew it was bravado talking. She didn't have the luxury of tracking whoever was behind the emails. She clicked on the highlighted link to open it and scanned the message. She could confirm her blood pressure was rising just by reading a freaking email. It could absolutely go straight through the roof with one click of a battery-powered mouse. "Target *me*, asshole, not my child."

Coming back here to this hotel had been stupid. She should have just kept going when she'd picked up the car.

"Get your butt on the road, sister." But where could she go? She'd traveled all over the states, with no rhyme or reason to where she went next. She wanted to bah, or gah, or maybe even arrr like a freaking pirate but she didn't dare; opening her mouth now would mean screaming, and that would wake RJ.

She shut down the computer and headed for the bathroom. With the water running in the shower, maybe she could muffle the sounds of her frustration enough that they didn't disturb her son's sleep.

Virginia

TEX CHEWED SLOWLY, not really paying attention to the food, and studied the photograph he'd printed out after Rexar had emailed it to him. "Who are you, Lily Mitchell?"

I know you from somewhere. How do I know you?

It was driving him nuts. A puzzle he couldn't figure out was rare. A person he couldn't find—even rarer.

The sound of his phone buzzing made him frown. He lowered the forkful of lasagna which had been aiming for his mouth. He loved the guys and the girl posse as Dude called them, but coming between him and the Italian food he'd been craving all week... it was a toss-up as to which would win. Even as he thought it, he knew it was a lie. If they called, he'd answer.

Every. Time.

"Go."

"Hey, Tex, it's Cookie."

"Hey, man, how's our girl?"

"She's why I'm calling..."

He immediately tensed. His brain took off at a million miles a minute. He pushed the plate of food aside and tugged his laptop across the desk. He flipped the screen from the facial recon search he was running for Rexar Mitchell, and his fingers hovered over the keyboard ready to fly as soon as he knew what was going on.

"Hit me. Where. When—"

"Tex, bro, relax. Fee's right here next to me."

Relief slammed into him, so hard he reared back in his chair, his prosthetic leg thumping off the desk as he did. For once he didn't even notice the jolt of pain which would normally have knocked him on his ass.

"Thank fuck."

"Fee just wanted to talk to you."

"Lead with that next time, dumbass."

"Sorry."

But while Cookie didn't sound one bit sorry at all, and Tex was so damn relieved that he could hear the happiness in his friend's voice.

"Sure, Gimme our girl, let me talk to her." He could hear murmuring on the other end of the phone.

"Hi."

"Fiona." He heard the relief in his own voice. Hell, that wouldn't have taken a rocket scientist. "How are you doing?"

"I'm good. I promise." Her voice was hesitant.

"Before this goes any further let me make this clear. Don't be embarrassed. Don't be upset. When PTSD sucker-punches you, all you can do is ride it out as safely as possible."

"But I…"

"I'm not done." His voice was filled with affection, laced with a side of sternness. "You never have to apologize to me when your demons stalk you. All you need to do is promise me, you will call me if you need me."

"Okay. Deal." She whispered softly.

When he heard her inhale, he knew she had more to say, so he waited for her to gather her thoughts.

"Thank you for looking after me when Hunter wasn't here to do it."

The only thing that sucked about living so far away was Tex wasn't able to give her a big hug. Instead, he had to settle for whispering back, "Anytime you need me, I'm here. If you call, I'll answer."

"Tex is the shit show supervisor." In the background he could hear Cookie reassuring her that everything was okay. "He doesn't mind what time of the day or night it is; if I'm not here and you need someone, you call him, baby."

I think he's more of a miracle worker than a shit show supervisor," Fiona replied.

"That, too."

He couldn't help himself teasing them. "As your shit show

supervisor, I feel it's my solemn duty to give you this week-end's safety brief." He put on his best impression of Wolf's voice. "Don't add to the population, unless that's in your future plans. Don't subtract from the population in the continental United States." He could hear Fiona giggling at his tone, and it sounded like Cookie had spewed something, probably coffee.

"Eww, Hunter, it's in my hair."

Yup, coffee for sure.

He continued on. "Don't end up in the hospital, or in the newspaper, and please avoid jail at all times. Staging a breakout is getting expensive these days. Should you end up in jail, please establish dominance quickly, to make sure you are still in one piece while I send around my Stetson like a mime on the street, to collect enough bail money to get you out."

"Stop, Tex, I can't breathe."

Mission accomplished. Fiona laughing so hard she could barely speak made his heart happy. He'd take it any day of the week and twice on a Sunday over the terror and fear in her voice from the last time he'd spoken to her on the phone while she was holed up at that hotel near San Francisco.

"Okay stopping, I'll behave."

"Sure, you will," Cookie muttered. "We just wanted to say hi and thank you…"

"Don't you dare finish that sentence, bro," he warned.

"Have a good weekend, Tex."

"Bye, you two." He hit *end* on the call and tugged his lasagna toward him, once again scooping the forkful toward his mouth. His hand paused before he got the food into his mouth and what had been bugging him slapped him upside the head. He returned the fork to the plate.

"Shit. It can't be that simple—can it?"

He logged back into the hotel security systems he'd used

for the hotel Fiona had been staying at. This right here was the reason hackers left backdoors open for themselves. You never knew when you might need to use them again. Scrolling through the files he'd saved he searched for the one from the day Cookie had gone to pick up Fiona.

"There you are."

Tex glanced at his phone. He could call Rexar. No, he would wait until he confirmed it. Clicking the mouse twice, he opened the video footage for the link. In his head he replayed the conversations he'd had with both Fiona and Cookie at that time. Hearing their voices had gone a long way to settling the unease he'd been battling within himself.

On screen he could just make out Fiona throwing herself at Cookie before the door closed behind them. He watched the pregnant doctor waiting in the corridor. The room next to Fiona's opened a crack before a woman appeared. He tapped the mouse to freeze the screen. The quality was beyond shit and fuzzy as all get out. He tilted his head to one side, his eyes flicking from the photo in his hand to the screen.

"There you are."

He backed out of the camera system and went to the front desk registration systems. Maybe the name she'd used there was one she'd used previously, or he'd be able to track her based off it. Pulling his second laptop toward him, he went back into the security system and started pulling footage.

"This is going to take forever." He stuffed a pencil into the corner of his mouth and chewed on it. While he waited on his program to do its thing to get him into the booking system, he started looking at video footage.

On screen, he found her again. She smiled at the doorman and she and the small child with her entered the hotel. Tex split the screen in two and pulled up the cameras for the outside of the hotel, his fingers flying over the keys as he combined the necessary codes to pull everything with Lily's face, and went back to the image of her entering the hotel less than an hour ago.

"Ding, ding, ding, it's a boy." A quick look at the time-stamp confirmed they were probably still at the hotel. He reached for his phone and punched in the number from memory.

"Hello?"

"I got her."

CHAPTER ELEVEN

"You shittin' me?" Rexar dropped the duffel he was carrying and braced his hand against the window of the airport building. His knees decided they weren't working today. A full-on knee strike was called for and both of his were turning up with bells and whistles on. "You're sure it's her?"

"Nope, I'm not shitting you, and yes I'm sure it's her." Tex sounded annoyed. "Get your ass to San Francisco stat. I'm going to send Wolf Steel up there to make sure she doesn't rabbit."

She's in California, holy fucking shit. What were the chances?

"Bro?"

He waved off Kentucky's question and focused on Tex. "I'm just getting on a flight to San Diego," Rexar told Tex. "Is there a way to make sure she doesn't leave until I get there?"

"Not unless you have an arrest warrant and a cop," Tex said. "Want me to send Steel on ahead, or do you want him to wait for you?"

"Shit, I don't know. One sec." Rexar glanced over his shoulder at where Kentucky, Mike, and the rest of the boys were waiting on him. For once, the concern in their eyes didn't rub him completely the wrong way.

"What's going on, Rex?" Mike asked the question the rest were probably thinking.

"Tex found my wife and kid... Keegan, my *kid*."

"Congratulations, it's a boy," Tex immediately answered. "At least going off what he's wearing, that's my guess."

A son, I have a son. Holy fucking shit. Those knees which had been on strike a few seconds before now completely gave up the ghost and he slammed them into the concrete as he dropped onto them.

"A boy."

"Where?" Mike asked loud enough that Tex obviously heard him.

"Give the phone to Mike, man. He sounds like his brain-cells are working more than yours right now."

Oh, the fucking irony. But as he had no words—none, nada, zip—Rexar did as he was asked and held the phone out to Mike. "Talk."

"Fuck, okay." Mike put the phone to his ear, "Hey, Tex. Talk to me, because he's giving me exactly nothing."

He paused, clearly listening to what Tex had to say.

"In a hotel near San Francisco." Mike clicked his fingers and gestured to Kentucky. "You're sending Wolf Steel up there with a crew, to make sure if she moves, they can tail her. Roger that, one sec." Mike pulled the phone away from his ear, "Ken, we ain't goin' to Coronado; get us flights to San Fran, stat."

Kentucky narrowed his eyes at Rexar as if he'd planned this shit to happen today, huffed out a breath, and nodded to Mike. "On it. Hunt, you're with me."

"Copy." Caleb grabbed his duffel, fell into step with Kentucky, and they disappeared from view into the terminal.

"Hmm, sure. Uh-huh."

"Words, Mike," Now that he'd managed to remind his legs how to work and his lungs how to breathe, it was making him crazy that he couldn't hear what was going on. "Fuck, Gimme the phone back." He made grabby fingers with his hand.

Mike met his gaze and nodded. "Handing you back to Rex," he told Tex. "Good to talk to you, Keegan. Yup, later."

Rexar took the phone, "Hey, sorry…"

"If someone else today starts off with the sorry shit, I'm going to lose my damn mind," Tex grumbled.

"Sor—fuck—go on."

"Ha," Tex snorted. "Okay, I have her at the hotel until tomorrow morning. But she may bug out during the night."

"Shit. Tex, man, I have no words."

"Yo," Ken's call was followed by a sharp whistle. "They have one flight, and the gate is closing in twenty minutes. Move your asses."

"I—"

"I heard," Tex assured him. "Go. When you get to San Fran, call me and I'll give you Wolf's number."

"Thanks, man." He grabbed his duffel and took off at a fast jog toward the terminal door. For the first time in forever he wasn't stressed about getting to the security gate. He didn't give one flying monkey, never mind two, about emptying his pockets and going through the scanner. He just wanted everyone in front of him to hurry the fuck up so he could get his butt on the plane, and the plane in the air. Would the pilot let him fly? He didn't think so. Maybe he should ask… but he dismissed it as a ridiculous notion. He knew better.

Focus, Mitchell. You need a plan for when your butt gets on the ground.

"Remember, we change in Denver and get the connecting

flight to San Fran." Tate grabbed his duffel off the x-ray table and stepped back to put on his boots.

"Fabulous. You're telling me I get to do this all over again in a couple of hours." Rexar grabbed his shit-kickers off the tray and his duffel, then stood next to Tate with his butt against the wall to put on his own boots.

"Pretty much." Tate lifted one shoulder. Rexar envied him his ability to blend into places. Tate with his five-foot, eleven-inch height and slim build didn't stand out in regular places like airports and stores.

"Thought you had a date?"

"Changed my mind." Tate replied.

"You mean she blew you off."

"Nope."

"Mommy, why does that man have ouches?"

When the child's words filtered through the noise of the airport, he glanced at Tate, and both as one scanned the area looking for someone bleeding or with a bandage.

"Can I ask him if I can kiss it better?"

"No sweetie, I don't think the man wants to be bothered." A woman's voice—he was assuming she was Mommy—replied.

Rexar spun toward the voices, searching the area between him and the couple and their daughter. "I don't see anyone, do you?"

"Nah, man," Tate muttered. "C'mon, if there's someone in trouble, let security deal with it. We have a plane to catch and your wife to find."

"Yeah." Unfortunately, even though Tate's words made sense, the unease roiling through his body made him take another look.

"Man, can I kiss your ouches better?"

The tug on his pant leg confused him.

"Molly, come back here." The mom hurried toward him. "Leave the nice soldier alone."

Holy shit, she means me.

He glanced down at the little girl looking earnestly up at him. "Hi."

"Hi, man. You has ouchies."

"I suppose I did have." His fingers went to the deep furrow which now ran from the corner of his right eye to his ear and then down to the corner of his lip. "But they don't hurt anymore."

"I kiss them better."

"You don't need to, little miss." He crouched down to her level, not wanting to scare her by towering over her. Not that he thought she was scared of anything given how she'd just marched right across the room and tugged on his pant leg.

She pointed at herself, poking her chest. "Molly, not little miss."

Was his son like this child? Or rather had he been at the same age? It was the only thing keeping him in place as Molly's fingers traced the worst of his scars.

"Okay, you don't need to, Molly, they don't hurt anymore." He reassured her again.

"I'm so sorry, sir. Molly hasn't learned the art of..."

"Don't worry about it, ma'am, I have a son a little older than her. She's good." He managed a smile for them both. Shit, would his scars be the first thing his son noticed about him? He hoped not. But this encounter with Molly now put the possibility on his list of shit to prepare for.

The airport announcement system crackled into life with a ding. "Final call, United Airlines, flight 648 to Denver, the gate is now closing. All remaining passengers, please make your way to gate A2 immediately."

"You ready, Mitchell?" Kentucky came to a stop next to him. "We've got a plane to catch. They're closing the gate."

"I'm coming. I heard it, too." He tugged on one of Molly's pigtails. "Have a nice flight, little one."

"I's going to see the mouse."

"You are, huh?"

"Yes." She nodded with her hair flying. "And the princesses."

Would he have the chance to take his son to Disneyland? Damn, he had a lot of catching up to do.

"Have fun." He turned away at another call from the guys but paused and looked over his shoulder when Molly's mother called after him.

"Thank you for your service, sirs."

"It was our honor." Fuck so much for not drawing attention to themselves. Thankfully Kentucky didn't mention it as they headed toward the gate at a fast pace.

"Five bucks," Caleb muttered. "Five bucks, that it happens again."

"I don't know, Cal, he can't be that…." Tate trailed off, snapping his mouth shut as if he didn't want to test fate. "I'll take you up on that five bucks though."

"Ha, I thought you might."

Rexar was tempted to mutter some choice words when, just as the boys were betting on, airport security came to a stop next to Bryan.

"Excuse me, sir, can you step out of the line?"

"Sure."

"Hah, hand it over, dude."

Caleb smacked Tate on the shoulder hard enough that he took a step forward.

"Jeez, can you guys fricking behave for five minutes until we get out of here?" Kentucky grumbled. "It's like traveling with a bunch of five-year-olds."

"I feel that," the second security guard replied. "They remind me of my cousins on a family trip."

Getting through security took forever when you traveled as a pack. Even though he'd already half expected Bryan to get himself pulled out of the line for an extra check. The delay frustrated the shit out of him when all he wanted to do was get his butt to the hotel and check she was still there.

"I turn off my phone now, right?"

"Think so." Caleb shifted his duffel from one shoulder to the other. "We're getting on the bird, so you can't do any tech voodoo with that thing."

The security guard's head whipped around to look at him.

"If your big mouth gets me searched, I'm going to kick your ass."

"You and which army?"

"Dude, I'm a Sailor; we don't need no army to help us open a can of whoop-ass."

"Damn straight," the security officer muttered. "Maybe I'll just look at this one instead," he turned toward Caleb.

"Check his ball sack too," Rexar advised.

"Shut the fuck up, Mitchell."

Whoops, maybe he'd pushed Kentucky too far. His commander's hand whipped out to smack both on the back of the head with one swipe. "Y'all are a bunch of assholes, shut the fuck up, stat." He repeated, "How copy?"

Sometimes the man was just a damn spoilsport. Did he not know, Rexar at least was acting like this because standing in line to go through security was fucking with his brain? Either way it didn't matter, he supposed, and answered the only way acceptable to Kentucky.

"Yes, sir."

"Copy that."

"Keep pouting, Hunt, and I swear to fuck, seeing as we don't have latrines," Kentucky whispered furiously, "I'm having the boss send you down to the barn for shit cleaning duty the second we get our asses home."

"Yes, sir, I'll behave, I swear."

"My ass." The second the words were out of his mouth, Rexar squeezed his eyes shut. He knew better, damn it.

"You'll be joining him, Mitchell."

"What?"

"You heard me." Kentucky pulled out the small notebook he kept in his top pocket and scribbled a note.

Well, fuckballs almighty. There went his next week. Once Kentucky scribbled a reminder of some transgression, there was no getting out of it.

Kentucky passed out boarding passes, "I couldn't get us seats together, so watch your mouths and don't get us arrested," he ordered. "Mike, Rex, you are in front of me. We board from the back of the plane."

"Roger that." He could behave for just over two hours, get through security again and deal with a second two-hour flight…right? He hoped so, because if he didn't, he'd lose sight of Lily and his son. He didn't even know his son's name. By tomorrow night, he *would* know it. Nothing and nobody was going to stop him.

Virginia

TEX SCANNED page after page of reports and files. Now he had a location, a hotel, a face, a name, and a throwaway credit card number used to book the hotel room. Tracing Lily Mitchell, aka Lily Yelverton's steps backward was ridiculously easy.

"I'm missing something." He massaged his thigh. Sitting at this desk for the last two days straight wasn't helping his leg any. It hurt like a mother—he needed to get up and stretch it some. But then it was a puzzle and he had to figure it out.

He flicked through the screens looking for the file Noble

Bauer had sent him on Rexar's capture and subsequent rescue from Section 209. Something smelled as bad as a dog who'd been skunked there, too.

"Besides being married, there has to be a crossover that I'm not seeing." He hit *print* on both files and grabbed a highlighter pen. Maybe if he highlighted what pinged on his radar, it would stand out to him. "I thought I'd left this stuff back in high school." He grabbed the paperwork off the printer and got to work. He would figure this shit out... a quick glance at the clock told him he didn't have much time before Rexar made it to California. He'd made it through four pages when his phone dinging pulled his attention away from the task at hand.

Wolf: In situ, confirm target is still at location?

His computer hadn't pinged to say Lily's hotel hallway had any movement, but he took a second to scroll back through the footage from the last half hour and checked the code to make sure it hadn't been tampered with before responding.

Tex: Confirmed.

Wolf: Our incoming?

He flipped over to the airport arrivals page and scanned for the flight information.

Tex: thirty minutes from LZ.

Wolf: Mozart and Benny will pick them up.

Tex: Copy.

That should have been the end of the conversation, but there went his instincts again, knocking on the door of his brain insisting there was something he was missing. He typed out a message, deleted it, and tried again. There was no way to say it without raising suspicions. He wouldn't leave Wolf and his men in the wind without having all the intel Tex had. Even if that intel was just his guts doing summersaults.

Tex: Keep a handle on Rex if his people don't do it.

Wolf: He's gonna be a problem?

Tex: My gut says there's more I'm not seeing.

Wolf: got it.

Thank fuck. He'd worked with this man often enough that Wolf picked up on his unease and didn't question it. Ice was one hell of a woman, and Wolf a lucky guy. A relationship such as theirs may not be in his future... but it didn't mean he didn't regret that he'd never have one like it.

"If wishes were horses, beggars could ride. Get your ass back to work."

He picked up his highlighter and for once took his own advice. He'd figure this shit out. He just hoped it was before he found out he'd messed up by finding this woman and child for Rexar Mitchell.

CHAPTER TWELVE

The second the seat belt light went off, Rexar popped the clasp, opening the restraints. If he could have gotten away with not using it at all, he would have. Anything restraining him these days took multiple rounds of breathing four square to keep from revolting against it.

"You good, Mike?"

"No," Mike muttered under his breath. "I need to get outta this tin can, stat."

"I feel that in my balls, man. Just give it a second for most people to get off before we move," he whispered in return. "If there's a stranger behind me, I might lose my shit."

He figured putting the delay on himself would be easier on Mike. If this turned out not to be Lily, he'd see about going to Italy with Mike. That Drax lived there too would make it a plausible option. But at least Mike wouldn't have to do a transatlantic trip, commercial, by himself. He made a mental note to speak to Kentucky and Dalton about it later.

"Yup."

He inhaled and wrinkled his nose against the smell of people. Two hours on a tin can as Mike called it, made for almost as much body odor as living in a containerized housing unit with the guys for a week straight while waiting on orders. "Four square, bro, Four square."

"Copy that."

In sync they inhaled for a count of four. Then held it for a count of four, before releasing it for four, and then waiting for another count of four before doing it all over again. As ridiculous as some people might think it was, four square worked. They'd perfected it in the military to slow their nerves and breathing. Avoiding panic in combat was always a good thing.

"Another ten to go," Kentucky whispered through the gap in the seats from his position behind them. Clearly, he'd overheard the whole conversation.

Rexar figured that didn't matter though. Ken knew the score with both of them, and he'd be an idiot not to keep track of how his guys were doing. Out of the corner of his eye, he started counting people as they moved past his seat.

"Three more," Kentucky confirmed.

Rexar elbowed Mike. "C'mon, dude, what do you say we pop smoke and blow this joint?"

"Jeez, Rex, don't say that too loud or you're gonna get us arrested," Kentucky grumbled.

"Ha." He got to his feet and hunched his shoulders and head. Smacking his skull on the overhead locker wasn't something he wanted to try today, or any day. He glanced over his shoulder to make sure there weren't any stragglers and made eye contact with Kentucky.

Kentucky quirked up one eyebrow, silently asking if they were both okay.

Rexar nodded, yes, we're fine. There was no way he'd freaking admit his stomach was a whole jamble of nerves. And he knew jamble probably wasn't even a word, but he also didn't care—it was now.

He dragged a duffel out of the overhead locker and knew by the feel of the handle it wasn't his,

"That's yours, Mike."

"Thanks."

He grabbed the other bag and turned toward the door of the plane. This was it. As soon as they made it through security and out of the airport... he wasn't sure what would happen then, but the world could just bring it on. He. Was. Ready.

Finally, they made it to the head of the line and one by one handed over their IDs to the person behind the desk. Rexar strode after Kentucky with Mike next to him as they walked through the arrivals gate.

"Yo, Smith." A voice yelled and as one they turned toward it.

"Mozart, good to see you."

Rexar made short work of cataloging the features on the tall, muscular man Kentucky smacked hands with before dragging him into a bro hug. His dark hair was just a shade too long to be within normal Navy regs, so he was going to take a wild-ass guess and put him in the Naval Special Warfare category.

SEAL.

Yes, one of the Brotherhood for sure.

The man had high cheekbones and dark eyes. His face was split by three deep scars on the right side.

"Ken, we gotta scoot. Benny's double parked," Mozart said. "The lot is jam-packed, and someone's waiting on a tow truck near the other door, so it's mayhem out there."

"Sure thing." Kentucky nodded to them. "You sure you can fit everyone?"

"Yeah, we borrowed a van." Mozart turned and strode away toward the door. "Which one of you is Mitchell?"

"Me."

"I have something for you from Tex when we get to the van."

"Thanks." *What the hell? Had they grabbed Lily already? Shit.* He'd wanted to see her face when she realized he wasn't dead. That her friends in fucking Iran hadn't succeeded. "Lead on."

They stepped out into the late evening sunshine, and Rexar flipped his mirrored shades down over his eyes. Mozart hadn't been wrong. Everyone in California appeared to have converged in the arrivals parking lot of San Francisco International Airport. Horns blared. Voices rose and fell in arguments and swearing at being blocked from moving forward or back.

"Holy shit."

"Yeah," Mozart moved along at an easy gait. "Benny's over here. I can see the top of the van."

"You mean the daffodil-yellow monstrosity?"

"Yeah." Mozart grinned and smirked. "I figure there must be something going on this weekend, because everyone and their mother were hiring vans."

"If you brought me out here," Bryan muttered, "and San Fran is going to get hit with the big one, I'm telling you now, you gotta explain that shit to my momma."

"Aww, are you scared of a little shaking?" Tate teased. "Wuss."

"Hell fucking yes," Bryan grumbled. "I may be from Kansas, but I'm no witch and I'm not looking to get a house dropped on my head."

"That was a tornado, dumbass." Mozart slid back the door of the panel van. "Or do I need to start callin' you brick or something?"

"Brick, I like that." Kentucky settled himself into one of the bench seats. He reached into his top pocket for his notebook and scribbled a note. "There, you just got dubbed."

"No. Nope. What the fuck?" Bryan complained, "That's not how this works."

"Hell, yes it does," Benny called over his shoulder. "Why the heck do you think he's called Mozart?"

"Don't ever sing karaoke down in Coronado," Mozart advised. "You end up with weird-ass monikers and I've got the only good one in the bunch."

He slammed the door, shutting Bravo team and Mike into the rear of the van and climbed into the passenger seat next to Benny.

Rexar listened to the banter back and forth. While they hadn't met these two men before, or at least he hadn't, most military teams were similar. Let them throw a bit of snark and shit, back them up when they needed it, and let them mutter and complain and you were pretty much on the path to a solid friendship.

"How are we gonna get out of here?" Benny scowled at the minivan which clearly didn't see his turn signal as he went to merge into traffic.

"Fucked if I know," Mozart muttered, "but don't jump the curb because it's a hundred dollar fine and Wolf will freak."

"Yeah, not doing that." Benny replied.

Rexar scanned the van but didn't see whatever it was that Tex had sent for him. "Hey, Mozart, you said you had something for me?"

"Oh yeah, one sec." Mozart's head disappeared as he bent down to pick something off the footwell. "Here."

He took the envelope Mozart held over his shoulder. and turned it over. "Did he say what this is?"

"Not to me anyway." Mozart pointed to a minuscule gap in traffic and Benny somehow managed to fit the nose of their van in there.

"Wolf said Tex said whatever it is he's cleaned it." Benny ignored the asshole who blasted him with the horn.

"Cleaned as in laundered?" Caleb asked. "If Keegan is sending him cash, where's ours?"

He ignored the conversation going on around him. If Tex had sent him this, it was important. His fingers fumbled with the flap, but he didn't dare rip it open. Opening it carefully, he peered in, and his breath caught in his throat. "Holy shit."

"You say something, bro?" Mike leaned over his shoulder.

"It's photos." He slid them out of the envelope. They were clearly stills taken from security camera footage, but to him they were enough to sucker punch him. "My boy." His fingers traced down over the little boy's face.

"Holy fuck, he looks like you and Drax." Mike nudged him with his shoulders. "The Mitchell genes run strong in him for sure."

"Yeah." The tiny bit of niggling doubt that Lily had been lying about this too evaporated. There was no way on earth this boy was anything but his son.

"Well, he's either yours or Drax's." Mike grinned at him. "And considering we all know which side of the street Drax lives on, I'm going to guess he's yours."

"Yeah." He flipped through the other papers, not pausing to look at Lily's picture. He didn't want or need to get pissed all over again.

Or devastated.

Shut up, don't go there.

He busied himself with flipping through the file Tex had sent him. Jeez, Tex should have writing on the outside of the envelope—guaranteed to give heart failure, or some kind of similar warning. Especially for the last fucking page—a birth certificate—for his son. Rexar James Yelverton.

"She's using my—my mother's maiden name?"

She has some fucking audacity.

He packed up all the feelings swirling inside him, and somewhere found a piece of mental twine to tie them all together with a pretty fucking bow, and stuffed them into the box in his head where he hid everything he wasn't quite ready to deal with yet. After pushing the papers back into the envelope, he tapped Mozart on the shoulder. "What's the plan?"

"Get you to the hotel, then we're waiting on Tex, I think."

"Let's do it."

"Working on it, man, I'm working on it." Benny finally got them out of the airport and turned into traffic which thankfully was running at a decent pace for once. "ETA about twenty minutes."

He could wait twenty minutes. Maybe. "Sounds good."

CHAPTER THIRTEEN

Lily got to her feet and arched her back. This cleaning everything from top to bottom each time she moved was playing hell on her back. If she ever got to the point where she didn't have to run anymore, she would hire a cleaner and pay her double. She never ever wanted to see another bottle of bleach or furniture polish...ever.

She poked her head out of the bathroom to check on RJ. Maybe she should just check out in the morning, like a normal person. But old habits die hard, or so they, whoever they were, said. She'd been running for years and knew the people who were chasing her were either lazy or she wasn't where they wanted her to be just yet.

If they'd wanted to catch her, they could have in Memphis, when she'd had pneumonia. They were herding her. She knew it. She just didn't understand where or why. All she could do now was make sure she stayed ahead of them.

"Fuck you, CIA. Find someone else to terrorize."

Her gear was ready, everything was packed and waiting at the door. "I'll leave at six AM." God, talking to herself wasn't a sign of madness as she'd always thought. There was no one else to give her advice so she was asking herself the questions which needed answering and hoping she was logical enough to come up with a decent response. She set the alarm on her throwaway phone and curled up on the bed next to RJ. Six AM, she decided. That would have to be soon enough.

"Momma?" RJ's voice filtered into her dreams. "Momma, why you crying?"

"I'm not crying." By the wetness on her cheeks, she knew she was fudging the truth, buried her face into the pillow. "Momma just has something in her eyes."

Every single time she closed her eyes at this time of year, she dreamed the same dream. The picnic on a rooftop hotel, the dancing under the stars, and the hot sweaty nights spent exploring each other's bodies. But even her dreams couldn't offer her peace, because just when she would get to the point where she could almost touch him, the images in her head would turn from beautiful and bittersweet into the nightmare of the knock on the door a military wife never wants to get. One which changed her life forever.

"I don't know," RJ said with more maturity than any four-year-old should have. "When my eyes leak, we call it crying."

Lord, he had Rexar's snark. His little mini me. It was so fucking unfair that they never had the chance to know each other. She felt RJ moving on the bed and heard his feet hit the floor. She didn't dare move until she heard the bathroom door close. Sitting up in the bed, one glance in the mirror told her RJ was right. She'd been freaking ugly crying in her sleep. Her eyes stung. Her nose, as red as freaking Rudolph the Red-Nosed Reindeer's.

"Wonderful." She grabbed a tissue and blew her nose, just as she heard the toilet flush, "Don't forget to wash your hands, buddy."

"I doin' it."

"Good boy." She forced herself out of bed and fished her phone out from under the pillow. "RJ, did you turn off the alarm?"

"Yes, Momma, it was shouting."

"Shit."

"Momma, that's a bad word."

"It's a grown-up word, that's what it is." She kissed the top of his head. Eight o'clock, she was hours behind. She waited until she closed the restroom door behind her before she repeated, "shit," soft enough that her son with dog-like hearing abilities couldn't hear her.

It took her five minutes to do her morning routine and go back to the bedroom, "Turn on the TV for a bit, buddy, I've got to clean up before we go."

RJ didn't answer but grabbed the remote and put on the TV. An advert for Big Bear Holiday Cabins filled the screen, before cartoons came on.

She'd listened to that annoying jingle so much all week, that she mouthed along with the words. Who on earth would want to go to Big Bear at this time of the year? Up above the clouds they'd be snowed in for sure. Unless skiing and snow-boarding was your jam, this time of year, Big Bear Lake wasn't the place to be.

If you don't want someone to find you, Big Bear Lake might be just the place to go.

I'm an idiot. Why didn't I think of that?

Google is free, see how long it takes.

She grabbed her phone and typed 'distance from San Francisco to Big Bear Lake' into Google maps. Eight hours, and as it went back the way she came... maybe she could make it work. She clicked into the website and searched for availability.

They have vacancies. It's a sign... we should go...right?

"Hey, buddy, how would you like to go build a

snowman?"

"Really?"

"Yes." She quickly filled in the booking form and paid for it with a prepaid credit card she hadn't used before and heaved a sigh of relief when the system flashed with a green button confirming their reservation. She took a screenshot, then pushed the credit card back into her purse. "I'm just going to clean the bathroom, then what do you say we go find some snowsuits and go find somewhere to build that snowman?"

"Yay." RJ bounced out of his chair and jumped around the room, squealing.

"Shh, there might still be people sleeping. Inside voice, okay?"

He lowered his voice by a couple of decibels. She wrinkled her nose and huffed out a breath.

More freaking cleaning. Will it ever end?

Probably not. But she could live in hope, right?

After a round of scrubbing, she shoved everything into the suitcases and took one last look around the room. "Let's go buddy, we have to find a Goodwill with some snow gear."

* * *

THREE FREAKING GOODWILL stores later and she finally found a snowsuit which would fit RJ. She'd found a hot pink and orange one in her size at the first store. But each kid-sized one they'd come across had either been three sizes too big or at least two sizes too small. She made a mental note to rig the snow boots she'd picked up for RJ the same way she'd done for the tennis shoes.

"What do you think, bud? Do you like it?" She held her breath waiting for his answer. Internally wincing as he stuck his hand down the back of the suit's neck. "My neck's itchy."

"We'll ask the lady for scissors and take off the label, okay?" She'd figured that would be the case. Even with his own clothes or wearing something new, until the label was taken off, RJ was convinced it itched.

"'Kay, Momma."

She unzipped him and helped her son out of the suit, then got to her feet.

"Let's go pay, and go find a laundromat, because these clothes need washing before we wear them."

"Me no wants cooties."

It was such a typical boy thing to say, that she snorted a laugh. "Yeah, me neither."

She checked the tag for the price and blew out a silent breath of relief. She had enough cash on her and wouldn't have to use yet another prepaid card. With the emails she was getting she didn't want to leave yet another trail.

"RJ, do you want to stop by the book section and pick something to read for the trip?"

"Yes, please." RJ bounced in place but didn't leave her side as they walked across the store to the shelves which lined the opposite wall. Maybe she could find something for herself to get lost in, too.

"Ma'am, you have such a well-behaved child."

The man's voice behind her made her jump. She'd been watching, trying to make sure nobody approached them. How had she missed the tall muscular dark-haired man?

"Thank you." She tensed when she took in his wide shoulders and muscular physique. Her instincts screamed that this man could be dangerous if needed. She told RJ, "Go check the books, I'll be there in a minute." RJ didn't need telling twice and thankfully made a beeline for the bookshelves.

She stepped after her son, keeping her body between him and this man, while giving herself room to fight if she needed to. She flicked her gaze around the store and landed back on the man, who had a strange look on his face.

She widened her stance, moving one foot slightly behind the other, and bent her knees. Which wasn't as easy as it sounded when you were trying not to make it obvious what you were doing. "Can I help you with something?"

"No, ma'am." The man picked up the ugliest vase she'd ever seen. "I'm just buying something for my wife."

"And that's what you're going with?"

"Um, you don't think it's pretty?" He held the vase out at arm's length, turning it this way and that. "I think it might be an antique and worth some money. Don't you think?"

"I think, if your wife has any smarts, she'll whack you over the head with it." She couldn't help herself and gave her honest opinion, "and tell you to wake up and smell the roses. It's ugly as sin and it's probably haunted." She glanced over her shoulder to make sure RJ hadn't disappeared from view.

"My wife has a pretty good nose for smells." He held the vase to his face and sniffed, his eyes widening as he jerked away from the vase, almost dropping it in the process. Served him right; the idiot probably got a whiff of some old dear's perfume which was dropped in there by a ghost about a hundred years ago.

"Sir, you may be better taking your wife for a day out to go putter around some flea markets and stores and let her pick her gift," she advised. "Otherwise, if you buy something that's haunted, I see a couch in your foreseeable future."

"Ah, my Caroline would never send me to the couch," he told her.

If he was flirting with her, then she was going to neuter him on his Caroline's behalf, even if the only Caroline she'd ever run into was probably miles away in Riverton, and this most likely wasn't her husband.

"She'd send me to the basement instead."

"If you're flirting with me, then I will make it my business to tell Caroline," she promised, "and I'll help her neuter you, cowboy-style."

He actually winced and pressed his thighs together as if he could protect an important part of him, which she had no desire to see. "You know my Caroline?"

She didn't blame him for looking all kinds of confused. She had absolutely no idea how this conversation had gone from haunted vases to neutering him as he spent the next God knew how many nights in the basement.

"Not unless she lives in Riverton and is spunky and funny and loves her girl posse with the fierceness of a terrier."

Confusion crossed his face, but she didn't have time to figure out why.

"Have a nice day." The conversation was over. She passed the first shelf of books and paused mid-step.

"Is that?" She slung the cold-weather gear over her shoulder and ran her finger down the spine of the book which had caught her eye before plucking it off the shelf. "What are you doing here, my beautiful?"

Inside she did a happy dance. When was the last time she'd had the luxury of reading a Caitlyn O' Leary recent release? She didn't dare use social media anymore and missed the shenanigans of John O'Leary reading excerpts from his wife's books during their Facebook Lives in Caitlyn's group.

"*Her Wild Warrior.*" She turned the book over, but only skimmed the blurb. "Darn it, it's book three." Not that it would stop her from buying it, mind you. Reading book two would have to wait until she found a copy. But she'd loved Kostya and Lark's story in *Her Selfless Warrior*, so there was no chance of her passing up this opportunity to have this book to reread until the pages fell apart. Another quick glance at the shelves confirmed there were no other romantic suspense books. One would have to be enough until they moved on from Big Bear. She didn't dare use her precious pre-paid cards on the online bookstore many people used. It was way too easy for someone to hack that system and trace an IP back to her location. Any decent hacker could do it. There was also no way in hell she was going to a pirate site—her one remaining laptop didn't need any viruses either.

"Momma?"

"Did you find some books, buddy?"

He proudly held up two large-sized books. "Yes, Thomas comics."

"Awesome. Let's go pay for them and go find that laundromat." She glanced around the store, making sure Mister In-Danger-Of-Losing-His-Family-Jewels had really left before making a beeline for the counter.

"Good morning." The girl behind the counter tucked her bright pink braid behind her ear and stood out of the chair she'd been sitting in.

"Hi." Lily put the clothes and her book on the counter. "Pass me those comics," she asked RJ and took them when he passed them over. She placed them on top of her own book, "Just these, please."

"Would you like a bag?" the girl asked.

"Yes, please." She watched as her items were scanned and frowned as the girl paused to scan the back of her book. She better not tell her Caitlyn's book wasn't for sale or she may do the one thing she'd avoided since Rexar died and make a scene, drawing attention to herself and RJ.

"I finished book two in that series yesterday," the shop attendant said. "I have it in the back, if you'd like it, too?"

Was she serious? "Really, you, have it?"

"Yes, we do. We had two of book three, so I borrowed one

of them." The girl pushed the books into the paper bag. "Let me go grab it for you."

"Thank you." This could not be happening. Good things rarely happened to her. Finding not one but two of your favorite author's books at Goodwill ranked right up there with awesome ice cream on a hot summer's day.

"Here it is." The girl turned it over to check the price and tapped it into the cash register.

"Thank you so much." Lily resisted the urge to snatch the book right out of her hands. "Did you enjoy it?"

"So much." She picked up the snowsuit and glanced at RJ. "Is this for you?"

"Yeah, but I no like the tags."

"I can fix that, easy." She grabbed a tiny seam ripper and used it to cut the thread holding the tag in place. "Just the neck one or do you want me to grab the one down the side, too?"

Lily smiled at the woman; it wasn't often she was surprised by people anymore. But twice in the space of the last five minutes this person had surprised the heck out of her, not only by being generous with the book, but by treating RJ like a human being and not an annoyance.

"Go on," she encouraged him to answer.

"Sides too, please."

She went to work before she replied, "You got it."

"Thank you." Lily said.

"I'm not the biggest fan of tags either. They make my skin itch just by knowing they are there."

"Me, too."

"That's fifteen even with tax."

Lily handed over a twenty. "Please keep the change and buy yourself some coffee for your break."

"No, no, you don't have to do that."

"I want to," Lily insisted. She wasn't exactly rolling in

cash. Her funds were starting to run low, and she'd have to pick up some design work online soon. But for now she could afford to buy a coffee for a person who'd gone out of her way to spread a little sunshine.

"Can you tell me where the closest clean laundromat is?"

"Sure, I can there's one on the corner if you go left out the door. It's the one I use."

"Thank you, so much." It was a relief to have a recommendation. Because some of the places she'd found online hadn't always been the cleanest. And washing clothes in washers full of cat hair was just ick. She'd rather wear the clothes straight out of Goodwill than spend the week itching again.

"Have a nice day, ma'am."

"You, too." She gathered their shopping and turned toward the door. "Thank you so much for the books."

"Bye." RJ called over his shoulder.

"Bye."

CHAPTER FOURTEEN

It was one hell of a morning for sucker punches. Rexar had thought he'd gotten all of those over with the previous evening on the trip from the airport to the hotel. But fate—that bitch—wasn't done with him yet. The first real look, with his own eyes and not a photograph, at his son and he'd struggled to breathe so much that Wolf and Kentucky had asked if he was choking.

Sometime overnight, the trucks Dalton had hired for them, after hearing they were working out of a panel van, had been delivered. Now they were ready to follow his damn wife wherever she went.

He watched her and his son entering the third Goodwill store that morning and it wasn't even ten o'clock yet.

"We should grab them when they come out."

"You are not grabbing a woman and child off the streets of San Francisco," Wolf growled. "Even if that woman is your wife."

He knew he was correct, but damn, he was so tempted. Grab his child and run, let her see how it felt to live in hell for years. The only thing stopping him were the men here standing next to him, along with the possibility of years in jail.

"I'm going in there," Wolf said.

"What, no, I'll go."

"Your wife thinks you're dead or still in Iran, unless she still has contacts over there," Wolf said harshly. "If you go in there she'll keel over in shock, and you do not want your kid seeing that." He pointed at Kentucky, "Get his ass under control while I'm gone, because if not I'm calling Tex and we are outta here. I will not risk our security clearances."

"I agree," Kentucky called after Wolf as he slammed the door behind him and crossed the street to the store.

Shit. He'd fucked up. *I should get better at keeping my thoughts to myself.*

"Rex, get your shit together," Kentucky ordered. "Because Steel is right. You are acting like an asshole."

"I know." His thumb flipped through the pages Tex had sent him. Overnight, he'd memorized his son's face and every word on his birth certificate. "How did she manage to register his birth, with a false name?"

"That's a question for one of the T's," Kentucky shot back. "You want shooting or fighting, or keeping your ass outta jail, that's my wheelhouse. Trev and Tex have dibs on internet shit."

"No lie." His finger caught on more than one sheet of paper and the next time he flipped it over, it came to rest on Lily's file. "Fuck."

"You can't avoid it forever, bro." Kentucky the asswipe was pretending he was all sage and shit. Hadn't he said he was only good for shooting and fighting a couple of seconds ago? "You need to look at that file, because we never go to war without all the intel, and this, brother, is a war no matter how you look at it."

"You don't got to be right all the time."

A phone rang behind him and Mike answered. "Yo, yeah, he's here, one sec." He nudged Rexar on the shoulder. "It's Drax for you."

"Thanks." Freaking wonderful, just what he needed—his older but shorter twin giving him shit. "I'm here."

"You didn't answer your phone, shithead. Why are you avoiding me?"

He pulled the phone away from his ear when he realized it was on speaker. "I'm not."

"I know you, Rex," Drax reminded him. "Don't add lying to me to the list of shit we're gonna talk about."

"I don't have time to talk now."

"I'm Santa Claus," Drax snorted. "I'm making a list and checking it fucking twice."

Rexar could feel his twin's frustration even over the phone. "I don't want to look."

"Because you know you fucked up and not her." Drax said.

"Wait, what the hell are you talking about?" There his idiot brother went talking in riddles again. "No."

"Liar."

"Fuck you."

"Hell no." Drax dropped his voice low. "You don't get to say that to me. You aren't the only one all kinds of fucked up about what happened, Rex. Read the damn file, now."

"Fine."

"Now you sound like you're two years old and not an operator."

Trust his brother to call it like it is and not let him keep his head buried up his ass. "Ugh, I'm reading, I'm reading."

"FYI, he's not." Mike called.

"Shut up." Rexar punched Mike. Not as hard as he'd like, but enough to have Kentucky rolling his eyes again.

"I'll wait while you read it," Drax muttered. "Take all the

freaking time in the world. It's not like I'm waiting to go wheels up in about twenty minutes."

"You're going out?" Mike asked. "Is Cas going?"

"Cas is flying the damn helo, of course he's going," Drax grumbled. "He's not sitting around waiting on you, moping his ass off."

"Whoa, bro, that's cold." He huffed out a breath and turned over the page.

"Someone please say a prayer for my twin or something, because he's suffering from I don't listen for shit syndrome, and like Zenko, I fucking resent being forced to be the reasonable one in this family."

Drax grumbling and muttering was so freaking normal it should have been a balm to his soul. But it wasn't, because for the first time since the fucking Iranians had tortured him with photos of Lily, insisting she was the one who betrayed him, he took the time to look at her face.

"She betrayed me."

"What?" Mike leaned in to look at the photo of Lily and his son. "She looks like your average suburban mom. Did she cheat on you?"

"No. When I met her, she was a CIA liaison for the DOD working out of Vincenza," he explained. "She's the reason I got busted doing that undercover job."

"Being CIA doesn't mean she betrayed you, bro." Drax said dryly.

"I spent months staring at her face, when those bastards taped my eyes open as they sent electricity slamming into me to make me talk." He shook his whole body in an attempt to keep himself from going back there. But damn it, he failed, and he was right back in that room, his chained hands hanging over the meat hook, with only the tips of his toes keeping him from dangling on his full weight.

She told us you are a spy.

Your wife told us where to find you.

She hates you.

Lily told us you are the one who pulled the trigger which took the life of our commander.

She told us you need to die. Maybe we will give her that wish.

The steel of the blade to his face was cold, in sharp contrast to the fire burning down his cheek.

Mike's soft nudge made him jerk, thankfully snapping him out of the flashback. "Hey. You okay, bro?"

"She told them where to find me. How to recognize the spy in their house." He locked down the tiny spark inside him, which even after all these years insisted that wasn't possible. Lily wouldn't do that to him. "They proved..."

"Who did?" Drax interrupted.

"Two Zero Nine."

"Fine upstanding people who we'd trust with national secrets." Kentucky's sarcasm wasn't unexpected. It's what he'd thought at first, too. Until they'd showed him the emails from Lily giving everything from his undercover alias to the clothes he was wearing at the fancy shindig he'd been attending.

"Normally, I'd think as you do—"

"Shithead," Drax cut him off again, "I'm paying a fortune for this international call, because Keegan called Noble. He has concerns—"

"Excuse me?"

"Shut the fuck up and listen, my minutes are running out."

"Sorry."

"Keegan said you need to read her file. Really *read* it and don't just see what you want to see. Read between the fucking lines. Just because something was proven over there doesn't mean it's proven on this side."

"What the fuck does that mean?"

"I'm not the one looking at her file." Rexar clearly heard Drax's frustration over the phone. "You are."

Maybe he should send it to him and have Drax fucking read it if he thought it was that damn important. He was here to find his son and make sure that traitorous bitch didn't raise him.

"Read it and call me back."

"He's gone." Rexar scowled at the phone. He didn't see how it would change a damn thing. Lily had betrayed him. She'd sold him out; there was nothing John Keegan could find which would prove otherwise. But despite the conviction in his soul, he did as Drax had practically ordered and started to read the damn file.

"Look at that file like you would any file that comes across the war room table," Kentucky advised. "Take the emotional shit out of it."

"I don't know if I can do that." Admitting it sucked. But he'd never been one to shy away from the truth, even when it sucked.

"Then hand it over." Kentucky made a give me motion with his hands. "I don't know her from that stray cat on the street. I'll give it to you straight."

He chewed on the corner of his lip and huffed in annoyance at himself. He should be able to do this.

"We haven't got all day," Kentucky grumbled. "Hand it the fuck over, because if you think I'm snatching a kid—any kid, even yours—you've lost your damn mind." He snatched the file off him. "And I'm telling you now, Wolf and his men will lose their shit if you have more planned than finding your wife."

Understatement of the year.

This right here was why he hadn't pushed every button to find her before now. There was still the tiny bit of stupid hope which lived inside him, that he was wrong. *Stupid, right?* Facts didn't lie.

"I'm going to read it out," Kentucky said. "Y'all just listen to it, and tell me what you think."

"Go ahead," Mike replied before he could say no.

"Lily Marie Waters, born April 25th aged thirty-five."

Rexar squeezed his eyes shut as Kentucky went down the list of his wife's attributes. He knew all this information; he didn't need to hear it again.

"Recruited to the CIA out of college."

Yup, she'd told him that.

"Liaison to the DOD," Kentucky read. "Based out of Vincenza Italy, for an op involving Iranian activities in Afghanistan."

The same job he'd been pulled for to go undercover. He could still remember walking into that war room and taking a seat at the round table. Lily had been standing with her back to him, watching drone footage on screen of what looked like an outpost in the Hindu Kush. COP Wild Wolf, if he wasn't mistaken.

"She pulled everything together for that op you were on," Kentucky said.

He fucking knew that too, thank you very much. "Then?"

"Nothing."

"What do you mean nothing?"

"I mean," Kentucky flipped the papers over, "then nothing on the work side." He moved onto the next stapled bunch of paperwork, scanning the page as he'd done with her resume.

Rexar frowned. It was so weird that she'd stopped working right as he'd gone missing. The Lily he remembered had loved her job. They'd spent months going over intel for that job, falling in love as they'd done so. A stupid move on both sides, but unavoidable.

"This one is where Tex tracked her." Kentucky interrupted his musing into the past. "Zurich, Berlin, Madrid, Marrakesh, Mexico, Texas, and about fifty different small towns in-between."

"Sounds like she's running." Mike said.

Yup, running in case she got her ass caught for being a damn mole.

"Why run then?" Kentucky asked. "Rexar was already listed as KIA. There's nothing in the file to show she turned. The CIA would list that shit, at least where someone with Keegan's skills could find it, right?"

"You'd think so…"

They can both just shut their mouths.

"…Sounds to me like they cut her loose, or something else made her rabbit," Mike continued.

Mike has lost his mind. She ran because she knew she was the only one with that intel.

Along with everyone else in that room and on that team.

Shut up.

"Does the CIA have a policy for pregnant analysts?" Kentucky asked. "I thought it was just pull them out of the field and put them in an office, but maybe that's now and not then."

"Should be about the same for everyone else," Mike said, "But I'm sure we can get someone to verify it pretty easy." He pulled out his cell and shot off a text. "Trev will tell us."

All the time they were discussing what happened when the CIA needed to take care of a pregnant employee, the wheels in his head were finally starting to spin.

"Mike, do you happen to know if Shaun mentioned the name of the fucker who screwed him over in the 'Stan?"

"You mean the asshole behind that weapons shit at COP Wild Wolf?"

"Yeah."

"Col. Long, I think." Mike tapped his chin with his phone "No, Lang, Col. Lang."

"Fuck." He squeezed his eyes shut.

"What? Spit it out," Kentucky ordered. "Steel is on his way back from the store."

Rexar glanced out the window and spotted Wolf's easy loping gait and he crossed the lot to the truck. "Lang was also on that task force in Vicenza."

"We already know he was playing for the other side," Mike said. "I'm still not convinced he was the reason me and Jared were fucked over, too. I just can't prove it."

"He's dead, right?"

"I don't know," Rexar admitted. "You'll have to ask a Panther that intel." Former Delta Force Team Panther had been fucked over by Lang. Matt Garrett's capture at COP Wild Wolf a couple of months before he'd been captured in Iran, had set the wheels in motion for the job in the first place.

"I'll do that." Kentucky made a note in his little black book and stuffed it back in his pocket.

"If." Mike held up his hand in a wait gesture, as if he expected Rexar to protest the second the words were out of his mouth. "If Lang was involved, do you think your wife got burned by the CIA?"

Fuck.

Shit.

Damn.

And to quote an Irish family member:

Bollocks.

The door of the truck opened, and Wolf climbed into the truck. "She's buying snow gear, books, and going to the laundromat over there. If anyone wants food, now's the time to run across to KFC and grab some."

Sometimes all a beaten soul and a bruised heart needs is a chance, and the opportunity to figure its shit out.

Lily. Lang. Iran.

They all kinda rhyme, don't they?

"I'll go grab food," Mike said. "Ken, get your ass out here and come with me."

"Why?"

"Because you're paying."

"It's Mitchell's wife we're after, not mine," Kentucky argued. "He should pay."

"Get your fucking ass out of the truck before I drag you out and you aren't pretty enough to go visit your Doll-Face before we go home to Montana."

"I thought you were going to Italy."

"Cas is fine. He's going on a job," Mike groused. "He don't need me. Rexar does. Out."

He thought Kentucky was going to refuse, but his commander finally moved his butt and got out of the truck.

"Steel, what you want to eat?"

"Some kinda snack box. Will you ask my men…" He reached into his ass pocket and pulled out his wallet.

"Put that the fuck away," Rexar ordered. "Here, use this card." He grabbed a pen and scribbled a number on the back of Mike's hand. "Get them whatever they want."

"And you?"

"I'm not hungry."

"Fuck off," Mike muttered and turned away to make his way to the other truck.

"He seems pissed with you," Wolf said. "They both do."

He was going to ignore that question unless he pushed it. "Tell me…"

"Your woman is sassy as fuck, and she obviously knows my wife."

"Excuse me?" That couldn't be possible.

136

"That's what I thought." Wolf pulled out his cell. "I'm calling her now." He punched in the numbers. "Hey, Ice, it's me." The man's whole face lit up when he listened to whatever his wife had to say.

Ice? Why would a man call his wife Ice? There has to be a story there.

He made a note to ask Wolf about it later. He wanted to hear what this Ice had to say about Lily.

"Do you know anyone called Lily, has a little boy about four called Rexar?" He nudged Rexar with one finger and pointed out the window at the Goodwill store.

Rexar's breath caught in his throat as he saw his estranged wife and his son. The boy was holding onto his mother's hand but given the way he was almost bouncing as he walked, Rexar was going to assume he was excited about something. This time the smile on Lily's face slammed him in the heart.

I fucking loved you!

I still do!

"You don't, huh? Weird. It sure sounded like she knew you." Wolf said and launched into a story about how Lily had threatened to neuter him cowboy-style.

He listened to the one-sided conversation, but his focus was on Lily and their son. His hand went to the handle of the truck. He should go out there now instead of sneaking around watching them like a creeper. They were right there. Right. Freaking. There.

"Don't open that door, Mitchell, unless you wanna do this whole reunion right there in the laundromat."

Damn it, Wolf was right. He released his fingers and sat back into his seat. He'd waited this long. He could wait until this could happen somewhere more private.

CHAPTER FIFTEEN

"Finally."

Lily spotted the first sign for a turn off for Big Bear Lake. Her shoulders and butt ached from driving so long. All of the weather apps said the snow was less if she took the farthest exit. It had been so long since she'd driven on snow, maybe she was an idiot for choosing here, but Christmas in the snow sounded pretty damn awesome. She didn't have presents, and she needed to stop for groceries. But hopefully this would make it up to RJ for missing out on the Christmas she'd planned in her head for their rental in Riverton.

"Do you..." She trailed off when a quick glance in the rearview mirror showed her RJ's head tilted to one side and his mouth open as he slept in his car seat. She didn't need to pee after all, she could wait for the next rest stop. She reached for the dial on the radio and turned it up slightly and hit the button to flip through the stations to look for a local one. Hopefully it would give her weather updates.

Another hour further down the road and the GPS lady on the phone warned her she'd be turning off the highway in one mile. Seeing the sign for a rest stop she hit the turn signal. There was no guarantee she'd be able to find one on the road up the mountain. She needed gas and desperately needed to pee. But the deciding factor was if RJ slept much longer, he wouldn't sleep tonight and he'd be cranky if he missed the first time they encountered snow. "Hey, sleepyhead, do you need to potty?"

"Sleeping."

She grinned at his annoyed tone. Sometimes he was so like Rexar it wasn't funny. But in this instance, he was all her. His father had been one of those annoying people who could jump out of bed as soon as his eyes popped open. She needed an hour to get her wits about her. Although since she'd had RJ, she was a lot better about it. Having a two-year-old bouncing all over the bed tended to do that. Now that he was four, he didn't do the jumping on the bed as often.

She pulled the car to a stop at the pumps. "Come on, bud. Start waking up so you can come in the restrooms with me as soon as I've finished pumping gas, okay?"

"No, sleeping."

She shook her head, got out of the car, and pushed her prepaid card into the machine. She'd call him again when the tank was full.

Three blacked-out, kickass trucks pulled in behind her, clearly waiting for the pumps, too. She scanned them and drew her eyebrows together as a figure in the front of the closest one ducked his head down.

Rexar?

She shook it off, but yet the ache in her heart reminded her she'd never ever stop missing him.

I'm losing my mind. I thought... Drax, maybe that's Drax. That has to be it. It has to be his twin. Dead people don't drive in trucks.

She finished pumping gas and tried to reassure herself that she was seeing things. Until another thought slammed into her.

Shit, does he know about RJ?

"I don't need to pee." She hung the pump handle back on the holder, twisted the cap shut, and got back in the car.

"Momma, you said we need to potty." RJ straightened in his seat, his closed fists rubbing the sleep out of his eyes.

She started the engine. "I was thinking we might wait until the next one."

"I need to go."

Shit.

"Okay, just let me move the car closer to the door." All the time she watched the truck behind her, trying to make out the face of that man.

"Momma?"

She pulled herself together as much as she could and put the car in gear. "Sorry." Thankfully, the people in the truck hadn't started honking the horn at her. She'd been sitting in place at the pump for longer than was normally necessary after pumping gas. She eased the car into gear, fiddling with the stick to get it into first, before moving off.

Parking in the spot closest to the door, she reached her hand into the side panel of the door for the Glock and stuffed it into her purse. If that was Drax Mitchell and he somehow knew about RJ, there was no way in hell she would let him take her son from her.

She stepped out of her car and glanced at the trucks by the pumps. A man had emerged from the rear and shoved a credit card into the machine.

Do I know him?

She squinted in his direction and decided she didn't.

You're imagining it.

But the way her stomach roiled and threatened to throw up the water she'd been sipping on the road, told her there was more to those trucks than she knew.

Is it Drax sending those emails?

Even just thinking it made her heart ache. Rexar would have been devastated if Drax was the one keeping her running. The one chasing her and their son. It didn't bear thinking about.

Oh, baby, I don't want to have to shoot your brother in the balls for threatening our son.

"Momma." RJ had unbuckled himself from his seat and stood with his nose pressed against the glass of the door. "I really gotta go."

"Sorry." She opened the door and helped him out. "Keep holding my hand, okay? I don't want you to get run over by a truck."

"Ok." He did as she asked without argument, which was a relief. She cast one more glance over her shoulder and hurried into the store and found the women's restroom. Maybe they'd be gone by the time she came out.

"You waits here." RJ pointed to the spot outside the stall, where she normally stood while he did what little boys needed to do.

"I'm going to be in the next stall." Thankfully he wasn't old enough yet to insist on using the men's room by himself. There was no way she was ready for that just yet. "Don't come out of yours until I call, okay?"

"I got to wash my hands," RJ called.

"Just this once, they can wait until I'm done." She briefly closed her eyes. She was probably being overly cautious but doing anything less wasn't an option. She heard the toilet flush in RJ's stall and hurried to finish herself when she heard a latch give. "Stay in there another minute," she reminded him.

"I am. That not me."

Oh no. She hadn't heard the outside door opening. When did someone else come in here? She fixed her clothes, grabbed her purse, and hurried out of the stall.

She scanned the bathroom, and seeing one closed door, she cautiously tried to look under it without seeing anything. A pair of women's shoes reassured her it wasn't Drax at least. She moved back to RJ's stall and called, "You can come out now."

"Excuse me?"

"Sorry, ma'am, I'm just talking to my son." The elderly tone of the lady's voice reassured her further and she flipped on the faucet.

"I can't reach, Momma."

"Gimme a sec to dry my hands and I'll lift you up." Normally she brought a folding stepstool with her into restrooms, but with all the uncertainty over the men in those trucks, she'd forgotten it.

"We didn't bring my step."

"Yeah." She flipped on the faucet for him, and lifted RJ up so he could stick his hands under the flowing water.

"Rud-a-dub, rud-a-dub."

"Rub, not rud, remember?"

"Yeah. Do." RJ giggled. "I just likes rud more than rub."

"Do you now?" She placed him back on his feet and grabbed some disposable towels and helped him dry his hands.

"I do. Thank you, Momma."

"You're welcome." She took the chance she had to hug him close and press a kiss into his hair. "Let's go find some snacks and then we'll see about that snow."

"Yay." RJ turned toward the door, stumbling to a stop when it slammed open, almost hitting him on the nose. "Oops, sorry, mister."

"Out." The tattoo-covered man in biker's leathers scowled at her kid.

"Leave him alone." Lily grabbed RJ's shoulder and tugged him behind her.

"Get the fuck out into the store, bitch." He raised his hand and her eyes lasered in on the handgun.

Stupid, you should have listened to your instincts. Coming in here was a bad, bad idea.

"Okay." She slammed as much fear and timidity into her voice as possible. Not that it took much effort, mind you. With RJ behind her to protect, terrified was pretty darn appropriate for what she was feeling.

"Momma." RJ screamed behind her, ripping her focus away from the asshole with the weapon point at her nose.

"I'm here."

"Momma!" her son wailed again. Despite her training that warned her not to take her eyes off the biggest threat in the room, her mothering instinct to check on her child took over. She barely had time to see the woman holding a struggling RJ against her chest before her head exploded in pain.

God, I hope that was Drax and he'll protect his brother's son was her last thought before everything went dark.

CHAPTER SIXTEEN

Rexar's eyes widened as he made eye contact with Lily at the gas pump. He ducked his head down, breaking their connection. Shit, did she recognize him?

He punched his fist into Wolf's side. "What the fuck did you pull in right behind her for?"

"We need gas, dude. Letting someone else go ahead of us would have looked weird," Wolf grumbled. "And don't fucking punch me again."

"She's studying the truck. You see that, right?" Mike said from behind him. "Did she recognize you?"

"I don't know." But he sure recognized her. He wrapped his fingers into the hand holder on the door. If he didn't have something to hold on to, he was getting out of the truck right now, and they would be doing this in one hell of a public place. No matter how much he didn't want to.

Fuck, she's more beautiful than I remember.

Motherhood suits her. I always knew it would.

But then his memories and brain were kinda fucked after Iran, so that didn't say much.

"I don't think she knows it's you for sure though." Wolf

opened a pocket on the dash and pulled out a card. "Mike, you're on pumping duty."

Mike snagged the card out of Wolf's hand. "You got it."

"She doesn't know you, right?" Wolf flung one hand over the back of the seat and half turned to look at Mike.

"No, she doesn't know him," Rexar answered before Mike did. "Unless she met them at a different base, she never met any of my team at Camp Darby or in Zurich."

"Good, then Mike, you're up."

"Sure." Mike shifted in the back of the truck. "My ass will be grateful for the reprieve of me sitting on it for fuck knows how many hours."

When Lily moved her car out of the way and parked it near the door of the store attached to the pumps, Wolf moved his truck forward and took her place. Mike did as he'd been asked and jumped out to fill the tank.

Rexar craned his neck, trying to see through the gas pumps to see if he could catch a glimpse of them. He craved it. Needed it. Wanted it. So badly he could taste it.

"There they are."

"I think she recognized you," Wolf said softly. "We should go into the store and see."

"Hm-mmh." He made a noncommittal sound as he didn't know how to approach her. But he certainly didn't want an audience of strangers when he did. "I think we should wait until we get to where Tex said she'd booked."

"Big Bear Lake." Wolf sighed. "My happy ass is just thrilled to be doing that drive on those shit roads a few days before Christmas. If we get snowed in, you get to explain to my wife why the first time I'm not deployed or on duty since we got married, that I'm not home."

"She'll be thrilled not to have all the pens and shit that come with a uniform in her dryer for the Christmas season."

"No," Wolf muttered. "No, I can guarantee you, she probably won't."

The grumbling growl of motorcycles set his teeth on edge. He could hear them all the way from the highway. When six bikes pulled into the forecourt and went straight to the door, he winced. A woman climbed off the back of one hog and entered the store, while the men huddled together, clearly in conversation. It kind of reminded him of being in one of the countries which ended with 'Stan when something was about to go down.

"Something's off." He nodded toward the bikers, seeing Mike's attention was riveted on them, too. "Do you feel it, too?"

Wolf leaned forward to get a better view. The frown on his face told Rexar the answer, but he gave the other man time to give his opinion anyway.

"I agree, they are up to something."

Both realized their instincts were in good working order at the same time.

"Weapon." Rexar called it, as the bikers pulled sawed-off shotguns out of the saddlebags hung over the back of their bikes.

"Shit," Kentucky muttered. "This was not meant to be a fucking showdown at dawn. Do you think she knows them?"

Since he'd read the damn file as both Tex and Drax had insisted, he'd been running through the intel over and over in his brain. Knowing someone was right and admitting it were two whole different ball games.

"I've never known Lily to go to a biker bar or even mention a bike." As much as he'd wanted this reunion to be somewhere private, it wasn't worth his son's safety. "Call the cops."

"Thank fuck," Wolf said on a rush of air. "I was starting to think you were gonna be a dick about it."

While he understood Wolf's relief at his request, he had security clearances for him and his men to be concerned about. He himself didn't have that constraint. It would probably be better if he had, as he could feel the rage building inside him, coiling like a snake, ready to strike.

"My son is in there." He pulled on the door handle to open it, but Mike's weight against it from the outside kept him in place.

"And his mother."

He swallowed hard; Wolf's reminder hadn't been necessary. Even if she had fucked up somehow, she was still his wife. His. If someone hurt her…shit, and him losing it…was high on the list of possibilities for what could happen. He didn't have time to consider what that meant just yet.

"Yeah, her, too." He knocked on the window. "Mike, let me the fuck out. I've gotta go in there."

"Fuck off. Plan first, fight later," Mike called back.

He pushed against the door with all his strength. "Get off the fucking door." He was going to kick his damn ass, just as soon as he got out of the fucking truck.

"Hey, Mozart, we got a problem. Tell the guys to get ready."

He tore his gaze away from the building to see Wolf on the phone.

Good call. You should have thought of that, too.

He could see Mike's hands moving and recognized the sign language they used on Bravo. Good; he was telling the others what was happening.

"Yeah, park along the front of the building as if we're just gonna go in to use the john," Wolf ordered. "Stay fucking frosty. I don't want no damages to any of you, or Ice will have my butt. There'll be nothing left by the time Command or Tex get involved." He tapped Rexar on the shoulder, "You hear that?"

"Yeah." Now that he'd managed to lock down the panic and rage, he agreed with the plan. Running off halfcocked would get everyone in trouble.

The bikers moved from their huddle and walked into the store, leaving one to guard the outside. That they were doing this with three trucks at the pumps told him there was more to this than meets the eye. There had to be.

"Maybe they'll just rob the place and go with no trouble," Kentucky said as Mike got into the truck and Wolf rolled it forward.

The first shotgun blast filled the air.

That was not a good plan. That better not be the plan, or he was going to be so fucking pissed it wasn't funny. He didn't care that the truck was moving, Rexar tumbled out and hit the ground running.

"Fuck."

"Get the fuck down!" The biker on guard outside pointed his sawed-off at him, waving it around as if it were more intimidating that way.

"Fuck off." Rexar could hear the guys behind him, but he kept his focus on that weapon. He slammed it to one side and hit the asshole with a flying punch, sending him stumbling backward with blood flying out of his nose.

"Take care of him." He yelled the order over his shoulder and kept going.

"He's gonna get himself killed."

Yeah, don't give a fuck as long as they live.

It turned out the beast that BUD/s and the Navy had trained him to be—the one he'd thought was dead—was only sleeping inside him. That bastard came roaring up from deep down in his soul, determined to protect those he loved at all costs. He reached behind his back for the weapon he'd stashed there, slid back the rack, and came to a stop with his back against the side of the building next to the door.

"Thank fuck, I thought you were going to do a stupid and run in there without looking," Mike muttered as he slid into place just behind his shoulder.

"The fucking Iranians didn't take all my braincells." He took a fast look in the window and jerked his head back as he saw the one inside the door start to turn around toward him. "Just most of them."

"Tex is getting us eyes on the inside." Benny slid into place behind Mike, with two more of the men on the opposite side of the door. "Wolf has him on the line."

"Roger." Eyes on the inside would be pretty freaking awesome. "Keep us in the loop."

"You got it," Benny replied. "We got one against the door, another in front of the till, there's two gone toward the restrooms." His voice trailed off. "Repeat that, Wolf?"

That did not sound good. He hadn't thought it was possible to tense up more than he already was. He was wrong. "My woman. My kid?"

When Benny didn't answer him, he drew his eyebrows together and glanced past Mike's shoulder, "Tell me."

"She's down, one of them has your boy."

He had to pull on every ounce of training he had. Every single ounce, to prevent the bellow of rage which burned in the back of his throat from escaping.

"Switch out," Mike demanded. "I go first, then you."

"Or me," Benny agreed.

Hell no.

"No."

"I need to take out the fucker blocking the door," Mike whispered furiously. "You need to get to your kid and your wife."

"You're too close," Benny chimed in. "You focus on them, we clear the way for you." He handed the phone past Mike's shoulder to him. "Tex for you."

"Mitchell, I swear to fuck if you get my people killed by being a dumbass, you are on my blacklist." Tex didn't wait around for pleasantries like hello or even go, as was typical for him. "Get your ass behind Mike and Benny."

"But…"

"*Now*, Mitchell," Tex demanded. "That's an order."

He'd spent too many years following orders to not obey one from a man he respected now.

"Yes, sir."

He motioned to Mike and Benny. When they stepped away from the wall, he slid into place behind them.

"For now, your woman is spitting mad, and your boy is wriggling and wailing like the SEAL cub he is." Tex's words tamped down the fear enough that he could focus on what needed to be done.

"Your woman was out for a few minutes, but the idiots didn't tie her up properly while she was down. Just zip-tied her hands in front of her."

And there went his new-found calm flying right out the window like a cigarette from a trucker's semi on the highway.

"She was knocked out?"

"Don't snarl at me, save that shit for the tangos," Tex ordered. "All I'm saying is don't count her out yet. From the way her bound hands are in her purse, she's probably armed. But I can't see clearly from the angle of the cameras."

"Lily may be armed," he told the others softly. "If we'd driven down from home like I wanted to, at least we'd have had some flash-bangs."

"I got you, bro." Benny dug into one of the pockets of his pants and came up with one of the devices. We did drive, so I stashed some in the rental; that's why I had to go back after we dropped it off. I almost forgot to take them out."

"This right here, is why I knew I liked you," Rexar

muttered. In his head, he mentally flipped the switch. Mission mode activated. Husband—or rather estranged husband and father—was officially on lockdown and the SEAL was freed from his cage. "Okay, Keegan, you call it, and I'll follow orders."

"Is good boy an appropriate response?" Tex was doing what Rexar had remembered from when he'd worked with him on Teams—trying to lighten the mood and break the tension.

"Hell no."

"Hah." Tex snorted. "Send Benny around the side and have him toss the flash-bang in on my count." Rexar opened his mouth to protest, but snapped it shut again when Tex added on. "It's the furthest point from your son."

"And my wife."

The silence coming from Tex told him everything he needed to know.

"Shit," Rexar said.

"I'm sorry."

"Don't worry about it." At least Lily would recognize what it was…he hoped. His son on the other hand must be terrified. He quickly passed the intel on to Benny who nodded and took off around the side of the building.

The second he disappeared, Rexar realized that Benny couldn't hear Tex's countdown when he didn't have a phone. As much as he wanted to be first in that door, the damn door wasn't opening until Benny tossed that flash-bang. He looked around the corner and saw Benny about halfway down the building. Snapping his fingers grabbed the other man's attention and he nodded in acknowledgement.

"This shit would be so much easier with comms units."

"Bluetooth would work too," Tex replied.

"Blue what?"

"Never mind. I forgot I was dealing with a technophobe

for a second, I'll make sure it doesn't happen again," Tex said. "Benny is in place, yet?"

"Yes, sir, he is."

"On my count then, three."

Rexar made sure Benny was paying attention and held up three fingers, giving him a starting count.

"Two."

He dropped a finger, following Tex's countdown.

"One."

And he dropped another, letting Benny know to be ready to throw.

"Go. Go. GO."

Rexar closed his fist and the second he saw Benny's arm rear back, he spun on his heels and took off toward the door. "Go, go, boom."

Two heartbeats later, all hell let loose. The flash-bang boomed, and Mike slammed open the door at full force, knocking the biker standing in its way clear off his feet. Before the man could recover, Mike landed flat on him, grabbing the back of his hair as he did so, and smashed his head into the floor.

Fuck, yeah! Nice one, bro.

Rexar jumped over Mike and the biker, his sole focus on finding his wife and son. He half stumbled when he spotted her tied up on the floor right next to the window. Shit, her eyes had to be burning. As if she felt him watching her, her eyes popped open. But he didn't have time to do anything about the stunned look on her face.

"Drax."

Did she just call me D's name?

"Left," Tex ordered in his ear. "Your kid is near the freezer, close to the restroom doors. I'll keep an eye on your wife. Benny will be with her in about ten seconds."

"Roger." With the reassurance from Tex that she'd be

looked after, he spun away from Lily and made a beeline for the back of the store. All around him chaos reigned. Men yelled, a woman screamed, but he pushed it all to one side, blocked it out to focus on the one thing he knew mattered more than anyone else. His son.

With his handgun at ready position, he edged up to the end of the aisle. Ignoring the burning in his eyes from the residue left over from the flash-bang, he glanced at Mozart and nodded when he held up three fingers. They may not have been on the same SEAL team or even been Green Team brothers, but some hand signals were universal across all Teams. He nodded once to say *yes, ready on your count.*

The second Mozart's fist closed he swiveled out on a side-step from the aisle. Knowing Mozart was on his six meant he could keep his focus on the asshole with a sawed-off fucking shotgun pressed against his little boy's head. He took a split second to scan his son's face. The closed eyes worried him, but he couldn't allow himself the luxury of worrying about it yet.

"Drop it, asshole," he ordered as a round of 'clears' filled the store behind them. "You hear that? My brothers have taken down everyone."

"I'll kill him right here and don't give a fuck."

"You kill my boy, and you die right here, right now. Because I also don't give a fuck."

"You—" the man narrowed his eyes and stared at him, his mouth dropping open in clear surprise.

Suddenly Rexar knew, he just fucking *knew*. It wasn't Lily these people were chasing. It was him. Lily and their son were the bait.

Fuck. Fuck. Motherfucking fuckity fuck.

His guts told him that his Wild-Ass Guess was spot on. Jesus, WAGs were never ever meant to turn out true...

"Take a good look, motherfucker. Dead men rise from the grave to protect their own."

The biker's face paled. Hell, Rexar could see his hands shaking from right here.

But then his son opened his eyes and stared at him. Their gazes locked, and his son screamed.

"Daddy!"

How the hell does he know who I am?

"Focus, Mitchell," Mozart murmured behind him. Clearly, he was shaken enough by hearing that name coming out of his son's mouth that the other SEAL noticed. "I've got him dead center, if needed."

"You need any more confirmation, asshole?" Rexar asked the biker. "The boy is mine. I protect the ones I love, even if it means putting stupid fucks like you in the ground."

"I'm telling Momma you said a bad word."

"You're gonna hear a lot more of them, kid," Mike called from somewhere off to the right. "And don't that beat all—a Mitchell to the bone. Not an ounce of fear in him."

Hah, Mike wasn't looking at the fear in his little boy's eyes.

"I'll ask you again, dumbbutt." This time he made an attempt at keeping the language clean for his kid. He had so much to freaking learn on that front. "Do you need any more confirmation that he's mine and that I'll put you down like a sick pony if you don't let him go right the heck now?"

"Hell no. I'm not being paid enough to deal with a goddamned ghost." The asshole released his son and placed his shotgun on the floor. Then raised his hands in a clear, I give up gesture.

His kid, bless him, shot toward him like his butt was on fire.

"Daddy."

"I got the tango right in my crosshairs," Mozart reassured him. "Get your boy."

Kentucky stepped out of the aisle behind the biker, kicking the weapon out of his reach.

"Me, too."

Rexar swept his son into his arms and retreated into the aisle filled with cans of peas and carrots, hunching over him as much as possible given the limited cover available.

"I got you son. I got you."

"I knewed you come, Daddy."

Huh. How do you even know I exist?

"You did, huh?"

"Yes." His head bumped under Rexar's chin. "Where's Momma?"

"We're going to find her right now," Rexar promised. "She's right over here waitin' on us." Thankfully his son wasn't struggling and seemed content to be carried by him.

Holy shit, I'm carrying my son.

Shit, don't drop him.

He paused at the other end of the aisle to check that the way was clear, and nodded to Benny and Caleb when they waved him out. Caleb flanked him until they passed where Benny was protecting Lily.

"Thanks, I got this, go help them."

"Yes, sir." Caleb gave him a chin lift and went back to the spot he'd been guarding.

"I think there's one more," he advised Benny. "I didn't hear a clear from Tate yet."

"On it."

The second Benny took off to locate Tate and the target he'd been dealing with was when reality slammed into him.

This woman, this child, him. Holy shit, this little corner of the store contained his family.

My. Family.

CHAPTER SEVENTEEN

A blinding flash of light and an extremely loud bang was the first indication that shit was going to get real. The sharp pain in her ears and burning in her eyes told her she'd been way too close to that flash-bang as it detonated. But tied up with the guard on the door's sawed-off shotgun directed right at her meant she didn't dare move yet.

The device made her eyes burn and ears ring, dazing her. It took longer than she ever planned on admitting for her to scoot out of the line of fire and into the corner between the counter and the wall.

"RJ, Jesus. RJ."

The front door of the store exploded inward, one man taking down the guard.

The next man made her sore eyes widen painfully in shock.

She stared at him, her mouth moving, but no sound emerging. She knew him… it had to be…

"Drax?" That *was* him in the truck at the pumps.

He narrowed his eyes at her, nodded, and kept moving,

heading toward the back of the store, closer to where she'd last seen RJ.

She struggled against her bonds. Tugging and pulling as hard as she could at the zip-ties. Was this all about Drax taking his nephew? What the fuck? Why now? How did he even know RJ existed? She'd certainly never told him. There were so many things to think of, but she didn't have time.

I must save him.

She ignored the men fighting around the store and kept struggling to get free. Refusing to give into the panic. Instead, she focused on the momma bear fury at her cub being threatened. Every time a weapon fired, or the sound of a fist hitting flesh registered, she flinched.

RJ. Have to get to RJ.

She managed to wriggle around enough to get her legs out from under her butt and to sit with her knees raised. Putting her bound hands over one knee she yanked sharply.

"Stupid movies make this shit look easy. Break, damn it."

"Right?"

She snapped her head up at the sound of his voice. Drax strode toward her with RJ in his arms.

"Give him back. You can't have him."

She yanked her arms harder and but the damn tie didn't give. There was no way she would ever let him take RJ away from her.

"Here." Drax leaned down with RJ arms. "Stay down, keep him safe. I got you." He pulled a knife from somewhere on his body, shifted his grip on RJ, and sliced through the zip-tie holding her wrists together.

"Momma, it's Daddy." RJ whimpered. He dove out of Drax's arms and into hers. She caught him midair and tugged him into her lap.

"That's not Daddy, baby, that's your Uncle Drax." She regretted ever showing him the freaking photos of her and

Rexar. It had been a stupid move. She could see that now. But he'd asked where his daddy was, and she'd shown him the photo album and told him all about his hero daddy. "Remember, your daddy has a twin."

Drax spun away, putting his back to her and RJ. "Get as far into the corner as you can, I'll stay in front of you both."

"Is my daddy," RJ insisted, "mine." He jabbed his finger into his chest. "Mine."

She didn't have time to deal with what RJ thought right this second and instead focused on doing as Drax asked. She scooted backward with RJ in her arms, turning them toward the wall, curling over her son to protect him from any bullets which may still be fired.

"I think we got them all," Drax said. "The guys are sweeping up now."

"Okay." Her mind was scrambling to keep up. They'd gone from washing their hands in the restroom... "The woman... she's one of them."

"What?"

"The woman," she repeated. "She's the one who grabbed RJ in the restroom." She glanced over her shoulder at Drax. "Make sure she doesn't leave."

He studied her for a minute before he nodded and turned away again and yelled, "Bravo one, the broad is a tango, lock her down."

"Roger," a man's voice called from deeper in the store.

She could feel RJ's fingers playing with the buttons on her shirt, just like he used to when she was feeding him when he was a baby and he was trying to comfort himself enough to sleep. But her focus was on the man standing behind them. She couldn't believe it. It could not be a good thing that her brother-in-law was the one standing there, protecting them the only way he could. With his own body.

"You called him RJ?"

"Yes."

"I love that." His voice was soft, as if he didn't want to share the moment with anyone else. "Rexar James is a mouthful."

Oh my God, he knows RJ's full name.

How?

In her head she snorted at that stupid question she'd asked herself. Drax had more connections and intel sources than she could have ever hoped to have. If he knew about her then finding RJ's birth certificate would have been a piece of cake.

Deal with it later.

Yes, she would deal with it later. But first she needed to know her foe, and Rexar and talking hadn't exactly belonged in the same sentence together. All she really knew for sure was when she'd needed him after Rexar died, Drax hadn't come. His family hadn't come. And she hated them for it. They left her alone.

Well, they don't get to march back in here almost five years later and try to take my son.

She'd birthed him. She'd raised him. Alone. He was hers and with Rexar dead, hers alone. Even though Drax faced away from her, she studied what she could of him. Those shoulders of his were narrower than Rexar's had been. His back tapered in at his waist, similar to how Rexar's had. Drax's hair was sprinkled with gray, whereas Rexar's had been jet black. There were so many similarities, her heart ached, and so many differences her soul wept.

She scanned down his arms and paused on the scars showing from under the rolled-up sleeves of his shirt. Something about one scar on the back of his left arm ticked at the back of her mind but she couldn't quite make it fit with what she knew to be true.

The burn is just like the one Rexar got from the oven. How weird.

Her hands stroked over RJ's back, soothing him, keeping him as calm as she could. Who was she kidding, she was soothing herself, too. She'd about lost her mind in the ten minutes between when she'd come around at the front of the store and when Drax had placed RJ in her arms. He wouldn't have done that if he meant to take him from her. She hoped not. RJ was all she had left of Rexar. Oh, she knew it was selfish as her son was also all Drax had left of his brother. But he was her son first.

She turned back to look at that burn again. It was almost identical to Rexar's.

It's not possible.

Twins don't injure themselves in the same manner.

A scar like an upside-down J was unusual in the first place. She remembered the night Rexar had gotten it. She'd been baking a cake and had forgotten about it when he'd distracted her and carried her off to bed. The smoke alarms had screamed at one AM and they'd both bolted for the kitchen. He'd refused to let her take it out with the oven mitts and had used a tea-towel instead. She'd told him it was his own fault when he'd burned his arm on the side of the oven door opening as he'd pulled out the cremated remains of the cake and dumped it outside the back door.

She'd never forget the smell of burning skin or his cursing in pain. The muttering and bitching which had followed had been pretty epic too, and the start of their one and only argument. Which in turn had resulted in their only round of makeup sex. For the record, that sex had also been pretty damn epic.

The more she studied that scar, the more she knew—just knew—she was missing something. She remembered Rexar

161

saying he and Drax were close... but it was impossible for a twin to have the exact same burn as his brother...right? *Right?* She wasn't insane or crazy. What she was, was confused.

There is one way...

It's not possible.

He's dead.

Col. Lang said he died in Afghanistan.

It's. Not. Possible.

"All clear." A man walked toward them, pushing the man who'd punched her in the face in front of him, just as she heard the sound of police sirens filtering in from outside the store.

She frowned at the man when she could make out his face. They had been following her. She'd been so stupid. Let down her guard and now it was going to cost her everything. She swallowed down the anger, pointed a finger at him, and with her voice dripping in ice, said, "You, I know you from the Goodwill store."

"Yeah. Yeah, you do." He at least had the grace to look sheepish. "I'm Matthew."

"Caroline's husband." Her cheekbone ached and she couldn't ignore it anymore. She touched her fingers to the side of her face, gently probing the sore spot.

"Who fucking hit you?" Rexar's twin elbowed Matthew out of the way. He cupped her jaw, tilting her face up toward his, and drew his fingers down over her eye. Almost but not quite touching the bruise she knew was there, his fingers traced its outline in the air.

For someone who worked in the field as he did, she was surprised he hadn't noticed it until she'd drawn attention to it.

"It doesn't matter." Was it ridiculous that she could feel the rage pouring off him? She thought so. Paranormal stuff like she read about didn't happen in real life. That was for stories and the movies. As much as she could dig a big bad shifter like most women, it just wasn't a thing in her world. And if they did exist, she had enough crappy stuff in her life —today being a perfect example of said crappy stuff— without adding a big bad alpha male to the mix.

"Nobody touches my *wife*," he muttered the word softly. "Who hit you, darlin'?"

Darlin—God, how I missed hearing that name from him.

Her eyes widened painfully as the words he spoke started to make sense.

Wife?

Not. Possible.

I have a concussion. That's it. My head is playing tricks on me.

"Rexar."

Silly woman, your husband is dead. You cannot go around imagining his twin is him. That's just all kinds of ick.

"Yeah, darlin' it's me, Rexar."

"No." He was lying. He had to be. Why was he lying?

He's not.

Shut up. He is, he has to be.

Rexar warned you.

She reminded herself of that last conversation before he'd taken off from Zurich. She'd bawled all over him. He'd wiped her tears and promised her he'd be back. Working for the CIA, she should have been able to deal better than most first-time wives, and she'd been so mad with herself that she hadn't held it together until he was out of sight.

Don't believe jack if you don't see a body.

"Don't believe jack if you don't see a body." He repeated the words she was hearing in her head.

I'll call you when I can.

He picked up a lock of her hair and rubbed it between his thumb and forefinger. "I'll call you when I can."

Don't let that stray cat in the damn house.

Then he freaking winked at her just like Rexar had that last day. "Don't let that stray cat in the damn house."

Oh! My! God!

"Weapons down! Put your weapons down. Get on the floor."

The doors slamming opened and cops yelling was the last thing she remembered, as for the second time in under an hour, everything went dark. Except this time the punch was to her heart and not her head.

Rexar had walked away. Let her believe he was dead, and never looked back.

CHAPTER EIGHTEEN

"Sir, you need to step back and give me room to work."

"I need to make sure she's okay." Rexar tightened his arm around RJ, banding it under his butt, and had the other on the center of his back to try and make him feel more secure and safe. His son's arms tightened further around his neck. He hadn't thought strangulation could ever feel so good, especially not with his background, but in this instance it did. RJ whimpered, and he stroked his hand up and down.

I hope to fuck I'm doing this right.

He tried for an apologetic smile in the direction of the paramedic working on Lily. But given how the man swallowed hard he was guessing it either came out as a scowl or a grimace.

"She just fainted and dropped to the floor."

"She got punched too, I'm thinking." The EMT lifted one eyelid carefully and then the other, checking her pupils.

His jaw tightened at the reminder. The only thing keeping him from looking for the asshole responsible was he didn't know which asshole was the one to kick the shit out of.

"That man hit my momma."

"Which one, son?" Rexar wasn't above exploiting his son for information. Although going after the fucker, right here, right now, with all the cops about, probably wouldn't be a good idea. Unless he wanted to get arrested, and wouldn't that be a fabulous impression to leave on his boy?

"Don't tell him, baby."

"Momma." RJ pulled his tearstained face from where he'd been hiding it in Rexar's neck and struggled against his hold. "Daddy, lets me go, Momma..."

"I see her, bud." He shouldered the EMT out of the way and leaned over the gurney. "How are you feeling?"

"How...?" She coughed and winced. "It's not possible..."

He understood her confusion. If anything, her reaction confirmed what Drax and Tex had been trying to convince him of for days.

"Later, I promise." He was not going to get into details here. He silently begged her not to push right now. To wait until they were somewhere private. He did the only thing he could hope would work and changed the subject.

"Tell me how you're feeling," he demanded.

"I—I don't understand."

"She's clearly confused." The EMT wrapped his fingers into Rexar's shirt and tugged hard on the material in an attempt to move Rexar. "Get out of the way. I need to check my patient."

He froze the man inside who'd been tortured and wanted to lash out now, who wanted to get those hands off him. The father who'd only held his four-year-old son for exactly twenty-seven minutes of his entire life didn't want to put the child down so he could do the lashing out.

"I wouldn't do that if I were you."

Thank fuck, Kentucky, I owe you a bottle of booze for the save.

"He doesn't like to be touched, and the only reason you

aren't heading for a lifetime subscription to the morgue is he has his son in his arms," Kentucky said. "Let him go now."

The hands on his back disappeared. Not wanting to distress RJ any further than he already was, he forced the tenseness to leave his body. He looked at his wife and scowled again. Jeez, at this point if the wind changed, he was fucked and would be stuck with a scowl permanently on his face.

"Lily..."

Tears leaked out of the corners of her eyes.

"Momma's crying," RJ announced.

"I see that." Fuck, he didn't know what to do. One side of him wanted to strangle her for leaving him there. For not knowing he was still alive. Which was unfair. He knew it now; he just didn't know how to convince all of himself that the Iranians had lied as they'd beaten him. The other side wanted to gather her up into his arms and take that devastated look off her face. Both sides warred within him, and he froze.

What do I do?

She might have...

But the paperwork Tex sent says she didn't.

Fuck.

Fuuuuuck.

"Give me the boy," Kentucky ordered, interrupting the voices in his head as he tried to figure out what to do. "You look after your wife."

"No. He stays with me." There was no way in hell he was letting RJ out of his sight. Not yet. It was too soon. Even to send him with Kentucky, a man he trusted almost as much as he did his twin.

A distressed sound from Lily made his eyes narrow in confusion. Was that fear on her face?

Shit, is it something I said?

No. He stays with me.

Fuck.

"With us." He watched her face when he amended what he'd just said. "He stays with both of us. He's ours."

He recognized a flash of relief when he saw it, but it flitted across her face so fast, and was gone again so quickly, that he almost missed it. But it was enough to tell him that for once he'd managed to remove his size fourteens from his mouth without causing too much damage. He hoped.

"Sir, you really do have to move." The EMT turned to Kentucky. "You are going to have to make him move if he won't let me do it or I'm going to call the cops over here and have them do it. My patient comes first."

"Careful, man, he's been deployed a long time." Kentucky blew out a long slow breath, clearly searching for patience. "Then we stop for gas, and he finds his wife stuck in the middle of a robbery. She's hurt and his kid has a gun to his head. You gotta cut him a little slack here."

"I'm fine." Lily shifted onto her elbows. "My head just hurts a little."

Fine? Fine was never ever a good word when it was coming out of Lily's mouth. Ever. He'd learned that the hard way.

"If you pull it out a little then I'll stand on the other side of the gurney."

"I'll take it." The EMT nodded. "Thank you." He stepped back to allow Rexar and RJ to give him room to do as Rexar had asked. He flipped up the lock on the wheels and pulled the gurney away from the walls of the ambulance. "Can you fit in there?"

"Yeah." He'd make himself fit. "You want to sit on the end of the bed, bud?" He dipped his head down to look RJ in the eye.

"Yes."

"That's okay, right?" He should have asked the EMT first but hadn't considered it until the words were already out of his mouth.

"Yes. Fine." He was guessing the EMT's *fine* was completely different from Lily's.

He kept his eyes both on his wife and son as the EMT worked the pump on the blood pressure cuff. He leaned over the bed to get a look. Not that he knew what the numbers were—that's what medics were for where he came from.

"Is it okay?"

"A little high, but that's to be expected, given what's going on." He jerked his thumb over his shoulder where the cops were still trying to figure out the mess, which was the aftermath of a bunch of off-duty operators taking care of business.

"Hey, Smith, you're up."

"I'll be back." Ken waved an arm to acknowledge Wolf's call. "Please don't get arrested before Steel's commander gets done over there. I gotta give my statement."

"No promises." Rexar put his hand down to Lily's and turned his palm over. "But I won't do time."

"Fuck. Don't piss me off, Mitchell, because this weekend is just a fun ride in the 'all kinds of fucked up' rodeo."

"Watch your mouth around my child." Lily pointed a finger first at Kentucky and then Rexar. "Warn the other idiots over there that if I need to remind you all multiple times, then you and me," She scowled at Rexar and winced when it clearly hurt her face, "are going to have bigger problems than we already do. Do you understand me?"

"Yes, ma'am." What else was he supposed to say? He agreed with her. But on the other hand, a bunch of operators getting creative with words to ensure they didn't swear...

maybe he should think of selling tickets for that show. He'd be loaded before the end of next week.

"You are lucky, ma'am. It looks like you got away with a mild concussion and a black eye."

Knowing she was going to be okay should have filled him with relief. Instead, knowing she was hurt because of him filled him with rage all over again.

"She can come home with me?"

"I'd prefer if she went to…"

"No hospital, I'm fine," Lily said.

My ass you're fine.

He wouldn't call her on the lie in public though. It had never been his style, and now with the trailer load of guilt he was hauling behind him, he wasn't about to make it his style now.

"Just stay here with RJ for a couple of minutes and rest, okay?"

"You won't…?" Her eyes darted to the EMT and back to his face again. She didn't need to finish the question for him to know what she was asking.

"No. I swear it on him, I won't." He checked over his shoulder to see what was happening with the guys and spotted Wolf walking toward them, "I'm going to have to go give a statement, too. Wolf will stay with you until I'm done."

"Wolf?"

He searched his brain for the man's real name, which escaped him right this second.

"Matthew, ma'am." Wolf came to a stop next to the open door of the ambulance. "Caroline's husband, remember?"

"Yes, I remember." She rubbed her temple with her fingertips. "And I'm still tempted to neuter you cowboy-style."

Given the way Wolf's face morphed into a grin in

response to Lily's smile, Rexar knew there was a story behind that. He would find out what it was, because wanting to thump Steel for making Lily grin like that was just all kinds of wrong. Right?

"I'll be back shortly," he told Lily.

"I've got them, Mitchell, I promise," Wolf reassured him.

Rexar figured he probably understood what it was like to have a wife, considering he did have one. He also knew from Tex and spending time with the operator over the last day and a half that he was as good as his word.

"Thank you, I appreciate it."

"You're welcome. Now get your—" Wolf glanced at RJ and made his language suitable for a child, "—rear-end over there, before the commander sends someone looking for you."

Rexar nodded. The last thing he wanted was the commander sending someone to fetch him. That was never a good thing. Throw in the fact he wanted this bit over with so they could figure out what came next, he lengthened his stride.

"Commander." He greeted the older man, and winced internally when he recognized him. Fuck, he'd been warned by the DOD not to disclose what happened, and to get them off his back and gain the freedom he'd earned, he'd agreed. "Good to see you, sir."

"Holy shit." The commander stared at him for a few minutes with a confused look on his face. He tapped his closed fist on his chin a couple of times, the wheels clearly turning in his brain. "Wait, are you the twin?"

"No, sir."

The commander sat heavily into his seat. "How?"

He didn't bother trying to stop the snort, and bitterness filled his tone. "It's probably still classified."

"Shit." The commander got to his feet and held out his hand. "I'm happy to see that the bullshit on the grapevine was wrong for once." Thank fuck he was going to let it go, he hoped.

"Me too, sir." He sat on the seat that Commander Hurt indicated. "But do you mind if we catch up later? My wife is hurt, and my son is upset."

"Of course." The commander grabbed the notepad and pulled it closer to him, "Start at the beginning and walk me through it from your point of view."

"Yes, sir." He launched into what happened from the time they'd pulled into the gas station behind Lily's car. By the time he'd repeated himself at least three times, and answered fifty billion questions, he was fidgeting in his chair. Which he knew made him look suspicious as fuck.

"Commander, what happened isn't going to change, no matter how many times you tweak how you ask your questions."

"Am I pissing you off, Mitchell?"

"Yes, sir, you are." He figured honesty was the best policy here, so he gave it to him. "You're pissing me off more than my twin does."

"That much, huh? Drax is pretty hard to beat on that score," the commander deadpanned, then grinned at him. "I've been practicing; does it show?"

"Yes, sir, it does. Outdoing my brother is pretty impressive." Out of the corner of his eye, he spotted a uniform and jerked around.

"I'll take that as a compliment." Commander Hurt didn't miss where his focus was directed, "Easy, son, it's just the cops taking the trash out."

He ignored the curiosity at his reaction to someone unexpected in his peripheral vision in the commander's eyes and voice, choosing instead to stuff his hands under his thighs. If he was sitting on them, he might not be tempted to get out of this chair and…

Those assholes have answers I need.

"Mitchell," the commander snapped.

"Yes, sir?"

"Sit your ass down in that chair right there, and don't move until they are gone," he ordered. "Then we're done, and you can go back to your family. That's an order."

"Yes, sir."

The years of torture in Iran hadn't come nearly as close to breaking him as the next five minutes sitting there watching the answers he needed drive off in the back of a patrol car did. The second the last one disappeared from view, he got to his feet.

"Thank you, sir. I appreciate the order." He figured someone who'd been around the block as many times as Commander Hurt had been would understand the cryptic comment.

"You're welcome." The commander also got to his feet. He once again held out his hand and Rexar grasped it. "It's really good to see you, Rex."

"You too, sir."

Thank fuck that's over with. He strode across the parking lot and paused mid-step when he saw that the ambulance was gone.

"What the fuck?"

A sharp whistle, and his head snapped around to the left, where he spotted Kentucky waving at him.

He jogged across the lot to the truck. Relief slammed into him when he could make out the little, short legs sticking over the edge of the rear seat of the truck.

"Mozart and Benny are driving Lily's car to Riverton," Kentucky said. "Wolf has invited us to stay the night."

"Okay." He climbed into the truck next to RJ. "Thanks, Wolf."

"No problem." Wolf glanced at his watch. "But Ice has dinner on, so can we get moving?"

"Sure." He ruffled RJ's hair, unable to keep from touching him. "You okay, Lily?" He asked her over RJ's head.

"Yesh."

"The EMT gave her some over-the-counters." Kentucky shut the passenger door on the truck and tapped his hand on the dash, telling Wolf they were ready to roll. "They seem to have made her a little loopy."

"Aspirin?" He checked for a seatbelt for RJ, and had to dig around under both his wife and the booster seat thingy RJ was sitting in to get it out from where it was stuck between the seats.

"Yes."

"Figures." He scrunched up his nose, remembering a train trip to Rome where she'd failed to mention that aspirin made her feel all kinds of icky and she'd been mortified that he'd held her hair back while she puked. "Do we have a barf bag in case she throws up?"

"Seriously?" Wolf met his eyes in the mirror.

"Yeah." Rexar frowned at the seat RJ was in, and the belt in his hand. "Pull over, I think this is meant to secure his seat."

"Shit." Wolf whipped into the hard shoulder. "None of us have kids..."

"I've only seen a carseat a few times," Rexar admitted, "so I don't know how it works either." He tapped Lily on the shoulder to get her attention. "Lily, how do we close RJ's seat?"

"I dids it, daddy," RJ chimed in. "See?" He tugged on the three-point harness securing him into the seat.

"Awesome job, bud. Do you know where this seatbelt

goes?" He kept his voice even. That lily was smiling at him a bit lopsided as if she were drunk concerned him.

"Momma fixes it under my butt."

"Under your butt, huh?" He opened the door and climbed out of the truck, squatting down to look under the booster seat. Kentucky joined him and Wolf leaned between the front seats to look, too.

"How many SEALs does it take to strap in a car seat?" Lily giggled.

"Shit, bro," Kentucky sounded concerned. "We wouldn't have let her take the meds if we'd known this would be the reaction."

"As long as her concussion doesn't cause any complications, I've seen this before." He tilted his head down and spotted the small white square on the side of the seat. "This looks easy enough. Ken, you push the belt through here, and I'll close it from the other side."

"Okay."

"Everything okay?" Caleb called out the window from where he'd pulled the other truck in behind them on the hard shoulder.

"Yeah, we just got to secure RJ's seat." He rounded the bed of the truck and opened the door on Lily's side.

"Use the seatbelt," Caleb advised. "Push it through the metal bars underneath, snap it into place, and make sure it's not kinked underneath. It's not rocket science."

"Why didn't you tell dumb and dumber here that before they put him in the seat?"

"What am I, the dumbass whisperer?"

He offered a response which only involved one finger and leaned into the truck.

"It's just me." He paused in front of Lily for a second.

Nope. You're still mad with yourself and with her... no kissing her.

"Can you reach it?"

Kentucky's question jerked him back to reality, and he leaned down, almost laying his head in Lily's lap to see under the seat.

"Yup, got it." He took the buckle and snapped it into the holder. "Did it tighten enough?"

Lily's fingers stroked through his hair a couple of times and he jumped back, smashing his head on the top of the truck door.

"I think so." Kentucky snickered.

Of course the asshole hadn't missed that. Why would he? Rexar went back to his side of the truck with every intention of punching his team brother, but the fucker was already in his seat with the door shut by the time he made it there. He slammed the door after himself and settled for smacking him on the back of the head instead.

"We're good to go, Wolf."

"Good, because I'm starving," Wolf grumbled. "This is one of the many reasons my wife and I don't plan on ever having kids."

"Keeping them safe is more than I'm good for, that's for sure," Kentucky agreed. "I run around after a bunch of operators who act like five-year-olds on a daily basis. I don't need to do it when I'm off the clock, too."

Rexar leaned his head back on the seat and turned his head to look at Lily, only to find her in a similar position—watching him back over RJ's head.

"It's the drugs," she whispered. "It's just the drugs, and this isn't real."

"It's real, Darlin', as real as our son is," he promised her softly. It fucking killed him that a single lone tear fell and he couldn't fucking wipe it away without hurting her. The emotions rioting through him were so overwhelming that he needed to close his eyes. He had to. If he didn't, he'd be the one crying and he didn't know if he was ready to handle that yet.

When he opened them again, Lily had turned away from him.

Shit, he didn't want that either.

CHAPTER NINETEEN

Lily swallowed against the burning in her throat.

This cannot be happening.

She'd always considered herself one of the most logical people she knew. But not anymore, because somehow, she'd fallen asleep and was having some heart-wrenching dream of a parallel universe. Or maybe it was just the aspirin and all the Monster she'd consumed on her drive down from San Francisco which was screwing with her reality.

He left me.

Devastation slammed into her soul. She felt vomit rising in the back of her throat and swallowed hard against it. There was no way in hell she was giving Rexar the satisfaction of seeing what he was doing to her. She remembered that feeling from when she'd thought he'd died. Seeing him now brought it all back. The nights alone in their big bed, with her tears soaking into the pillow. The early mornings staring at a coffee mug she couldn't bring herself to put away in the cupboard, and she didn't want to fill it with coffee, because being pregnant she couldn't freaking sniff it without the same burring in her throat and the churning in her stomach.

How many nights had she sat on the floor of the closet in the dark with his shirts pressed to her nose, just so she could remember his smell? And all that time, he'd just walked away from her and RJ and didn't look back, not once.

Did he even care that her heart was no longer whole? It was a jigsaw puzzle of pieces which no longer really fit together properly. RJ had cemented those broken pieces into some semblance of fixed, but yet the scars remained. They would always be there, a stark reminder of how stupid she'd been to not protect her heart in the first place.

She'd known better than to let Rexar in under her defenses. She'd talked herself out of just jumping him and throwing caution to the wind. Multiple times. But then she couldn't help herself. When he'd turned that megawatt lopsided smile of his on her and combined it with that hella sexy drawl. He'd wooed, coaxed, and promised her the world until she'd been so lost under his spell, she hadn't known which way was up anymore.

He just left me.

I was such a fool to think he ever cared.

She peeked at him again out of the corner of her eye. The bastard was watching their son with a stupid grin on his face, like he hadn't just taken her world, spun it around a billion times in the washer, and stomped it into the ground for the second time.

Rat bastard.

She would not let him see how much it hurt. Hell no, he didn't deserve that. He needed a solid kick in the balls, preferably from a mule who could kick a lot harder than she could. He should have those balls ripped right out of his sack and fed to something which didn't choke on them. She wasn't cruel after all; whatever poor animal she fed them to didn't deserve to suffer just because Rexar Freaking Mitchell was an asshole.

He better not make RJ fall in love with him and just take off like a jackass again. If he does then I swear next time I will find him, and I don't care that he's almost twice my size. I'll make him cry for his momma like a freaking baby.

"Five more minutes," said the driver who'd introduced himself as Matthew, but most of the others called Wolf.

"Me needs to potty," RJ piped up.

Bless him, he'd been so awesome today. She knew there would probably be nightmares. But she could deal with nightmares. She snorted in her head. She was an expert at the horrors which came in the dark. If she couldn't help RJ herself, she'd figure out a way to get him into therapy. It may not be a bad idea anyway.

"You heard Mr. Matthew; we'll be there in five minutes."

"Don'ts gots five minutes."

She clamped her hand over her face to suppress the laughter when the truck sped up. Clearly, the driver didn't want an accident in his truck.

"Shit." Matthew slammed his fist on the steering wheel as sirens and flashing lights filled the window over her shoulder. "Sorry, kid, you're going to have to hold it a little longer." He rolled down the window.

"Do you know why I stopped you?"

"No,"

"I has to go," RJ wailed. "I cant's stop it."

"What's the matter with the boy?" The cop leaned in the driver's window and Matthew in turn leaned so far over the man sitting next to him that he was almost in his lap.

"Me has to poop." Big fat tears rolled down RJ's face. "I feels it coming out."

"Oh, um." The cop's eyes widened. "I, uh, see the urgency, sir. Do you have far to go?"

"About four blocks that way." Matthew pointed to a side street on the left. "I swear I'm just trying to keep the rental clean. I didn't even look at the speedometer."

"Mr. Maffhew, I needs to go poop *now*."

Lily searched through her pockets looking for a tissue to wipe away the snot and tears streaming down his face.

"Here." Rexar beat her to it. "Let me clean your face, bud."

"Daddy, me needs to poop."

"I know. We'll be going in a minute, I promise." Rexar mopped up RJ's face. "Just as soon as the nice policeman says we can go."

And there it was—that tone which said I'll fix everything that's wrong in your world if only you let me take care of you. She wanted so badly to warn her son not to trust it. But she just couldn't bring herself to voice the words.

"Go on." The cop finally had mercy on them. "Don't let me catch you speeding through here again and keep it under the limit until you get home."

"Thank you, sir." Matthew waited for the cop to step back before they moved again. "Two minutes, RJ, then you can poop. Just please don't do it in the truck."

"If he does, I'll clean it up," she promised. There was no way she'd allow these men to get mad with RJ for something he couldn't help.

"Darlin', we've all been in his position a time or two," Rexar said. "None of us care except that it would upset him." He nodded to RJ as Matthew hit the turn signal and pulled into the driveway of the cutest house she'd ever seen.

"We're here." He opened the door of the truck and jumped out. By the time he turned around, RJ was already out of his seat and headed after Rexar.

She refused to acknowledge the ache that RJ had turned to him and not her. RJ had never in his short life turned to someone else before.

He's just growing up is all.

But even her reassurance to herself made her heart ache. She trailed after the men as Matthew led them into the house.

"Ice I'm home. Tell me the bathroom is free; we have an emergency."

"Is everything okay?" A woman rushed out of a door which seemed to be from a basement.

There is no way it's her. It cannot be the same Caroline, can it?

"Yeah, we have a little man who needs the latrines, stat."

Matthew's wife's face when she smiled wide completely transformed her from girl-next-door-cute to beautiful in the most serenely happy way.

"You know where it is." She planted a kiss on his jaw. "Welcome home."

Maybe this was the one man on the planet who didn't need to be whipped into shape. He paused a second to kiss his Ice back, then his fingers trailed across her jaw.

"Come on, RJ."

RJ reached for Rexar and grabbed his hand to follow Matthew down the hall.

"Just in there, little man."

"Thans." His lisp was back and while she found it adorable and had missed it when he'd grown out of it, hearing it now told her how stressful today had been on her suddenly too-grown-up little man as Matthew had called him.

Rexar made as if to follow him into the bathroom, but RJ propped his hands on his hips. "No, Daddy, you waits here."

"Are you sure?"

"I gots this."

Despite not wanting to, she couldn't help but smile at the interaction between them both.

"I gots this, Daddy," RJ repeated and slammed the door in Rexar's face.

Go, son. Put that jackass in his place.

"Oh my God, I know you. You were at the mall." Caroline laid her hand on her arm and Lily jumped. She'd been so engrossed in watching RJ and Rexar that she hadn't seen her approach.

Jumping hurt her head. "Ow."

"Oh, I'm so sorry." Caroline frowned when she got a good look at her face. "Did he do that to you?" She scowled in the direction of the hallway and Rexar.

"No, no." She held up both hands and showed Caroline the marks on her wrists left by the zip-ties. "That was the bad guys, the men here saved us."

"Are you sure?" Caroline asked. "Matthew?"

"Coming." Matthew appeared out of a door farther down the hallway from the bathroom. "Everything okay?"

"What happened?"

It was always interesting to her to watch couples interact with each other.

"Let me introduce you to everyone." Matthew sat on the couch and pulled Caroline onto his lap. "Down the hall is Rexar Mitchell and his son RJ. Lily…" he nodded to her, "is RJ's mom."

"Hi." Lily took the seat Caroline waved her to. "I think we may have met at the mall the other day."

"I was just saying that." Caroline smiled. "It's nice to meet-you meet-you, rather than, you know, just in passing."

"Same."

"The big dude hovering near the door is Caleb Hunt."

As nobody had introduced them to her either, or if they had she didn't remember, Lily also nodded when Matthew gave the operator who was clearly one of Rexar's team, a name.

"Hello."

"Ma'am."

Caroline glanced at her husband and waited for his nod, before she replied, "Caroline. We don't stand on ceremony here."

From the way his hand was planted on the small of her back, Lily knew it wasn't because she was asking for permission, but because she was checking the situation. There used to be a time when…

Nope, don't go there.

Not the time.

Definitely not the place.

"The short one next to him is Tate Sullivan."

"Ma'am."

"Pfft. These two are way too polite," Caroline grumbled. "I'm going to start looking for my mother if you all keep this up."

I like her. She has spunk.

From the incident at the store, she already knew Caroline was an awesome friend to have.

Someday, sometime…

"The one sniffing in the direction of the kitchen," Mathew told Caroline, "is Mike Rios, a former Green Brother of mine."

She knew most of the SEAL teams used colors, and Green Team was a training/evaluation unit within DEVGRU, or as the media called it, SEAL Team Six, where operators trained prior to selection to an operating squadron.

She studied Mike. From the interactions she'd seen between him and Rexar over the course of the afternoon, they seemed close. It was almost like they had a bond which hadn't been extended to the others on the team.

"Something smells amazing coming out of your kitchen, ma'am." Mike touched his fingertips to his forehead.

"It wasn't me," Caroline assured him. "I ordered from the bar we go to. All I did was put their cowboy stew in the crock pot to keep it warm because I didn't know what time you'd be here."

"Then we have Kentucky Smith." Matthew nodded to the man who rode shotgun in their truck on the way down from the gas station.

"Ma'am, thank you for your hospitality."

"My hospitality would feel a lot better if you all sat down." Caroline's smile took in everyone in the room. "Seriously, there's plenty of chairs."

"There is another one," Matthew told Caroline. "Bryan, but he's coming in with Benny and Mozart."

"BB's a backseat driver." Kentucky's eyes twinkled. I seriously hope all y'all have dot therapy on standby. If not, BB's either gonna be walking here or your boys will need those appointments."

"I'm sure they'll be just fine," Caroline said. "They drive with Matthew all the time."

"Momma." RJ came racing down the hallway with Rexar on his heels.

"Hey, hey." Lily snagged him by his sweater, gently pulling him to a stop. "What's the rule for indoors in someone else's house, buddy?"

"Company manners and inside voice."

"Yes." Even though she hurt all over she squatted down to eye level with him. "No running in the house, okay?"

"But Daddy said to race him…"

"Yeah, Daddy needs to remember his company manners and inside voices too." She ignored the snorts from the men around the room.

"If daddy fegets does he gets to sits on the step, too?"

"Absolutely. Timeout—"

"Isn't just for football."

"Good job." She gave him a hug and got to her feet. "Come say hello to Caroline and Matthew."

"I's knows Mr. Matthew." RJ grinned. "He talked to the policeman."

"Policeman?" Caroline nudged Matthew. "Did you get pulled over for speeding again?"

"Maybe?"

"Seriously, Matthew, another hundred-dollar fine?"

"Nuh-huh." He nodded to RJ when Caroline raised a suspicious eyebrow. "RJ got us out of it."

"Thank you, RJ."

"Yous welcome."

"Rexar, ma'am." Rexar kept one hand on RJ's shoulder and offered his other hand to Caroline. "Thank you for opening your home to us. I appreciate it."

"Don't make me regret it, Mitchell." Matthew said.

"We'll leave in the morning, if that's still okay with you, Wolf, and grab a hotel."

"I've got a hotel for me and the boys," Kentucky cut in. "I can book a room for you and your family."

"Um… wait." She was so confused. What on earth was happening? "We are in Riverton, right?" She waited for someone to confirm or deny it. When Matthew and Caroline both nodded, she continued. "I still have a rental over on Oak. It doesn't have much in it, but we should go there." Maybe RJ would get his wish and get to go home after all.

"You were living here?" Rexar narrowed his eyes at her.

Mr. Reincarnated Himself could just stuff a sock in his mouth and wait for answers to his questions. She had a whole bunch of them stacking up like flies on cow manure. There was no way she was doing this in front of complete strangers and especially not in front of their son. "We'll discuss that later."

His jaw could tick like a damn clock all it wanted. If he

187

wanted this to be a discussion then he'd better start remembering their behind-closed-doors rule.

"Why don't you all come in the kitchen and eat." If her opinion of Caroline hadn't been sky-high already, the woman jumping to her aid would have certainly done it. "The kitchen is small, but I promise the plates will be full."

"Dinner on plates?" RJ asked. "Real plates?"

"I was thinking we might go with paper plates." Caroline leaned down to RJ and whispered to him, "That way neither of us needs to do the dishes, as I think there may be grown-up talk coming, and I might want to go sit in the garden and watch the sun go down, what do you think?"

RJ cocked his head to one side, as if he was giving her question serious consideration. "Is smart thinking," he nodded solemnly. "No dishes and more fun, is a plan."

"Will you shake on it?" Caroline held out her hand. "Then help me in the kitchen? You can check the freezer to see if we have anything for dessert."

Did anyone else see how similar he and Rexar were? She'd always known it. From the very first day, with his big dark eyes and that black hair, he'd been Rexar's mini me. Right now, with them side by side, both looking curiously at Caroline, a thumb hooked into the loop on their pants… if the others didn't see it, then they had no business being on the working end of a weapon without corrective eye surgery.

"Deal." RJ pulled his thumb free of his belt loop and shook Caroline's hand. "Dessert is a deal."

"I like the way you think." Caroline nodded to the kitchen. "Are you coming with me?"

"Momma?"

"Go on, bud," Rexar replied before she could.

"Momma, may I?"

It was probably shitty to be relieved that he hadn't forgotten her in the excitement of Rexar being around, but she was anyway. Relieved and a little bit pleased. If that made her a horrible person then she could live with that.

"Of course, you may."

Lily perched on the edge of the chair and tried to ignore the ache in her head. Being punched sucked, do not recommend, zero stars. She just knew with RJ out of the room, that there would be questions...

"So..."

"Tex first." Matthew pulled his phone from one of the pockets on his cargo-style pants. "Then questions. I want him to hear this, too."

"Sounds good."

Of course it sounded good to him. She on the other hand was trying to figure out why the clock on the wall was moving. Was it possessed? It was right? It had to be... from a distance she could hear people talking; it almost sounded like one of those voices was a ghost calling her name. But she'd wake up from this nightmare soon, and find all of today had been a dream of some sort.... Right?

Please tell me it's a dream, or all these years have been a lie.

A lie.

CHAPTER TWENTY

Rexar listened to Wolf and Tex as they greeted each other, and Wolf gave a run down on what had happened over the course of the day. He'd found her. After so long he hadn't been entirely sure it was real. RJ having an emergency in the poop department had slammed everything home for him. This was happening. He had found Lily. Found his son. But now what? He glanced at where she sat out of the corner of his eye.

Is she swaying?

Fuck, she got hit on the head.

I'm an idiot.

"Lily?" He watched her for a heartbeat more, "Lil?"

"It's not possible." She stared at him with those huge green eyes of hers. "It just can't be possible."

"What can't?" He crossed the room and crouched in front of her chair so he was level with her face. "That I didn't die after you put me in that hellhole?"

She reared back from him, "What?"

"Did you think the Iranians would be easier than a divorce?"

"Mitchell, what the fuck?" Tex clearly had heard what he was saying through the phone, "Did you even read the file?"

"He did, kind of," Mike chimed in. "But I agree; Rex what the fuck?"

"I don't understand," Lily whispered. "What's happening?"

"Fucking aspirin, Jesus." He reached out to feel her temperature and she flinched away from him. He saw the exact moment she somehow found a rod of steel for her spine and straightened in the chair; her hand lifted toward his jaw. He refused to move as her fingers traced the scars. He wouldn't give her the satisfaction of knowing the revulsion on her face gutted him and told him there was zero point in them trying to figure this shit out.

"You are dead."

"Sorry to disappoint, darlin'. As you can see, I'm not." Her touch was still like freaking fire to his soul. It burned through his defenses faster than a bouncing betty would through a barbed wire fence. "Did you hope for different?"

Don't fall for that shit again, dumbass.

"What did you say?"

Now why did she have to go and be all upset, except for the fact he was still alive. That probably put one hell of a damper on whatever plans she had.

Crack.

It took a second for the reality of what had just happened to make sense. His hand went to his face, covering the scars, feeling the heat of the slap.

"Y—yo—you asshole." He'd always thought it was cute when she got so mad, she stammered. Now not so much, not when all that fury was directed at him.

"Guys." Wolf was already on his feet. "How about we bring the food outside and eat out there? These two clearly have shit to sort out and their kid doesn't need to hear any of it."

Fuck. RJ. How could I be so stupid?

"Thanks, man."

"Don't do stupid stuff in my house." Wolf pinned him with a fierce stare. "In this house we respect women, and we protect them. Even if it's friends' butts we need to kick. Got it?"

"Yes." What else was he supposed to say? He would normally agree with Wolf, but right now that feeling roiling around in his belly like a swarm of angry yellowjackets threatened to take over.

"Don't make me regret giving you time to figure this out."

Could he do this without losing his shit?

Maybe.

Maybe not.

But he could walk out that door if the switch on his PTSD flipped again.

"I won't. I'll sit on my damn hands if I have to."

"Not making me feel in any way good about this, Mitchell," Wolf deadpanned. "Try fu—freaking harder." Wolf made a swirling motion with his finger; follow me. He ordered the rest of the men in the room, "Grab a plate or a dish and put it on the table in the garden."

Rexar watched them leave while keeping an eye on Lily. The paleness in her cheeks worried him, but he... whatever he'd been about to think was cut off when Lily braced her hands on the chair and got to her feet.

"Where are you taking my son?"

He had to admire her guts. She was clearly struggling with the blow to the head, and the aspirin still coursing through her body, and still she was on her feet making a beeline across the room to where RJ had stopped on his way to the door with the salt and pepper shakers in his hand.

"They are going to eat outside."

"No." She turned her momma bear fury on him. "He does not leave my sight. If he's going out there, so am I."

"I can't run off with him, if I'm in here." He would do reasonable. "This is Wolf's house, his wife is right there, and those other men are my team. Do you seriously think any of them would allow something to happen to our son while we talk in here?"

"It's not you I'm worried about," she shot back. "He stays where I can see them."

Caroline stuck her head back in the door.

"Lily should come eat with us," Caroline said. "The talking can wait until later when RJ is sleeping."

"No." He'd waited for years for this showdown; it could not wait another second, or Caroline was going to be cleaning up body splatter from her pretty house, because he'd exploded in either frustration or... Well, he didn't know for sure, but given enough time he could come up with something. "We do this now."

"We aren't doing a damn thing, if my son is out of my sight."

"Ours..." he said softly.

"What?" She put one hand on the back of the couch and took a step to move past him, but he side-stepped, cutting her off.

"Our son, not just yours."

"Rex—" Mike interrupted.

"What?"

"You are missing something."

Could he not just fuck off for five minutes?

"I'm not."

"You are, dude." Mike must have put on his pair of brass balls today, because he wasn't giving up. "Why don't you want your son out of your sight?" he asked Lily. "Who's gonna take him?"

The implications of Mike's words slammed into him, and all the pieces of the jigsaw puzzle which were scattered across the metaphorical board in his brain, slotted into place. He lowered his head to look her in the eye.

"Who did you piss off? Who's chasing my kid?"

"Ours," she threw his words back at him, "our son, not just yours."

"Who?"

"I don't know." Her shoulders slumped and curled inward. She seemed so much more vulnerable than he'd ever seen her before. Even sitting on the floor of the gas station with her hands zip-tied in front of her, he'd never seen defeat like this on her face. "I just know that there is."

Disbelief, rage, and fear warred for pole position inside him.

"Are you serious?"

He didn't need to see her answering nod to know she was telling the truth. Of all the things she could lie about, he was goddamned sure RJ's safety wasn't one of them.

"Tell me everything." He grabbed her arm and pushed her into the couch. "Don't leave anything out."

The operator he'd been for so many years took control in his brain. This version of him would listen. This one wouldn't be a dick to her, and would believe what she said... he hoped.

"Don't try to play me, Lily, because I'm not the idiot you married anymore."

"I—" she stared at him for so long, he thought she'd changed her mind.

Out of the corner of his eye, he saw Mike gesturing for the others to leave. He snagged a ladder-back chair from the table behind them, placed it in front of her, and straddled it.

"Tell me, darlin' I'm listening." This time it wasn't a demand. Instead those words came out of his mouth in his soft, coaxing Carolina drawl, just like he'd used on that kitten he and Drax had rescued from the storm drain when they were six. It was just a damn shame; it had been a raccoon kit and not a cat. Their mom had freaked when they'd let it loose in her kitchen.

"I—"

"Deep breaths. I'll grab you a glass of water." Leaving her to even go to the kitchen was a risk, but he figured if he gave her a second to pull herself together, she might remember she'd been an agent, and how to give a briefing. That woman he knew, that one he could deal with... he hoped. This vulnerable version of his wife was so different from who he remembered her to be, and he struggled to know how to deal with this version.

He took longer than he wanted to find the glass, and then ran the water in the sink before changing his mind and opening the fridge to see if there was bottled water. He grabbed a bottle from the six-pack and loosened the top.

On handing it to her, he warned, "It's open."

"Thank you." She sipped some water and screwed the top back on.

Did she know how much his fingers itched to tuck that lock of hair, which had escaped from her braid, behind her ears? He didn't think so.

"I don't know who's following me." Her words snapped his attention from the hair on her shoulder to her face. "I just know that a couple of hours after the casualty officers and the pastor left, the phone rang..." She trailed off.

"Drax?"

"No." She lifted one shoulder. "No... I don't know. It could have been, but I don't think so. Unless your twin is the type to tell me it was my fault you died. That having me in your life distracted you."

"Maybe if he was hurting." He could see Drax lashing out.

But he couldn't see his commander Garrett Rockwell allowing it, or his momma for that matter. "But it doesn't sound like something he'd do." That couldn't be what put the look of fear in her eyes. "Go on."

"The man on the phone told me our child had to die, just like you did."

"You were barely pregnant; how did he know? I only knew because you'd emailed me."

"Yeah, once I'd calmed down enough to stop freaking out, that was my question, too." She picked at the label on the bottle, dropping shredded pieces into her lap.

"What did you do?"

"I searched the house."

"Why?"

"Because I should have done it every freaking time I went back to it." She lifted her eyes from the bottle and met his. "It's what a field agent is supposed to do. I guess because that house felt like home, I got lax in following protocol."

With that one sentence, she reminded him she wasn't a civilian, she'd been one of the CIA's top analysts.

"What did you find?"

"Can you ask an easier question?"

"Tell me." Damn it, he wanted to still be mad with her, but in his head he could picture her going through their house. Searching it. He could take a guess at what she'd found but he wanted—no, he *needed*—to hear her say it. "Please tell me what you found." He softened his demand.

"Cameras, wires."

Fucking assholes. It wasn't his people who'd have done that. There was no fucking way the Navy did that to him. Noble would never have allowed it.

"From where?"

"They looked Russian-made. I looked at similar ones enough when I was researching other cases for work."

"Not Iranians?"

She shook her head. "They didn't look like it. But in that part of the world, that doesn't mean very much."

"Truth." Something she'd mentioned earlier kept tapping at the back of his brain. "Why did you say field agent and not analyst?"

"I'd just been promoted." Sadness filled her voice. "It was my dream job. Vicenza was to be my last analyst role before going in the field."

"Well done." The words were out of his mouth before he could stop them. He remembered how much she'd wanted to make a difference in the world. "Getting a field role is hard. I'm so fucking proud of you." There was more truth to his words than he ever wanted to admit.

"Thank you." His praise did what nothing else has achieved. It gave her the confidence she seemed to have lost over the years, and she finally snapped into work mode. "The phone calls were coming in fast and thick, almost like an auto dialer. Sometimes there was someone there," she explained, "and I could hear him breathing. Other times, I could hear nothing. And yet other times, the asshole threatened our baby."

He hated to ask the questions. Didn't want to make her relive the horror. He knew the answers would threaten his hard-won calmness, but he knew they needed to be asked, so he did it anyway. "Did you call your handlers?"

"Yes, it's the first thing I did."

He'd been afraid of that. "What did they say?"

"To stay in situ." She snorted, "I was a new widow, and the trauma was playing tricks on my mind."

Why the fuck would the CIA leave her out there with her ass swinging in the breeze? Alone, undefended, vulnerable?

"Assholes."

"I thought so, too."

"Go on."

"After a couple of days, Braxton stopped taking my calls. They went to voicemail, and he never responded."

Rexar froze. He knew that name... where the fuck did he know that name from? Iran? Another mission... he filed it away to ask the guys about it later.

"Then someone followed me."

"What?"

"At first I thought I was crazy." She forged on as if he hadn't asked any question at all, "At first it was just a flash out of the corner of my eye. Then it was seeing the same man multiple times on a trip to the store for groceries I was never going to eat because I was puking so much."

He winced at the reminder of how much he'd missed but he didn't dare let it show in case he threw her off track.

"I checked the house and found more devices. Twice." She pinned him with a steely look, "It was time to leave."

He nodded in agreement. He'd have left after the first time. He'd have to remember to tell Drax that the house was compromised and not to use it anymore. Fuck, that pissed him off, but not as much as the words coming out of his wife's mouth did.

"Where did you go?"

For the first time she grinned at him. "I set my wanderer's soul free and took off on a trip across Europe with no rhyme or reason to my direction. If I saw a poster for a tourist site I wanted to see, I went and saw it."

"Smart."

"Rome. Madrid, Zadar, Berlin, Helsinki, Tallinn, Moscow for Red Square. Pula for the Roman ruins. Ireland for the fairy forts and the Aran Islands. Scotland for Glencoe. All of the places we'd wanted to see, I visited."

"Good girl." He'd seen some of them since he'd been rescued, following the minuscule trail he'd been able to find of her. He'd stood and watched the waves crashing on the rocks against the west coast of Ireland and wondered if she'd stood in that very spot, too, but knowing it probably was something he'd never learn, as he was years behind her. "And RJ?"

"I knew I had a limit to how long I could fly. When it neared that point, I had to make a decision. I changed my passport in Cork..."

"Why Cork?"

"Because that's where your mother's maiden name is from. Yelverton isn't exactly an easy one to find."

"Yeah." Her diligence was admirable.

"I changed my passport at the embassy in Ireland. My original was lost." She made inverted commas with her fingers as she said 'lost.' "By the time RJ was born, I'd established the name as mine. I wanted him to have something of yours and I didn't dare use Mitchell."

He rubbed his palm over his chest. Every word she was saying further confirmed his brain was fucked up. They reenforced how hard she'd been running and why... to protect their son. Now he felt like a fucking fool. He should have trusted her. Trusted himself. He'd fucked up and he didn't know if it was fixable.

"I believe you and I'm sorry I was a stupid dick to you."

CHAPTER TWENTY-ONE

Breathing could stop and you could still live.

All those books which mentioned the breath catching in someone's throat, hadn't prepared her for how much it would ache. Not one of them. She was going to have to drop some authors an email and tell them they were describing it all wrong.

"Wh—What?"

He cupped her face with his hand. "I said, I was a fool, and I'm sorry." Why did the scars tugging on the corner of his lopsided smile tug at her heart? "More or less."

She was not going to lean into him. No fucking way. She'd proved to herself that she was stronger than that. But goodness, did she want to.

"Why?"

"Because I…"

It was Rexar's turn to start explaining. If they wanted to figure out what was going on, they needed to be on the same page. She needed him to not hate her—they had to figure out how to co-parent after all was said and done. Somehow, they had to find a way to not screw that up; RJ's happiness depended on it. She just wasn't sure she believed him...yet. With his thumb stroking across her chin, she waited for him to gather his thoughts.

"When I was in Iran, they kept showing me your photo and saying you were the reason I was there."

"I wasn't." He needed to understand that. To believe it right down deep inside him. Anything else was unacceptable to her. "I would never do that to you."

"I'm starting to realize that."

Thank you, sweet baby Jesus.

She wasn't quite ready to forgive his stupid ass just yet, but knowing he believed her was a start she could live with.

"I searched for you."

"Because you wanted me back or you wanted to kill me for betraying you?" She was more than a little curious as to what his answer would be.

"Both."

She flinched away from the word and the man. Even though she'd guessed it, hearing it coming from his mouth was a whole different ball game.

"Why did you leave me? Were you undercover all this time?"

"Hell no. What part of what I said about being in Iran didn't you understand?"

"Because all you said was they kept showing you my picture and telling you that I was why you were there," she retorted. "I don't understand what that means."

"It means I was in section two-oh-nine of Evin Prison, and it wasn't a vacation to write home to momma about."

She could feel her eyes widening and there wasn't a damn thing she could do to stop them. "Section two-oh-nine doesn't exist."

"Wrong." His finger traced the scar down his face, and he stood out of his chair, tossing it to one side. For a second she thought he was going to grab her, but instead he tugged his shirt and pulled it out of his pants to expose his stomach.

Bile marched from her stomach to the back of her throat. The story of the pain he must have gone through was written in the scars crisscrossing his skin. Some she recognized as burns, others looked like knives, and there were at least three bullet holes. While she'd never be classed as a genius, she didn't need to be one to know he'd been tortured.

"How long?"

"Almost four years."

NO!

If that place existed, how was he here? The Iranians weren't exactly known for their cooperation in prisoner exchanges. Especially not with the United States.

"How did you get out?"

"Drax came for me."

She couldn't stop the vomit anymore and bolted from the couch, pushing him out of the way as she made a beeline to the door she'd seen RJ use earlier. *That better be a bathroom, or I'm going to vomit all over Caroline's floors.*

Kneeling on the floor in another woman's bathroom, puking her guts up—and the lock on the door which she'd used to keep her fears back. Her past and everything she'd felt for Rexar came tumbling out—emotions, fears, pain, and heartache exploded all over the toilet bowl.

Tortured.

He was tortured all this time.

Oh my God.

The pain...

The hand on her neck, and her braid being pulled back barely registered within her as she squeezed her eyes shut. For the record, closing her eyes didn't help either as her imagination took over and she could see him behind her eyelids. Had he screamed when they did that to him? She should have been there to comfort him. To save him.

"Shh, I got you. I got you." A damp cloth appeared in front of her, gently wiping her face like she did with their son's. She pulled the handle to flush the toilet.

"I got you," Rexar repeated. He tugged her until she sat across his knees as he sat on the floor with his back against the wall.

Lily couldn't hold it back any longer. She curled into his chest, tears leaking down her face where he couldn't see. There was little comfort in him rocking her back and forth.

They told him it was my fault.

Why?

Who?

I—I didn't." She hiccupped. Maybe if she did it enough, she'd remember how to breathe.

His hand slid up and down her back. "I survived. It's okay."

He was reassuring her. Was he insane? They said he was there because of her. She didn't know if it was true or not. But it felt like it was. And that ripped her heart out all over again and stomped it into the ground for good measure.

"What if it *was* my fault?"

"Your reaction tells me," he shifted her in his arms so he could peer down at her face, "if it was you, you didn't know about it."

"I'd never..."

"I know."

She wanted so badly to believe him. But the sadness in his tone made her wary. If he went through all that because of her, he would hate her. She'd been reeling from all the punches life was throwing her way.

"I thought you were dead." The wail came from so deep

inside her she didn't know it was possible for her toes to fuel a sound like that.

"I know darlin'. I did, too, for a bit." His chin rubbed across her hair, "I almost was."

"You were gone. Just gone. I wanted to die too, but I couldn't... the baby...yours..." Her words were broken by sobs as she tried to tell him what losing him did to her, and she wasn't even sure she was making sense. She turned, dropping a knee on either side of his, straddling him. In an echo of the past which nearly broke her, he raised his knees behind her back, trapping her against him.

"I know, darlin', I know." He cupped her face with both hands and lowered his forehead to hers. "We'll figure it out. I promise." A soft kiss brushed across her temple. "I swear we will find a way to make sure RJ is safe."

She hadn't told him about the emails and stiffened in his arms.

"What's wrong? Don't you want that, too?"

"Yes. No." She took a second to find the right words. "About a year ago the emails started."

"What emails?"

"The ones threatening to take RJ."

"Fuckers," he muttered against her hair. "Let them fucking try."

"But who? If we don't figure it out..."

"Shh, darlin'."

Damn it, he needed to stop being so comforting; this was too important. RJ was too important. "You don't understand..."

"A year ago is when Drax pulled me out of that hellhole."

The impact of his words hit her dead on. "Who knows you were rescued?"

"Family. Drax's team. Now this one."

That couldn't be it... "And?"

"The DOD."

"Fuck. The CIA, too?"

"Yeah. I had the fun experience of a couple of weeks of debriefing with both before they pulled my security clearance and cut me loose."

"If someone within the CIA or the DOD has decided you are too much of a risk..." her voice trailed off.

"They might come after RJ to draw me out."

She had to go. Now. There was no time to wait around.

"I have to disappear again. We need to go now." She struggled against his hold.

"Nuh-uh, darlin', we're not running." He refused to let her go. "If there's one thing I've learned the hard way it's that there is strength in numbers." He captured her wrists in one hand when she pushed against his chest. "Solo shit will get you in trouble every damn time. You've run and been running. It's time you learned what family is all about."

"But..."

"No buts, no maybes." His growl was a warning. "For RJ we stand together with the people we trust the most at our sixes."

"I don't trust anyone anymore."

"Do you trust me?"

Yes.

No.

I don't know.

Damn it, yes, I do trust him.

I shouldn't.

But I do.

"Yes."

"Then it's settled."

Not even close.

"Okay." If she thought either were in danger, she would leave. He believed he was captured because of her. With all the gear and surveillance equipment she'd found in their house after he was supposed to be dead... he may be right. She just didn't know why.

"Thank fuck."

She snuck a look at his face. Her eyes caught Rexar's, and time stopped. Both inhaled.

It shouldn't be this hard to breathe.

Breathe... Oh my God, I have vomit breath.

She scrambled off him, refusing to let him stop her. No matter how much she wanted to touch and be touched, it was not happening until she figured important things out.

Like where to find a damn toothbrush so I can kiss him until neither of us can breathe.

Shut up, girlie bits. You have no say.

None.

She ignored the cackling inside her head. Her inner self was stupid...just plain stupid.

"RJ, I have to check on RJ." She didn't wait for him to stand up, she just turned around and fled the bathroom as fast as she could.

CHAPTER TWENTY-TWO

Rexar stared after Lily for a full minute before he got to his feet. His brain swirling with all the intel she'd both given him, and the retelling of the sordid shit that was section 209, meant he needed to be sure he could get vertical without faceplanting immediately afterward. He knew she couldn't leave. The guys wouldn't let that happen.

"Rex?"

"In the john, bro." Trust Mike to be the one who'd come looking for him. "I'll be out in a second." He got to his feet and took a quick look at the toilet to make sure it was clean before flipping on the faucet to splash water on his face. The last thing on his stuff-to-do-today list was walking out into a garden full of operators with tear tracks all the way down the scars on his face.

"If you're drowning in the sink, I'm not giving you mouth to mouth," Mike called through the door, "so don't make me come in there."

He dried his face and hands and yanked open the door. "I'm a SEAL, water is my jam."

"Unless it's waterboarding, I'd probably agree with you." Mike muttered. "You okay, bro?"

"Getting there."

"Lily?"

"She's outside."

"Yeah, she almost tripped over me," Mike said. "I don't think she even felt me catch her before she took off like her ass was on fire." They walked down the hallway toward the living room, "What you say to her?"

"Showed her my scars." He figured by the wince on Mike's face that he got it. "I didn't know how else to explain it."

"Yeah, I get that."

"You, too, huh?"

"Yup." Mike's smile was wry. "Castiel punched a hole in the wall when he saw mine."

"I'll bet Noble was thrilled."

"Naw, bro, it was in Germany at the hospital, and Noble was delighted to have another round of paperwork to fill out."

"Hah."

They stepped out into the garden. His eyes narrowed when he spotted some people he didn't recognize.

"Who are they?"

"The rest of Wolf's team." He nodded to a couple who were talking earnestly to Lily. "Your wife knows Cookie's woman."

She'd mentioned a rental here in town, but that didn't necessarily mean she knew these people. Come to think of it, while he'd had his head up his ass, there had been a mention of her knowing Caroline, and he had a vague recollection of shopping being mentioned. But he didn't think that meant Lily and Wolf's teams' women knew each other that well.

"How?"

"Something about a lingerie store and a hotel." Mike shrugged. "Fuck knows for sure. You know how women are when it comes to shopping."

"Uh no. No, I don't."

"Then figure it out, bro, because with a wife, shopping and shit is in your future for at least the next fifty years or so." Mike slapped him on the shoulder. "Thank fuck the only store Cas is likely to drag me to is a weapons one." He grinned and turned away, leaving Rexar to his own thoughts.

Rexar leaned his shoulder against the doorframe and just watched her and their son. RJ bounced around close to her, blowing bubbles someone had given him. His kid's innocent laugher and his woman's smile as she chatted to these people wriggled in under his skin. Another couple of the reinforced concrete blocks which surrounded his heart, keeping it safe, tumbled off the wall he'd built to keep himself from feeling too deeply.

"Here, Mitchell." Kentucky held out a bottle of beer. "Get that down your neck."

"Thanks," He popped the top off and wiped the neck of the bottle with his t-shirt before swallowing down half the bottle in one slug. He watched Lily pushing food around the plate on the table in front of her.

She's not eating.

"You okay?" Kentucky asked.

"No," He dragged his gaze away from Lily and looked at the man who had become his friend. "But I will be."

"Good." Kentucky sipped on his own beer, "I'm not good at the talking and shit, so if you need something from me, you gotta tell me or I might miss it. Feel me?"

"Yup."

"Rex..." Kentucky rarely called anyone by their first name, never mind shorten it. That he did so now was important enough to give the man his full attention.

"Yeah?"

"Do you believe her?"

He gave the question the consideration its seriousness deserved. He really didn't need to think about it, his heart and guts knew the answer. They screamed it inside him.

"Yes I do."

"Thank fuck."

"You sound like you think I was gonna do something you wouldn't like."

Kentucky didn't dignify that with any response, not even his usual go-to snort of disbelief.

"If you are okay here for a day, I'm going to run down to San Diego to see Becky."

"Yeah, we'll figure it out," Rexar reassured him. The trip this weekend had been for Kentucky to check on his Doll Face.

"Hey, Ken?" he called after his retreating back. When Kentucky turned back to him with a querying look on his face, Rexar continued. "Thank you, for putting off your shit for mine."

"Family first, bro. every time."

"But your Becky is family, too."

"Not yet," Ken admitted, "but maybe someday."

Good, Kentucky deserved to have someone in his life who'd put up with his sorry ass. Although it would take one hell of a strong woman to do so. But he figured if anyone had that strength it was Becky. She'd survived the Organization; dealing with Kentucky should be a piece of cake...right?

He took another sip of his beer and kept his gaze on his own family. Holy shit, he had a family that wasn't his twin, his mother, or his brothers in arms. He frowned when Lily was still moving the food around the plate like her life depended on it. He remembered from before when she didn't eat she was nervous.

That won't do. She's going to need every ounce of strength for the war that's coming.

He drained the last of his beer and dropped the bottle in the trash and made a beeline for his family.

"Daddy." RJ spotted him before he'd taken two steps off the patio. "I gots bubbles." RJ swung the hoop and created a massive bubble which popped against his nose.

"Awesome job, RJ." He crouched down when his little boy flung his arms around his knees and hugged his legs. He scooped him up into his arms. "What do you say we go sit with Momma and have some food?"

"Okay."

Rexar grinned as he jerked his head to one side to avoid it being smashed by RJ's vigorous nodding head.

"Careful, or we'll hit our heads."

"Is okay," RJ told him seriously. "Momma kisses ouches better."

Oh man, she sure did. But it had been a hell of a long time...

"She does."

"Hi." Lily's smile didn't quite reach her eyes. He wondered if the others here saw that. From the concerned looks they were giving when she wasn't watching, he was going to take that as a yes.

"Will you eat with me?" Rexar asked.

"Ha..."

"Shut it, Hunter." The woman smacked her man on the chest. "It's romantic that he still wants to have dinner with his family, and it's sweet."

Hunter, who he knew was Cookie, folded his lips together and smiled fondly at her. "Sure it is."

"Men."

He placed RJ onto Lily's lap and tugged a chair closer to them both.

"Rexar." He reached across the table to shake Hunter's

hand. He didn't miss how Fiona snuggled into her man's side, so instead of offering her his hand too, he smiled at her. "Ma'am."

"Don't start with the ma'am stuff." She rolled her eyes at him, telling him whatever was going on with her was being handled.

"Sorry. What my momma didn't drill into me the Navy did."

"As long as it wasn't you who put that bruise on her cheek, I'll let you get away with it." Fiona replied.

"Fu—hel—shi—" he couldn't figure out which swear word he wanted to put in there, and cleared his throat, ignoring the snicker from Cookie. "No, it wasn't me, and the one who did it is in jail."

"Good, then you may stay." Fiona picked up a basket of bread rolls and offered it to him.

He snagged two rolls and a couple of butter pats. "Phew, that's a relief." He sliced the first roll in two and buttered it. "RJ?" he nudged his son with the roll and offered it to him.

RJ immediately took a bite and spoke around it. "Thank you, Daddy."

Lily smiled at him in thanks. This time the smile reached her eyes, warming him from the inside out. Good, at least he wasn't fucking up... give it a second though, and that was sure to change.

He buttered the other side of the bread roll and held it out to her. The smile in her eyes dropped while staying on her lips as if she didn't want anyone else to know she was displeased.

"Please, for me?" He whispered in her ear. "You had aspirin earlier, and your stomach will hurt unless you eat something." He already knew her stomach hurt. Probably a lot more than hurt, but he wasn't above using something he knew for sure would get her to eat.

She stared at him for a heartbeat but eventually took the bread. When she nibbled on the edge of it, he turned his attention to his own food. Around him the chatter and laughter of friends enjoying an evening in their backyard washed over him, comforting in its familiarity. Even though some of these people were almost strangers, there was still a connection. One forged on the beaches of San Diego through BUD/s and in the mountains and deserts of Afghanistan with the bullets of war flying over their heads. But for now, that connection was enough for him to focus on his wife and son and ensure he could look after them for the first time ever.

"Hey, Mitchell?"

His head whipped up to glance across the table, where Wolf spoke with Cookie and his woman.

"Tomorrow night we're going to Aces Bar and Grill, for our usual Sunday get together before we go to work for the week," Wolf said, "Do you and your woman want to come?"

"We have RJ." He glanced at Lily.

"You go, I'll stay with him," Lily said.

Not on your fucking life. There is no way I'm letting you out of my sight.

But he didn't dare say that. "Thanks for the offer, man, but we have RJ and..."

"We'll babysit," Fiona piped up. "That is, if you trust me to look after him." She stumbled over her words. "I mean, I know the last time you saw me wasn't very um, am, flattering, but I swear I'm not normally..."

"Fee, stop." Cookie hugged her into his chest.

"No, Hunter. You told me Lily watched out for me..."

"It was my fault," Lily interrupted. "Those men in the store were following me, not you. I caused your flashback." She added in a small voice, "It was my fault."

"No."

Hell no."

"Darlin'."

All three men spoke at once but paused when she raised a hand in a silent gesture, telling them to shut up and wait. Lily put RJ on his feet and handed him the bubbles and wand again. As soon as he was out of earshot she turned back to Fiona.

"It was my fault and I'm so sorry. When I saw you at the hotel, I didn't know who to call. There was no missing persons report. I could only watch over you and hope you were safe."

"Thank you," Cookie said seriously. "If ever you need me, you call anyone of us." He nodded to the others who had gathered around them. "You may be Rexar's woman, but you watched over mine; that makes you family. If you need us, call and we'll drop everything and come running."

"I agree," Fiona said. "If you want to go for dinner with the guys, then know I'll guard your son like you guarded me, even when I didn't know you were doing it."

Rexar swallowed around the lump in his throat. These men, these people, didn't trust easily, that they trusted his Lily mattered more than he could say.

"Thank you."

"Family." Cookie reiterated, "I mean that."

He nodded to the other SEAL, and leaned into Lily's ear. "I trust them if you do."

"You want to go?"

"I'd like to spend time with you," he admitted. "To get to know you again. What do you say?" He fucking hated the uncertainty in her eyes. Not being able to fix it... gutted him. But he waited her out, giving her time to think, all the while grateful that the others chatted among themselves, leaving them to it.

"Are you sure you don't mind looking after RJ, Fiona?"

"I'd be honored," Friona replied. "It means I didn't screw up our friendship before it has time to even begin."

"They can watch him here," Caroline offered. "That way it's not another strange place."

"Thank you." Lily smiled at the host who'd been so gracious to open her home to them. "Then I accept."

"Me, too."

Fiona's smile and the relief on Cookie's face was worth the indecision and time it took to agree. It was obvious to him, if not to anyone else, that Fiona needed this more than anyone knew.

"Thank you, Fiona," he told her.

"You're welcome." She smiled sadly at him. "I didn't think you'd trust me enough to do it."

"Stop right there," Lily blurted out. "Having a flashback isn't a reason for trust to be broken. My—our—son will probably see a lot more of those over the course of his life-time." Lily reassured her. "If I didn't trust either of you, there is no way in hell I'd leave him with you. I've never left RJ with anyone but one person before."

"Who?" Fiona asked.

"The day I met you all at the mall," Lily explained. "RJ had a birthday party playdate with a friend from down the street."

Rexar made a mental note to make sure RJ had time to say goodbye to his friend before he took them back to Montana. He hadn't known that was his plan, but he did now, and it felt so right there was no way it could be wrong.

"Thank you both." Cookie looked from one to the other. "We'll guard him with our lives."

"I know." He had a feeling Cookie knew more was going on than he let on. But he wasn't going to call him on it just yet.

The next couple of hours passed in a blur of talking, laughter, and teasing. Both teams blended seamlessly together. They'd been introduced to Abe and Alabama. He got a serious kick out of the fact they had two people named after southern states in the house. Mozart, Benny, and Bryan had arrived, introductions had been made, and everyone fed. By the time RJ was drooping and climbed up on his lap and snuggled into his chest, he'd pretty much decided this was the life he wanted for himself. Now he just had to figure out how to make it happen.

"Rexar?"

"Yeah, darlin'?"

"Caroline showed me the basement, do you want to help me put RJ to bed?"

"Yeah." His heart was about to pound out of his chest, but there was no way in hell he was going to show it. He carefully got to his feet and followed her into the house.

* * *

"Do you want to curl up on the other side of him?" Lily whispered softly in the room lit only by the cracked open door to the bathroom. "It feels wrong that you are over there on the chair."

"I'm just watching," He kept his voice as low as hers, not wanting to disturb their sleeping son. The poor kid hadn't even made it down the stairs before he'd fallen asleep in his arms. When Lily had climbed into the bed next to RJ, it had taken everything he had not to follow suit. Only the nightmares which haunted him kept him from doing it.

"What are you watching?"

He heard the rustling of the bed clothes, and when he shifted his gaze from his son's face to hers, she was sitting on the edge of the bed. "Both of you."

"Why?"

"Because I'm afraid this is all a dream, and if I sleep, I'll wake up and find today didn't really happen."

"Rexar."

Why the hell did she have to say his name like that? It played with his mind. Sent him back into the past. A past which should have been beautiful but instead was tinged with darkness.

"Rexar?" Lily whispered sharply.

"Yeah?"

"Get your butt into bed on the other side of our son and get some sleep," Lily ordered. "You cannot sit on the chair all night."

Says who?

He'd slept on the chair rather than a bed since he'd been rescued. Getting in one now seemed... he wasn't sure what the word was, but getting into bed was like inviting his nightmares in and that was one thing he didn't want to happen tonight.

"I'll have nightmares. I might hurt him."

"You won't."

"How do you know that?" Curiosity had him asking the question he wasn't sure he wanted the answer to.

"Because you wouldn't hurt a fly."

He snorted. "My military record says differently."

"Tangos, not family," she insisted. "But if you are worried, then sleep on this side of me." She patted the bed next to her.

"I might hurt you, too."

He huffed in annoyance, and RJ shifted restlessly in his sleep.

"Don't wake him, go back to sleep."

"We are going to talk about this." She climbed off the bed and padded across the room, stopping in front of him.

"I know." He thought the reason she'd come to him was to

219

argue further, but instead she surprised the hell out of him by pressing a kiss to his scarred cheek.

"Goodnight, Rexar."

"Night." He watched her going back to bed. "If I'm not here when you wake, I'll be on the patio out back."

"Why?"

"Because sometimes I need to see the sky to remember how to breathe."

"Okay. Patio. Got it." She tucked the covers around her and snuggled into the pillow.

What he wouldn't give to be able to curl around them both. Slowly the sounds of her breathing evened out. He counted off minutes in his head, just like he used to do in Iran.

At the two-hour mark, when the feeling of rats crawling over his skin got to be too much, he quietly climbed the stairs and let himself out of the house. Seeing the stars would fix the unease he couldn't quite place. Something was coming. He'd just keep watch until it got here.

He sank into one of the deck chairs, and plopped his stocking feet on another. Yup, stars, moonlight, and the sounds of the city settling down for the night. Even the flashing Christmas lights on the house across the street were soothing to his soul. Here, he could sleep.

CHAPTER TWENTY-THREE

"He's avoiding me." She sipped on the glass of wine Caroline handed her. "Thanks, I needed this."

"I gather things aren't awesome between you." Caroline curled her legs in under her. They had an hour before they were supposed to leave for the bar and grill. Cookie and Fiona would be there soon.

"Understatement of the year."

"Want to talk about it?" Caroline offered. "I mean I know I'm not one of your friends yet," she paused, "but I'd like to be."

"I don't have any friends." Admitting that sucked. "Not anymore." When Caroline looked at her curiously but didn't push, she was all kinds of confused. Normally people were nosey and would question that.

Caroline sipped her wine. As if she were reading her mind, she said, "I figure you'll tell me if it's any of my business or if you want someone to listen."

Do I? Yes. Yes, I do. More than anything.

"I met Rexar in Italy."

Caroline fingered the pendant on her necklace. "I'd love to go someday."

"It's beautiful." She leaned out of her chair to check on RJ. He was still running after the ball he and Rexar were playing with, and thankfully out of earshot. "We were both there for work."

"And he swept you off your feet?"

"Not exactly." She grinned at Caroline, "I made him work for it. I don't think he ever had to work to get a date in his life and I was determined I was working, not dating."

"But he won you over?"

"It's the runaway Vespa's fault," She said dryly. "It dumped me into his arms rather than in the canal, and he kissed me before putting me back on my feet then helped me get the bike out of the water before it sank."

Caroline's eyes twinkled as she fanned her hand in front of her face. "Swoon."

"Ha, his kissing skills are rather epic." She didn't think anyone aside from herself and Rexar knew their story. But she wanted to tell Caroline. Wanted her opinion on if she was opening herself up to another world of pain, now that it turned out he was alive after all.

"Not his muscles as he flexed them to retrieve your runaway Vespa?" Caroline wanted to know.

"Those, too." She checked on the boys again. "Before I knew it, we'd returned the Vespa to the rental shop and were kissing like a pair of teenagers on the sidewalk when we found out we were both staying at the same hotel."

"And the rest is history?"

"Not even close." She felt like an idiot as she admitted the next bit. "Before I knew it, he was taking me to meet his twin in Zurich."

"I can't picture two of him."

"Me, either. His twin wasn't there, so we made the best of

the trip. Got drunk way too much. Danced until my feet hurt. Multiple times. Then he got a call…" She trailed off.

"Standby?"

"Orders for twenty-four-hour wheels up."

"Shit." Caroline refilled their glasses. "What happened?"

"We got married. I still have no idea how he pulled that off. Then he deployed on the mission we'd both been working on back in Italy." She gulped another mouthful of wine. "My first clue something was off should have been when I wasn't called in, too. I just assumed it was a different mission."

"Oh no."

"Three days later, I had casualty officers at my door to tell me he was gone."

"I'm so sorry."

"Our marriage papers hadn't even been given to the relevant departments and already I was a widow, who'd just found out she was pregnant."

"RJ?"

She nodded. "I had to figure out how to go on for him."

"Wait," Caroline leaned closer to her, "I'm confused."

"About?"

"If neither of you had sent the paperwork in, how did the casualty officers know to come to you in Zurich?"

She paused her wine glass partway to her mouth. "Uh…" She turned everything over and back in her mind. Maybe Rexar had sent his paperwork in. That had to be it.

Caroline took charge and called for her husband. "Matthew, can you come here a sec?"

"Coming." He tossed the ball to Rexar and jogged across the yard. "Everything okay?" He bent down to plant a kiss on her forehead.

"If paperwork for a marriage wasn't submitted to the Navy, how would they know to send a casualty officer?"

"They wouldn't." He frowned, glanced at Lily, then turned his attention back to Caroline. "If one of his team or family knew, then there would be a whole ream of paperwork for benefits and stuff, but notification is made to next of kin. If there is no paperwork submitted, then next of kin would have been his twin or his mother. Maybe both."

Lily buried her nose into her glass. She knew this information. "Then how did they know to come?"

Matthew pulled out his phone and punched in a number. "I'll ask Tex to take a look. He'll see if there's anything on the records. He turned and went into the house to make the call.

"Tex is your tech guy?"

"Tex is family." Caroline tugged another chair closer to her with her foot, kicked off her flip-flops, and put her feet up. "He can find anything and anyone."

She knew, just knew. "He's the one who found me?"

"Probably. I don't know the details. Did Rexar not tell you?"

"Rexar Mitchell is known to be a lot of things." She muttered into her wine, "Hot, funny, sexy, a little bit wild under all that Southern charm, and he was one hell of an operator. But talking isn't a skillset he excels at. Grunting and chin nods are more his style."

"Caveman language." Caroline grinned at her. "Have you noticed it's contagious? When there's more than one of them, the words diminish, and the grunts increase."

"Oh, I noticed. I'd have to be deaf to miss it. It drove me nuts when I was trying to have a conversation, even over non-important stuff. You know, like what would you like for dinner?"

Caroline giggle-snorted wine out her nose. She chortled so hard that when Matthew returned from the house and looked at her with concern and tilted his head without saying anything, she had to hold her nose to prevent the wine making another exit from it again.

"I don't think I want to ask." Matthew winked at his wife and headed back to where Rexar and RJ were still playing ball.

"I give you exhibit numero uno."

"You are killing me. Stop."

Even when she'd had friends, Lily couldn't think of a time when she'd had so much fun, especially not with another woman.

I could get used to having friends if they were like the women in this family.

She watched Rexar grab RJ and pick him up, tucking him under his arm like a football and racing across the grass. Hearing her son's squeals of excitement was a balm to her wounded heart. He'd missed out on so much. They all had. Would they have a chance of a future? Only time would tell... but maybe...

"You know what might make him start talking?" Caroline asked.

"Hm-mm?"

"If we get all dolled up for tonight." Caroline jumped out of her seat. "I'm going to text Alabama and tell her to wear something to make Christopher swallow his tongue. Then you and me are going to find something to treat those two the same."

"Swallowing their tongues might make it difficult to get to the talking bit."

"But it also might mean we get more than talking." Caroline murmured, "Sometimes drastic needs require drastic measures."

"I don't have anything that isn't mom clothes..."

"You're about the same size as me." Caroline tugged her to

her feet. "We'll go shopping in my closet. I've bought some stuff for Navy balls and work parties which might do."

"I don't know…"

"It will be fun, I promise." Caroline practically dragged her down the hallway to the bedroom she shared with Matthew. "I promise if you're not comfortable, then you can take them off again. I have the perfect dress to go with your eyes. It might be a bit fancy for shooting pool and drinks at Aces, but I swear you'll look a million bucks while you do it."

She massaged her forehead and watched Caroline disappear into the closet. "I don't really know how to do girly stuff."

"Me either." Caroline stuck her head out the door. "Before Alabama and Fiona I'd never really had friends before."

How on earth was that possible? She was funny, welcoming, kind, sweet, and Lily had more than enjoyed being in her company all day. Not once had she felt the need to retreat to her room to regroup, which was unusual for her. What could it hurt to go along with her plans?

"Okay, but you're going to have to show me how this girly stuff works."

"We'll figure it out or call the girls as reinforcements." Caroline dumped an armful of clothes on the bed. "Look through those and see if there's anything you'd like to try on. I have to climb to grab a couple of boxes of shoes."

"Don't fall." The last thing she wanted was Matthew Steel pissed off because his wife had gotten hurt while trying to get something for her. "We have tall guys in the yard; one of them can pull down what you need."

"I have a stepstool. It's good, I swear."

"Okay." She was tempted to pull out the words her mother would have said to her, but figured they weren't quite to that place in their friendship yet. "If you fall off and break your neck don't come crying to me."

Caroline howled with laughter. "My mom used to say that," she called.

"I said that out loud, didn't I?"

"Yup."

Her big mouth was going to get her in trouble again one of these days. "I didn't mean to bring up…" she snapped her mouth shut when the other woman waved her off.

"Thank you for the memory." Caroline sat on the other side of the bed. "I lost both my parents a few years ago, and it's good to remember."

"I'm sorry you lost them."

"Do you have family?"

I should have guessed I was leaving myself open for questions. "No, I grew up in the system. The only family I had was Rexar and now RJ."

"Lily, you are one of us now." Caroline smiled and spread her arms wide. "You're the wife of a man who sacrificed and gave almost everything he had to serve his country. That puts you as one of a select few."

"Does that come with coupons?" She couldn't help herself from teasing her new friend. "Because feeding a kid, a growing boy at that, gets expensive."

"I'll bet it does." Caroline grinned at her. "It comes with friend coupons, will those do?"

"Yes." Oh yes, those types of coupons would more than do. More than Caroline would ever know.

"Pick something to wear." Caroline glanced at her watch. "Blow your man's socks off. He won't be sleeping on the patio tonight, I promise."

Ugh, she was crazy… maybe Caroline was correct. Rexar was so reserved now. Where had the ballsy, I-don't-give-a-fuck Special Forces operator who knew what he wanted and grabbed it with both hands gone? Maybe by dressing to the nines and reminding him of who they used to be when they were together would be the impetus to draw her fun-loving SEAL out of hiding inside himself.

Do I dare?

Is it worth it?

Yes, I do dare. He's in there, somewhere.

Oh, she did dare. The way her nether regions stood up and paid attention. She knew this was the right plan. Well, maybe it wasn't, but she wanted it to be. She took a deep breath and blurted out the words before she could change her mind. "My Rexar needs a kick in the pants. Will you help me knock him on his ass and take notice?"

"I thought you'd never ask." Caroline whooped. "Go shower, and meet me back here in fifteen minutes. Operation Blast From The Past is a go."

"Deal."

Three hours later Lily chewed nervously on the corner of her lip. She knew Rexar couldn't see her dress under her coat. He sat next to her in the rear seat of the Uber Matthew had called to take them to the bar. By the way his knee moved up and down, she could tell he was nervous, although she had yet to figure out why.

Then she got it; his team had gone down to San Diego to meet up with other friends. He didn't know Matthew and Caroline well, but she was grateful he hadn't insisted they go with the others. Breathing was good. Time out a relief. Starting a friendship with a woman who she clicked with, special. But seeing Rexar connect with their son—and RJ fall in love with his father—that was epic, and she wouldn't have missed it for the world.

"Do you think he'll be okay?" he asked.

She leaned into him to whisper back, "Yes. They brought popcorn, ice cream, and a movie. He'll have a blast."

"Why aren't you nervous about leaving him?"

"Do you trust them? Cookie and Fiona?"

"Yes." He answered without hesitation.

"There's your answer." She was conscious of Caroline on the other side of her. Matthew could probably hear them from where he sat at the front in the Uber. "You trust them, I've always trusted you. That didn't change just because you did a Lazarus and returned from the dead."

Caroline choked back a laugh next to her, but her husband wasn't so delicate about it. "She's got you there, bud." He leaned back to speak to Rexar. "But if you want to go home, then we go home."

He waited so long to reply that she thought all the time spent getting ready was for nothing. She could feel the indecision pouring off him. Did she dare offer support? Comfort? Shit, when had she become a ninny? Lily refused to allow her worries to exasperate his. She placed her hand on his arm. The warmth of his smile fixed some of the broken pieces inside her. When he turned his hand over with his palm up she didn't think or hesitate, just slid hers down to cover his.

"I'm good." Rexar's fingers closed around hers. "Good company, good food and new friends sounds like a good plan."

"Thank fuck, because we're here." Matthew pulled some cash out of his pocket and tipped the driver extra. "Let's go eat."

CHAPTER TWENTY-FOUR

"Wow." He fumbled with the coat Lily took off and almost dropped it twice while trying to drape it over the back of the booth.

Holy shit. Wow.

"Do you like the dress?" She twirled around, giving him his first good look at the emerald green. He didn't know what one called a dress which hugged her figure like a glove, but he approved. He so totally approved. *Just wow.*

"Cat got your tongue, Rex?"

Is she flirting with me?

He leaned in next to her ear and dropped his voice low, his damaged vocal cords adding some extra rasp. "Are you trying to kill me?"

He ushered her into the booth and ignored the knowing look from Wolf.

"Killing is not what I was aiming for, unless you mean killing a hot chicken salad."

He fucking loved how her voice had a hint of breathlessness. Even his dick stood up and took notice immediately. He shifted his stance to ease the tightness in his pants.

"Behave." He slid in next to her.

"What if I don't want to?"

Holy fuck, had some kind of switch been flipped on the ride over here and nobody had told him? He stared down at her. The smirk on her lips told him she knew exactly what effect that dress was having on him. She wanted to tease him. Hah, when had he ever turned down a challenge?

Game on, darlin'.

He laid his arm across the back of the booth, crooking his elbow, and ran the tip of one finger down the sensitive spot on the side of her neck. Just as he remembered, she shivered in response, so he did it again, just because he could.

"Hey Jessyka." Caroline smiled at the waitress. "How are you?"

"Hey guys, are there more coming?" She handed out menus and filled their glasses with water. "What can I get you to drink?"

"Yes, the others will be here in a couple of minutes." Matthew helped Caroline into her seat. "The usual, babe?"

"Please."

"Got it." Jessyka scribbled a note into her order pad. "And for you two?" She waited with her pen hovering over the pad.

"Beer for me please." He jerked in surprise and the table jostled because Lily's hand dropped onto his thigh.

"American?" Jessyka grabbed the glass nearest to her, preventing it from spilling across the table. "Tap or bottle?"

"Whatever American you have on tap is good, thanks." He grabbed Lily's fingers. If she kept stroking his thigh like that, there would be no dinner. Unless she was the entire menu. "What would you like to drink, darlin'?"

"White wine please." She smiled at the waitress and nudged him with her elbow. "It doesn't need to be fancy, just cold, and if you have a dry one, I'd love it."

"Will a Lindeman's Chardonnay work?" Jessyka asked. "I think the others might be too sweet."

"Perfect, thank you." Lily smiled at Jessyka and he felt the loss of her attention on him immediately.

He captured a lock of her hair on the opposite side from him and rubbed it between the tips of his fingers, tugging lightly.

"Yes?" She peered up at him from under her lashes. He had no clue what they'd done in Caroline's bedroom, but those lashes had grown.

Fuck. Lashes have grown, what the hell, dumbass?

You're losing it.

Loud cheers and hollers from the other side of the bar drew his attention to her. Having grown up in his family's bar, The Corner Pyrate, he was attuned to the sounds of a bar and knew when trouble was brewing.

"What's going on?" he asked Wolf.

"Pool tournament for charity." Wolf jerked his chin toward a poster on the wall next to the booth, "Me and the guys are down to play later too. Do you want in?"

"They'll let me?"

"Sure. When it's for charity they take players on the night."

"Sign me up."

"Me too," Lily said.

Fuck.

"You sure?" Wolf took the beer Jessyka handed him, and then leaned back so she could place Caroline's drink in front of her. "Lily, these guys here can play…"

Wolf stopped in his tracks when Rexar snorted. His wife didn't need any warning about playing with the big boys when it came to pool. He had more than one memory of Lily wiping the table with him in Italy and in Switzerland.

"She can handle a game or two."

Now that he was getting used to the weight of her hand on his leg, he didn't bat an eyelid when she flexed her fingers against his muscles. Having someone, anyone, even Lily, touch him was so damn weird. His instinct for everyone was to pull away. With her he didn't want to do it. He wanted her closer. If any of his team saw him now with Lily tucked in under his arm, pressed against his chest, they'd be putting down their beers convinced they were drunk and seeing things.

"Okay, sign them up," Wolf said.

"You got it." Jessyka smiled at them. "What names am I putting on the list?"

"Rexar and Lily Mitchell."

Jessyka scrunched up her nose as if she was thinking. She pointed the tip of her pen at him, "Are you related to Drax? You look quite like him."

Wasn't that a fucking kick in the teeth? Before, nobody would have doubted they were related.

"Yeah, Drax is my brother. Tell me he wasn't an idiot when he was here." If he was, Rexar was going to boot him in the ass.

"He was here a couple of weeks ago with Zenko and Noble."

He winced internally; they must have stopped off here when they'd come to see him in Montana. "I apologize for whatever trauma or damage the three stooges caused."

"They were well behaved. I swear." Jessyka grinned at him.

He smiled at Jessyka in disbelief and did an internal fist pump when Lily growled in annoyance. Ha, she still had a possessive streak a mile wide. That pleased him. It pleased him a lot.

"I know those three, ma'am, and it's not often you'll find

their names in the same paragraph as behaving, never mind in the same sentence."

"That's what my boss said, too. He asked if someone had possessed their bodies and could the aliens drop off the real versions next time."

"Ha, that sounds about right."

"Those three can't go anywhere," Wolf chimed in. "But I suppose when you have a reputation as a bunch of idiots who somehow defy the odds and get shit done, it's to be expected."

"Damn straight."

Rexar spotted Mozart coming across the floor, clearing a path for Alabama, who had Abe right up on her heels protecting her back as they moved through the rapidly filling room. He fucking loved that about these men; every one of them protected the women in their family. That was how it should be.

"Sorry we're late," Mozart said.

"No worries," He got out of the booth and tugged Lily after him to make room for the others. There was no way he was sitting in the middle. It would be a tight fit, but with Lily on one side of him and the other side free, he should be okay.

"You've got this." Lily stretched up onto her toes to whisper in his ear. "I'm not leaving."

Damn her, how did she know what he'd just been thinking?

"Thanks."

They waited for the others to get situated before Lily slid back into the booth and he took his place next to her. Thankfully, Jessyka went around the other way to take orders. He needed those couple of minutes with his nose buried in the menu to get his common sense back where it belonged— front and center in his head. He heard Lily ordering the hot chicken salad she'd talked about earlier, and quickly focused on the menu, so he was ready when Jessyka had finished scribbling that down.

"Is your mooing steak really served like a good veterinarian could revive it, or is it a play on words?"

"I can send the chef out to the field to chase one down," Jessyka deadpanned. "But it may take a while and you might starve in the meantime. But if you tell me how many minutes you want it done on each side, I'll let him know."

Lily leaned around him. "Just kind of show it the grill. I mean about thirty seconds on each side."

"Wow, um." Jessyka's eyes widened. "I might have to ask John to cook that one."

"My wife is kidding," Rexar said solemnly even though he knew she really wasn't. "If you ask him to give it two minutes on each side will that work?"

"Yes." Jessyka made note of the order. "I'll be back in a couple of minutes with your drinks."

"I'll come to the bar and grab them for you," Benny piped up. "It's busy tonight and it will save you a trip."

"Thank you, Kason."

"I thought his name was Benny?" Lily looked to Caroline for answers.

"Benny is his call sign." Alabama rolled her eyes. "Each one of them has two names so it can get confusing around here at times. "What's yours, Rexar?"

"He's T-Rex."

Damn it. He inwardly groaned. He was going to strangle her. Although he understood why she wouldn't think it was an issue when all of the other men had supplied theirs. He took a sip of his beer and waited to see what they would say.

"T-Rex?" Mozart studied him from under hooded eyes, "South Sudan?"

"Maybe."

"Hah." Mozart leaned across the table. "That was one hell

of a shot. Dude, you almost took my helmet off, left a furrow all along the side of it."

"You know him?" Lily asked, frowning.

"I never met him," Mozart denied. "Not until the day before yesterday anyway. But he's the one who shot the asshole who had a machete to my throat when we got jumped at that pipeline we were guarding."

A full body shudder ran through him at the reminder of who he used to be. "I'm not that man anymore."

"My ass," Mozart muttered. "It was my ass you saved that day. You'll never convince me you aren't that man anymore." He tapped the side of his head, "The only thing in the way of that man is all in here."

If you say so.

That man—T-Rex—had died on the floor of a rank and damp prison cell in Iran. In his place a shadow of him had risen from the grave. He'd never be that man again. No matter how much he wanted it. Craved it. Needed it. T-Rex was dead, and Rexar would never be that man again.

"South Sudan is a place of nightmares, man," he told Mozart. "Don't allow it in here tonight. There's pool to be played, and friendships to build."

"Agreed."

Thank fuck.

At that moment Benny arrived with the drinks, and Jessyka came with a tray of food.

"Kason is first up in your class of pool." Jessyka glanced at the watch pinned to her apron. "That's in about forty-five minutes. I can try and delay them if you guys need more time to eat?"

"We'll be ready," Benny promised. "Thanks, Jess."

"You're welcome. Enjoy, folks."

CHAPTER TWENTY-FIVE

If she'd known she'd be playing pool she probably wouldn't have chosen to wear this dress and would have gone with her skinny jeans and a pretty top instead. The look on Rexar's face made the inconvenience worth it though.

"He's good." She watched the man wiping the table with Mozart.

"Yeah." Rexar's voice rumbled against her ear. "He's the only one I've seen that's a concern."

"Still as competitive as ever, I see." She leaned back on the bar stool she claimed as hers when they'd finished dinner. She didn't worry about falling off it. The second he'd lifted her onto it, his front had been pressed against her back. Bracketing her, just like he'd always done before.

"That's ironic, coming from you."

She shivered when he pressed his mouth close to her ear, making sure no one could hear his words.

"Do you think they know what's about to happen?" she asked.

"Have you told anyone you were good enough to go pro?"

"No. You?"

"Hell no, darlin'. I'm looking forward to seeing you hand that jackass you were drawn against his ass."

"Babe, I was drawn against you."

"I know." She felt his chuckle all the way through her. "What will you give me if I win?"

"Me."

Ha, take that, tough boy.

"I don't know, darlin'. Lemme think about that one." His drawl was deep low and sexy as sin. God, how she'd missed it. When she'd heard him in her dreams the tone was never quite right. "Seeing as I married you, I think I already have you."

"Then a kiss." She pinned him with a sultry look over her shoulder, and swallowed hard at the heat which flared in his eyes, before he banked it and hid it from her again, "A real kiss."

Leaning down, he pressed their foreheads together, their mouths not quite touching, breaths mingling. She inhaled his scent deep into her lungs. And felt his breathing hitch when he took his next breath. She wanted to say something but didn't have any words that she was sure wouldn't break the spell being woven and wrapped around them. Everyone else in the bar disappeared. Somewhere in the back of her mind, she heard the thump and clatter of pool balls falling into pockets.

"A kiss, huh?"

"Yes."

"Just one?" he queried.

If she moved just a fraction of an inch she wouldn't have to wait for the kiss as their lips would be touching, her mouth on his, his on hers. "To start with."

"Then let's play, darlin'. The table is clear for us." He stepped back, putting space between them.

"Next up is Rexar Mitchell," the announcer called. "He's playing against his wife, Lily."

"Go, Lily." She thought that was Caroline and Alabama cheering her on but she focused on finding a cue which felt balanced in her hands.

"Rack 'em up, darlin'." Rexar dropped the balls on the table and snagged the triangle.

"Of course." She turned with the cue swinging. She made sure she wouldn't hit anyone, but a couple of people ducked out of the way anyway. She moved the balls around, placing the number eight in the center, and shifted it across the table to place it on the spot. "You want to break, or will I?"

"Ladies first."

She smiled at him, and rounded the table, making sure to brush against him—just to remind him who he was dealing with. "Sucker."

"Don't I know it." He swept his hand out, gesturing to the table. "Have at it."

She took her time chalking the end of the cue and blew the excess chalk off. She kept her eyes on him, watching his eyes darken in desire. The rest of the crowd disappeared. She kept her eyes on him for another heartbeat. When he nodded she stepped up to the table.

Lily lined up on the white ball and with a swift clean stroke, hit the center ball of the triangle square on with enough force that the balls scattered with a solid and a stripe shooting into the top pockets on either side of the table.

She ignored the hoots and hollers from the people watching. If she focused on them, she'd lose her concentration.

"Which one are you picking, darlin'?"

"Stripes are pretty, let's go with stripes." She smiled coyly at Rexar, enjoying how his mouth quirked up in amusement.

"Stripes are pretty?" He questioned.

"Yes, they are." She lined up on the white and in rapid succession pocketed the next two balls.

"You've been practicing," he accused.

"Why yes, yes I have been."

"You know, darlin', I could stand here and watch you shooting pool all week and never get bored."

She missed the next shot by a freaking hair. Damn him, and his sexy voice giving her compliments. She flushed when the people watching groaned at the miss.

"You're trying to put me off my game."

"Who, me?"

Did anyone in the room believe the innocent look on his face? If they did, they were freaking idiots.

He shucked off his hoodie and tossed it to Matthew. The rat bastard was going to play dirty—his smirk as he chalked up his cue confirmed it.

Two can play that game, she reminded herself. He bent low over the table and her mouth went dry. Oh, boy did he have a point about how easily one could watch the right someone playing pool all day. Rexar Mitchell in dark denim jeans and a t-shirt with a pirate on the chest…. Mind-blowing.

Every time he rounded the table, his hands wrapped around her waist and he moved her out of the firing line of the back of his cue. Did that stop him from dropping four freaking solids? No, it didn't, damn it.

As he lined up the next shot slightly to her right, she whispered, "Remember, a kiss is the prize."

She snickered to herself when the white ball shot from the end of his cue and into the center pocket.

"Oops, that's a rookie mistake, Rexar." His eyes flared when she teased him. This was fun.

He smirked in response. "Your turn, darlin'."

She narrowed her eyes at him, "You better not be letting me win, are you?" If he was… wait, was that a bad thing? Hell yes, she wanted her prize, his kiss, but she wanted to win it fair and square.

"Nope. Never." He spread his legs wide, and stood the pool cue in between them, with both hands wrapped around it. "I always play to win, darlin'... remember?"

"Shit, I remember," she whispered. It was when she saw his smirk widen from across the table that she remembered he could also read lips. She swiped her hand down over the skirt of her dress and she lined up a shot, then changed her mind. She was wearing a dress, damn it, and it showed off her cleavage nicely.

Let's see how you deal with teasing, babe.

She played the table, bending low as she lined up each shot—giving him an eyeful of her butt and boobs at every opportunity.

"Darlin'," he warned softly, his eyes dark. "Behave."

Hell no.

"What's the matter, hotshot?" She ran her hand up and down the cue, not even caring that there were others in the room anymore. Although considering how quiet it had gotten, maybe they'd all left. But she didn't dare take her eyes off Rexar; if she did...

"I'm trying to decide which shot I want to take next."

"Sure, you are."

She ignored his teasing tone and lined up on the purple stripe and knocked into position in front of the top left pocket. But damn it, it didn't drop.

"Damn."

"You have two shots," he reminded her. I sank the white."

When was the last time she'd been so distracted playing pool that she'd forgotten her advantage? She couldn't remember. But then the last time she'd played pool with Rexar freaking Mitchell, both of their commanding officers had been in the bar and there hadn't been any teasing or playing involved.

Where the purple had come to rest meant her next shot was either directly in front of Rexar, or she could grab the rest and try to take it from across the table. His smirk dared her to avoid him.

Snort.

As If.

Challenge accepted.

Lily sashayed around the table, her whole body moving in time to the background music. She paused next to him and leaned her cue against the table before gripping his arm.

"I need to take off my shoes to take this one."

"You're taller with them on." She could hear the confusion in his voice even as he steadied her so she could unbuckle the strap on her heels.

"I know." She kicked the shoes to one side, and stood on her tippy toes to line up her next shot, leaning right over the table, giving him an eyeful of her butt. Rexar's sharp intake of breath was probably loud enough for the whole bar to hear.

He stepped forward to stand behind her just as she drew back the cue. He leaned down to whisper, "The skirt on that dress is shorter than I thought while you were standing. Take your shot; I'm just preventing anyone else from seeing your ass."

"Hmm." And she missed the damn shot. "You did that on purpose."

"You did, too, darlin'. Be careful what you wish for," he warned. "There will be payback." He grinned at her and took his shot, sinking two balls at once. One into the bottom left and one into the center pocket directly in front of her, bringing them back to just one of his solids and the black on the table. He made short work of sinking the final solid and paused.

"Call it, darlin'."

"Mine or yours?"

"Ours. Same pocket." He leaned over the cue and pinned her with a stare that scorched the panties right out from under her dress. They were freaking soaking—how the hell could they be on fire, too?

She scanned the table looking for the most awkward shot she could find. "Bottom right."

He aimed the white at the black, sending it shooting across the table but it bounced off the sides twice before rolling to a stop an inch in front of the pocket opening.

"Damn."

There was no way he could have had the black come that close to dropping and have missed it on purpose. She grinned at him and chalked her cue, watching him stalking toward her.

"Remember, darlin', payback is a bitch." His eyes burned into her, scorching all the way through her dress.

She panted softly, not able to help herself, then twirled away to lean over the table.

"Payback, hotshot, goes both ways."

She sank the black, winning the game, and turned to smile in triumph at him as the people watching clapped and cheered her success.

"You win."

Holy shit. Every single muscle south of her panty line clenched hard at the smoldering heat in his eyes. "Yes, I did."

"You want to claim your prize?"

She glanced over her shoulder where the table was already being set up for the next players.

"Not here."

"Yeah." He lifted her onto a vacant bar stool and slipped first one shoe and then the other onto her feet.

"I can get them."

She started to lean down to tie them but stopped when his hand slid up her left leg, dipping under the hem of her dress to stroke the soft skin on the inside of her thigh.

"I know you can, Darlin', but let me take care of you just this once."

She nodded slowly. "Okay, hotshot. Show me what you got."

"That's for in a couple of minutes when I find a dark corner to give you your prize."

Her mouth went dry at the promise in his tone. She thought he'd better figure out those damn buckles before she kicked the shoes off again and told herself she could promise Caroline that she'd replace them if they went missing by the time they were done with the prize-giving.

CHAPTER TWENTY-SIX

Thank fuck he'd had the smarts to call Trev and ask him for a floor plan of the bar earlier today. There was no way he wanted this kiss which she'd won to be in front of people. He already knew once he started, that one would never be enough.

He lifted her off the stool and guided her through the crowd, aiming for the corridor where the ladies' room was. If the plans were right, there was a small supply closet just after it. It wouldn't be fancy, it sure as fuck wasn't a sexy place, but it would be private.

"Where are we going?"

"Closet."

"I'm not kissing you in the bathroom." She leaned her head back against his shoulder.

The trust she showed in allowing him to guide her through the people was a sledgehammer strike to that wall around his heart and another block dropped, lowering his defenses even further.

He pressed her against the wall, protecting her from the gaggle of women who emerged from the ladies' room.

"Wait until they go out into the bar," he whispered against her hair. But it didn't stop her twisting around to face him, her hands skimming up and down his back.

"I…"

The door closed behind the women and he wrapped her fingers into his, tugging her to the door the plans said was a closet. He depressed the handle and squeezed his eyes shut when the door didn't budge.

"It's locked."

"I don't care," Lily replied. "Please kiss me."

"You're as demanding as I remember." He pulled a Swiss army knife out of his pocket. "Keep an eye on that door and tell me if someone's coming."

"Okay."

It took him thirty seconds to pick the lock. He straightened.

"Darlin'?" He pushed the door open, and tugged her into the cleaning closet, shutting the door behind them, plunging them into darkness. "Sorry," his hands fumbled against the wall looking for a light switch.

"Give me your phone," Lily whispered.

"What?"

"Your phone, it has a flashlight."

It does? He pulled it out of his front pocket, searched for her hand in the dark, and placed it in her palm. "If there is one, I don't know how to turn it on."

"I got it."

his phone screen lit up, giving off enough light that he could make out her shape in front of him. Suddenly the light brightened, and he blinked rapidly against it. In the couple of seconds it had taken his eyes to adjust, Lily had propped the phone against a bottle of something with the light directed away from them.

"There." She smiled up at him. "Let there be light."

Fuck, she's so beautiful… I've got too many scars.

He lowered his eyelids, breaking the connection which had been firing to life between them.

"Don't shut me out."

"I…" Fuck, he'd promised her a kiss and he'd deliver. He never went back on his word. But this wouldn't be like how it was in his dreams. Nothing would ever be like that again for him. He swept her into his arms and spun them around, pressing her against the wall.

Her breath hitching sent the semi his dick had been sporting since he'd found her, back to full mast. Shit, he'd only just gotten it to calm down after the pool game.

"Kiss me," she whispered, her lips almost touching his. "Please, Rexar."

He cupped her face between his hands, using his thumbs to tilt her head up to look into eyes.

Her gasp killed him, and his mouth swooped down. One kiss. It only had to be one kiss. *Ha, understatement of the year.* Desire exploded through him at the first taste. When she met him kiss for kiss and pushed her tongue past his teeth and into his mouth, everything he was supposed to remember disappeared from his mind.

Her fingers twisted into his hair, his hands went to the back of her head, cupping it gently holding her to his mouth. She groaned, a low, sexy sound in the back of her throat that reverberated through him, and his hand moved down her body to her butt, his fingers digging into her ass cheek through her dress.

He poured all the angst and heartbreak of their time apart into this kiss. It would only be this one… he wanted her to feel everything. To understand—to know what she'd meant to him.

He broke off the kiss, panting, needing to breathe but not wanting to stop kissing her. Her eyes gleamed, luminous with desire, firing the already heated blood that pounded through his body.

I'm so screwed.

One kiss is never going to be enough.

He tried to draw precious air into his lungs, but got a noseful of strawberries, wine, and a scent which was uniquely her instead.

"You. Are. Mine," he growled, emphasizing each word.

"I know."

Fuck!

He needed a minute to think. They should not do it. He braced his hands, palms flat on the wall at either side of her head and pushed away from her.

"We shouldn't do this. Not here. Not like this."

She smiled at him, soft, gently, and tinged with memories. "That's not what you said in Italy."

"A lot of shit has changed since Italy, Lily." He panted, trying to control the emotions threatening to overwhelm him. He needed to find his equilibrium, and he needed to do it stat. "It would be sex." He leaned closer to her, unable to resist the need to be near her. "Sex in a cleaning closet."

"Are we talking hot, fast sex in a cleaning closet," she was fucking teasing him, "because I'm not adverse to that...just saying."

He couldn't freaking think when her fingers were under his shirt, stroking across muscles crisscrossed with scars.

"The first time you made me come was in a closet quite like this one," she reminded him. "I knew I wasn't supposed to touch you. I knew it was a bad idea." Her fingers flexed at his waist.

"I don't want to repeat history." He squeezed the words out past the lump in his throat. "I don't want to lose you, Lily, or RJ—and what's left of my soul." He'd played out this moment so many times in his head over the last two days, and yet his imagination hadn't lived up to how fucking important this would be. "I need for this to be real."

She leaned into him, pressing a kiss to the center of his throat, before tugging his head down toward her.

"This is as real as it gets, hotshot," she whispered against his mouth. Her stomach brushed against his dick. "Kiss me again."

Sparks seemed to fly between them, and he suddenly couldn't remember why he was resisting her and the connection they still had between them.

Connection my ass.

Love was a connection...right? Also need is a connection...right?

Even when he'd believed she had been the reason he was being tortured, it was Lily who'd come to him in his dreams offering a balm to the hurts. Why was he now talking himself out of claiming her as his again? She was right here in front of him and there was something in the center of his chest urging him to take what he needed.

He couldn't resist. He was tired of resisting.

Rexar stroked his thumb down her cheek and across her bottom lip. His other hand wrapped around her hip, pulling her toward him.

"This means there is no going back," he warned her. "You are mine, no more running. We stand together. Protect our son together..." He leaned in and pressed a kiss to her lips, sipping, tasting her. Fire raced through his veins and his dick pulsed with need. "Swear it."

"I swear it on RJ." Lily melted against him, parting her lips, and he took shameless advantage, pushing his tongue inside. His big hands wrapped around her and she looked up at him through her eyelashes.

"You're playing with fire, darlin'," he warned her. but damn it, her eyes seemed to grow darker.

"I want that."

Her husky whisper made an ache form deep inside him, and he struggled for control. Even with all the weight he still had to gain back, he was so much bigger than she was.

"What if getting burned turns me on more than I ever have been before?"

Snap. Snap. Ding.

There went most of the chains on his control. Poof, gone.

"Fuck."

He squeezed his eyes shut. Maybe if he didn't see her, he wouldn't... but she pressed against his body—all those soft curves, tempting and teasing him. Her hands wrapped around his neck and pulled him down for another kiss.

"I dare you, hotshot. I dare you to remind me how good it feels when you take me."

That control he'd been striving to maintain finally gave up the fight. Rexar took control of the situation, his tongue slipping inside to tangle with hers and his hands ran down her back to grope her ass. When she moaned into his mouth, a haze of lust chased all the concerns he had out the door.

As much as he'd dreamed of her in his arms again, the reality was a million times better than his dreams. But also, much more potent—stronger—wilder—hotter. He wasn't sure he would be able to find all the pieces of himself again if things went to shit this time. Did that matter when he had his arms filled with her and she had her legs wrapped around his waist, her dress bunched around his waist, and her panties hitting the bulge in his pants in just the right place?

Not a chance in hell.

She tightened her arms around his neck, her fingers clutching at his shoulders.

"I won't let you fall, darlin', ever." He pressed her against the wall, using his weight and one arm to keep her in place.

"Mmh." She moaned softly, her eyes at half-mast and filled with a mix of both lust and desire. "Rexar, please."

Her breathing turned into sharp, desperate gasps as he ground his dick against her. His fingers searched for and found the front buttons of her dress, popping them free one by one.

"Fucking beautiful, darlin.'" Her breasts were bigger than he remembered. He tugged at the material of her bra, barely waiting for her nipple to be free before her adjusted her in his arms and his mouth latched it, sucking and nipping with his teeth. The onslaught of sensations dragged a moan from her and she closed her eyes as she tilted her head back, thudding it gently against the wall.

Lily's hands touched every bit of exposed skin she could find until he couldn't take it anymore. He stroked his dick against her pussy, the denim of his jeans and her panties just enough to dull the sensation to prevent him from coming on the spot but not enough to stop the goosebumps rising along his skin.

He shivered as Lily's hands snuck between them, pulling and tugging at the belt on his jeans. The jingle of the buckle the only sound besides their soft moans and harsh breathing. Jesus, he was never going to survive her, survive this, with his sanity intact.

His mouth moved to the other breast, his tongue flicking back and forth, before he sucked it into his mouth and she squirmed against him. She would not rush him; now that he'd had one taste, he needed more. Craved it, craved her wrapped around his dick.

"Darlin.'" The pet name was more of a prayer than a word as she lowered his zipper and his dick jerked free of his pants. "You're killin' me."

"Do something, hotshot." She rolled her hips against him. If she'd felt amazing through his jeans, now with only her soaked, thin panties in his way the sensation was knee-droppingly wow. He scraped his teeth over her flesh, sucking hard against the ache he knew it caused.

"Rexar," she groaned, and he released her nipple with a pop and quirked up an eyebrow at her.

"Are you sure, darlin'? Right here against the wall?"

"Yes. Here. Now, damn it." She gripped his cheeks with her hands, forcing him to look at her, "Right here or I swear I'll make myself come and you only get to watch."

His lungs forgot what they were meant to do at that mental image. "Careful darlin'. Saying that to a man like me might get you in trouble." He sucked her earlobe into his mouth, nipping it with his teeth before releasing it to rasp in her ear, "I might make you follow through on that threat."

"Rexar..."

Her hips rolling against him, teasing him, combined with the pleading in her voice was too much to withstand. He reached under her dress, tangled his fingers in her panties, and ripped them apart at the seams.

"I'll buy you new ones," he promised before she could protest, "as many as you want."

The scent of their combined arousal wrapped around him. He wanted to bottle this smell, keep it for himself to be able to pull it out when the darkest hours before dawn fucked with his mind. There was so much he wanted to savor, to remember. But the sensations rolling through him, and her soft gasps and sighs as he teased, kissed, and played with her body didn't give him time to think.

Squeezing his eyes closed against the need in her eyes, he rolled his hips, rubbing his dick along her pussy to nudge at her clit. "So hot."

"More, please."

He did it again, and a third time. Loving the sounds she made in response.

Lily's head pressed back into the wall behind them, and she arched her body forward as he licked a dusky nipple, dragging a needy moan from deep inside her.

"Rexar." She rolled her hips against him, her wetness warm on his dick. Both moaned when the head nudged at her clit. "I'm... I'm not going to last, baby, it's been too long!"

Groaning low in the back of his throat, his fingers flexing on her ass, keeping her pressed against him, he froze. "Shit, I don't have anything..."

"I don't care."

"Darl..."

She tugged on his hair. "I swear, Rexar, if you stop now, I'm going to make the last five years seem like a fucking picnic."

He searched her eyes looking for answers—and found desire, heat, and need.

Thank fuck.

The last thing he wanted to do was stop. He smiled a slow lazy smile. "You're sure?"

"Oh, God Rexar. Please."

"I told you once, love always wins," he whispered in her ear. "Now I'll prove it this time around because we lost our chance before. Please let me prove to you that I'll never leave you again."

"Yes, God, yes." She sucked his bottom lip into her mouth, kissing him as if her life depended on it.

He knew his life depended on her never stopping. He shifted her in his arms and lined up the head of his dick against her opening.

"Ready?"

Her reply was a low sultry growl of her own.

He dipped the head of his dick into her opening, teasing both of them.

"Baby, I'm going to need words."

"Damn it, yes, more, now."

He fucking loved how demanding she was. Fucking. Loved. It. He lowered her body and pushed into her in one powerful stroke and they both sighed in satisfaction when he bottomed out, balls deep inside her, her pussy clenching around him like a vice.

"Fuck." He squeezed his eyes closed as he tried not to come on the spot. He'd missed this so damn much. Too much. He wrapped one hand around her neck, kissing her as he slowly dragged his dick almost all the way out, letting her feel every ridge before driving back in with a little more force.

"Yes, more, please."

The room filled with the sounds of their lovemaking as their bodies moved as one.

Rexar shifted his legs wider, giving them more room, and Lily pressed her head and shoulders into the wall to give herself purchase to meet him stroke for stroke. He could already feel the heat wrapping around his back.

Fuck. Her before me, every damn time.

"Touch yourself, baby. Let me feel you come all over my dick."

He felt Lily's hand slip between them, and when her mouth dropped open on a sigh as her fingers found her clit, he growled in satisfaction.

The movement of her fingers matched the rhythm he set as he pumped into her.

"Beautiful, baby, I love seeing you like this," he praised, and it wasn't long before he felt her muscles lock up and she clenched around him.

"Rexar." The sob sounded like it was ripped from deep inside her as she came.

"Oh, God, yes, love it. Baby." He pushed into her, sinking deep to fuck her through her release. He needed to give her more. But she felt too good. This between them was too much. Too perfect. He threw his head back and moaned, deep and growly, as he slammed deep inside her one last time, grinding against her, his cum pulsing.

"Lily." Her name was dragged from deep in his soul.

The next few minutes passed in a blur of soft kisses until the spell shattered around them, broken by a pounding on the door.

"Mitchell, hurry your ass up. It's closing time."

"Oh, shit." He eased her off his dick, both groaning at the loss, and placed her on her feet.

"I'm soaked."

"Me, too." He made sure she was steady before he stepped back to stuff himself back into his jeans.

"Um...."

"Yes, darlin'?"

"Where are my panties?"

She wanted *him* to remember? Was she crazy? He was lucky he remembered how to stand upright, never mind where he tossed her panties while they'd been otherwise occupied.

"I tossed them—somewhere."

"Oh no."

He winced as his fingers brushed across the sensitive head of his dick as he buttoned his jeans.

"Did you find them?" He turned to her.

"Yes, but you're going to have to grab them as I'm too short."

He followed the direction of her finger and grinned wide

at the pink lacy panties hanging on the corner of the top shelf.

"Sorry." He grabbed them and stuffed them into his pocket.

"Those are mine." She elbowed him. "Give them here. I'll put them in my purse."

"Nu-uh, I'm keeping them." He grabbed his phone and glanced at her—her tousled hair and that flush on her cheeks. "Damn, I want you all over again." He stroked a hand down over her hair, trying to straighten it.

"Am I a mess?"

"Totally." His mouth curved up into a smirk.

"Crap." She rummaged in her purse and came up with a hair tie. It took her less than five seconds to have her tangled hair in a messy knot on top of her head. He wrinkled his nose against how she no longer had that freshly fucked look.

"You wanna stop at the restroom and clean up on the way out?"

"Yes, please."

"Okay." He switched off the flashlight and stuffed the phone into his pocket. He opened the door and peered out, making sure the coast was clear, before he grabbed her hand and tugged her into the corridor.

"I'll wait here." He nudged her toward the bathroom door.

"Do not leave," she warned him before she did as he asked and disappeared into the ladies' room.

Hell no, I'm not going anywhere.

"My wife is pissed with you."

He whirled around at Wolf's voice. "Shit, don't sneak up on me. I could have hurt you."

"As if." Wolf had a shit-eating grin on his face. "Seriously, man, if your woman isn't smiling when she walks out that door, Ice will have your balls for breakfast."

"I'll be smiling." Lily appeared in the ladies' room door. "Blushing too, but tonight we're calling that smiling. Got it?"

"Yes, ma'am."

Rexar reached for her hand and huffed a relieved breath when she squeezed his fingers and fell into step next to him. By the time they'd gotten into the rideshare for the trip back to Wolf and Caroline's, his woman was genuinely smiling again. There'd been no knowing looks or teasing, thankfully. It would really put a dampener on Christmas if he had to murder someone on her behalf.

CHAPTER TWENTY-SEVEN

"Thank you so much for babysitting RJ." Lily smiled at Fiona. "Was he good?"

"Hunter is as big a kid as RJ is." Fiona's smile was wide. "The two of them wrestled and played for two full hours, before I got them to settle down and watch the movie." She grinned at Lily, "Both were out cold within five minutes of it starting."

"RJ just drops wherever he is." Lily watched through the window as Rexar peeled their son off Hunter's chest so the other man could get off the couch. "Nobody told me that. I freaked out so bad the first time he just dropped off to sleep in a sandpit."

"It freaked me out, too." Fiona nodded. "I made Hunter check his pulse. I had visions of me calling you in a panic to tell you I'd fucked up again."

"You know you didn't fuck up at the mall, right?" She impulsively put her arms around the other woman and hugged her, before letting her go just as swiftly. "Those men were following me, not you."

"Which men?"

Rexar's growl made her jump almost out of her skin. While she'd been hugging Fiona, Hunter had escaped the couch, and RJ had been placed back on it, thankfully without waking.

"Lily, answer me."

"Don't go getting all bossy, mister."

"You are mine." He folded his arms across his chest and scowled at her. "What men?"

"Do you need us to stay?" Hunter slung an arm around Fiona's shoulders. "We can if you want."

"Nah, man." Rexar gave them a chin lift. "Thank you for looking after our boy. I appreciate it. Me and my wife are going to have a conversation about continuing to keep secrets."

"I mentioned it."

"Must have slipped my mind." He nodded to the house. "Go put on your jammies and meet me back here, unless you want to bring RJ downstairs and we talk about it in the basement?"

"No, no, he's fine on the couch. If we try to carry him down, he'll wake up." She paused by the couch to check on her son and tuck the blanket tighter around him.

"Five minutes and I'll come looking for you," Rexar warned.

"Don't think that just because we..." she glanced at RJ, "... Just because we, you know, that you get to boss me around. That won't cut it with me this time."

The asshole just quirked up an eyebrow and kept his mouth shut. Then he even had the audacity to tap his watch as if giving her a countdown. "Jerk."

Yet here she was trotting down the stairs in her heels, just as he'd ordered. Because there was no way on anyone's planet that was classed as a request.

She sank onto the bed to tug off her shoes and whipped

the dress over her head. She still ached everywhere. Sex with Rexar Freaking Mitchell was one hell of a workout. More than any she'd done for years. Even when she'd struggled to lose those last ten pounds after having given birth.

He'd said meet her back upstairs, but he could wait until she had a fast shower. The cleanup she'd done in the ladies' room wasn't sufficient for her to be comfortable for the night. Dried cum, even Rexar's, was itchy. End of discussion.

She stepped out of the shower and bent over to drape the towel over her hair, twisted it, and flung it over her head as she straightened. She glanced in the mirror and reached for the nearest thing to hand, the soap dispenser.

"Eep."

"If this is how you plan on getting out of talking..." Rexar drawled. One shoulder leaned against the frame of the door. "...it's working."

"I don't..." Damn, the heat in his eyes as they moved over her naked body was so tempting. "Those men..."

"Don't matter right this second." He took a step closer to her.

Oh no, he didn't get to be a jerk and then come down here expecting to get laid for the second time tonight. That wasn't how this was going to work. She snatched the bathrobe off the sink and slid her arms into it, tying the belt at her waist.

"I don't know for sure that they were following me."

"Unless they are knocking at the front door, we can talk about it in the morning." He took another step, crowding her against the sink in the tiny bathroom.

"Rexar."

"Lily."

Shit. When he growled low and sexy like that she was screwed. She knew it, but the stubborn streak which had kept her one step ahead of the people who chased her wouldn't allow her to back down.

He reached behind his head with one hand and gripped his t-shirt pulling it over his head, and dropped it on the floor at their feet.

"RJ…"

"Is sleeping on the couch and I locked the doors and set the alarms."

Damn. Her brain worked furiously trying to come up with another excuse. "I just showered."

"I know." If anything, the heat in his eyes burned hotter. He braced his hands on the sink on either side of her and leaned in, his mouth hovering over hers. "Tell me no, and I'll stop," he promised.

"Caroline and Matthew…"

"Are all the way upstairs and can't hear us." His breath skimmed over the side of her throat as he whispered the words in her ear. "I'll never stop wanting you. Even when I hated you, every inch of me craved just one more minute with you."

Her body was wracked by a shudder she felt all the way to her toes. "You left me."

"I did." He nuzzled his nose into the crook of her neck, his breath hot against her skin, "Not because I wanted to."

"I know." She knew it and understood why it had happened now. But it didn't make the sorrow and suffering or the pain any less. She shifted her feet, making some room for herself to slip out past him.

He swiftly filled the space with his knees. "Tell me no," he leaned over her, and she bent her back over the sink so she could peer up at him.

Was he for real? Her nipples puckered and tightened against the flannel of the bathrobe. Thankfully it was thick, and he wouldn't notice…she hoped.

No.

What?

Are you crazy?

YES.

Not no.

YES. A hundred times yes.

"If you think I'll tell you no, then you've lost your mind." She barely had time to squeeze her thighs together before he pounced and snatched her up into his arms.

"Hey!" She beat on his shoulders when he tossed her over one and carried her to the bed. She bounced when he dropped her on the mattress and followed her down.

"This time we do it right," he promised. He pressed his lips to her neck just above the collar of the robe, trailing kisses along her collarbone as he peeled it off her. Between kisses his whispered promise sent desire racing through her. "I'm going to worship every damn inch of you."

"Wait." She pushed at his shoulders. "Did you lock the door?"

"The patio and this one," he answered distractedly, paying more attention to sucking up marks on her throat.

"No, this one." How in the name of anything did he expect her to be able to focus when his mouth was nipping at her skin? "Child in the house. Our child."

"Crap."

She missed his weight the second he scrambled off her. It only took five seconds for him to dash to the door and turn the key. She rose onto her elbows watching him. Her mouth opened and closed as he unbuckled his belt, kicking off his jeans on his way back.

Naked, fully aroused, Rexar would give any one of the statues she'd seen in Europe one hell of a run for their money.

"You distracted me," he accused, but she could hear the teasing behind the words. "I was feasting."

"Vampire."

"For you I could be." He dropped down over her, giving her most of his weight, but using his arms to make sure he didn't crush her. "For you I will be anyone I have to be."

"My hotshot hero," she murmured as he captured her lips.

"My sex goddess."

"Sweet talker."

His hands tugged at the belt of the robe and he spread it out around her.

"I think I won't take it all off." His gaze scorched her all the way to her toes. "If you try to escape, I may use it to tie you up."

"I dare you to try," she warned. "You'll be talking in a high-pitched squeak until at least next month if you do."

He chuckled against her neck and stroked his palm down her side, skimming over her breast, to rub over her belly. His roughened fingertips raised goosebumps all along their path. His fingers were followed by his mouth, offering a hot trail of kisses to drive her insane. Her fingers bunched into the bed covers, her back arching, searching for his mouth as he kissed everywhere but where she needed him.

Her elbow.

Her palms on both hands.

The inside of her knee. The top of her thigh, *so damn close…*

"Rexar."

"What, baby?"

"Kiss me." That breathless voice couldn't be coming from her. But she knew it was.

"Where?"

Damn him, he was going to make her say it. She could

stab him in the balls right now and there wasn't a female jury who'd convict her. "You know where."

The bastard laughed at her. He was kissing and giggling. *Fucker.*

"Where?"

Jerk.

She squeezed her eyes closed. She wanted it noted for the record that it was possible to be both mortified and aroused at the same time. Grabbing handfuls of his short hair, she tugged until he rose over her.

"Yes, darlin'?"

Him and his freaking sexy drawl.

"Kiss me," she growled.

"Oh, with pleasure," he chuckled, and dropped a kiss on her mouth.

He was fucking with her. "I'll make you pay for that."

"I'll look forward to it," he promised and claimed her lips in a slow, wet, deep kiss.

"You are making me crazy."

"That's the plan, darlin', that's the plan." He pecked her on the lips and went back to his exploring—lips, fingers, even his knuckles were used as torturous devices to give exquisite burning fire over every nerve ending.

Finally, she resigned herself to doing things on his time-line and relaxed on the bed. As if that was the moment he'd been waiting for, he kissed his way down her body, then huffed over her clit and her opening with his hot mouth almost, *almost* touching.

"Rex, please..." She no longer cared that she was whining.

He swiped with his tongue from her butt crack to her clitoris. "Mmh." He kissed, sucked, licked, nibbled, unleashing his tongue—his orgasm-inducing expert tongue.

"Yes." She fisted her hands into his hair, urging him to take more, to give her more of everything. "Don't stop."

He didn't stop. His tongue circled, sucked, flicked, and rubbed over her clit, driving her insane.

"Ahhh …"

He drew back slightly to blow over her mound before he was back again, his tongue lapping at her opening. He wrapped his hands around her hips, lifting her to his mouth while he feasted, hummed, and praised her.

It had only been how long …? An hour—two tops, since she'd come, but she needed this one more than anything.

"Rexar, please," she begged. "I don't want to come without you inside me."

"You'll get that, too," he promised.

"Make love to me."

"I am," he replied. One hand kept her pussy against his face, the other snaked up her body to tug and roll at a nipple.

"No. I want you inside me."

"Are you sure? I don't think you're sure."

Would it be murder or self-defense to kill him right this second?

"Please."

His sweet, exquisite torture didn't freaking stop until she arched against him, clenching hard as he lapped at her juices.

"One more," He peered up her body and grinned at her. His lips glistened with the evidence of her orgasm and started all over again.

It's so hot…

It's self-defense, she decided, and no woman on the planet would blame her for it either.

Twice more, he drove her to distraction and made her come.

Twice!

She didn't know she'd had that many orgasms stored up. That's what Henry her buzzy was for after all. Henry was fired. F.I.R.E.D. His pink slip was coming in the mail on Monday.

"Rexar, damn it."

"One more, darlin', just one."

"I can't."

"You can." He sucked her clit into his mouth and dipped his fingers inside her, curling and pressing until he was setting off sparks. The orgasm that she'd promised him wasn't there??? That sucker slammed into her out of nowhere. This time, he didn't lick and suck her through it, he lowered her hips and impaled her on his cock, pulling her toward him as he drove inward.

"Jesus, Lily."

Served him right; he'd driven her crazy for hours. She clenched hard around him. Squeezing and releasing. *Thank you, Kegel exercises, for your training.*

He tugged her butt onto his thighs, pumping into her, until both of them were breathing hard. "One more for the road."

He was fucking insane. He'd lost his damn mind. She was floating here on an afterglow of awesomeness. There was nothing left in her body to give. She didn't even have the energy to voice the words, just tossed her head from side to side as her body followed his lead.

His thumb pressed on her clit, rubbing and circling, almost to the point where it was painful on her sensitive skin. Keeping the fingers of one hand on her nether regions, he leaned over her and paused with his mouth hovering over hers. She could feel his breath mingling with hers. When he didn't kiss her immediately as she'd expected, she forced her eyelids to lift and looked up at him.

"Come for me." His order was followed by his lips taking hers in a deep kiss, a pinch on her clit, and his dick bottoming out inside her, and he ground against her, the head of his dick rubbing over a spot deep inside her, and everything behind her eyelids exploded into sparks of brilliant light.

"Jesus, Lily, I..." He ripped his mouth from hers and slammed into her once, twice, three times more, before burying his face into her neck and growing deep and low as he came.

Somewhere she found the strength to lift her arms and wrap them around him. She'd missed the weight of him lying on her so much.

His breathing hitched and he pulled his face from her neck. His big hands cupped her face, "Did I hurt you?"

"Only in all the right places," she reassured him.

"Looks like you need another shower."

"Yes, it does." She eyed him warily. "If I shower, are you going to do this all over again?"

"Three times in one day? I'm not sure I'm quite ready for that." He flopped over onto his back.

"I'm pretty sure it was about five." She lifted his arm and snuggled into his side. "I lost count around then."

"Mmh." He pressed a kiss to her hair, "Sleep, darlin'. If you wake up and I'm gone, I'll be on the patio. Okay?"

"Yes." She petted his belly sleepily. "But stay a minute, okay? I'm not ready for you to leave just yet.

"Sure."

CHAPTER TWENTY-EIGHT

"Whose bright idea was this again?" Rexar sidestepped to avoid standing on the lady with so many shopping bags that he could hardly see her under them and snagged the table before someone else got there first.

"Yours." Lily raised her hot chocolate to her lips and took a sip. "Santa shopping. I've done Santa shopping," she reminded him.

"I haven't." Where the hell did all these people come from? He'd thought Riverton was a small town. Every single one of them, except for Caroline, Wolf, and the others were here. "I'm kicking Wolf's ass for not warning me this was the reason he was spending the day decorating the tree."

"It's Christmas Eve." She licked at the corner of her mouth, capturing the cream. "Did you think everyone would be prepared?"

"No..." Hell yes; who the fuck left everything to Christmas Eve? His wife, that's who.

"Liar." She totally had his number. "You are always prepared for everything, so it blows your mind that this many people aren't."

"California is fucked if the big one hits," he muttered. "There won't be one single person who knows what to do. And the ones who do will already have headed inland weeks before it."

He'd thought this was an awesome idea when Wolf had dragged the tree and boxes of decorations in from the garage. He'd been all fired up about making this Christmas a special one for his family.

I was such a fool.

He drained the last of his coffee and placed the mug back on the saucer. "How many more stores?"

"We just have to get something for Caroline and Wolf and pick up dessert for tomorrow."

"Where's the dessert store?"

"You mean the bakery?" She picked up her chocolate chip cookie and split it in half, then quarters, popping some into her mouth.

"Mmh." He nodded.

"We're sitting in it."

"You mean if I get a gift for Wolf and Caroline, that we don't have to go anywhere but back to their house?" It couldn't be that easy to end this fresh kind of hell could it?

"Yes."

"On it." He yanked his phone out of his pocket and punched in the only number on speed dial. "Hey, Trev, it's me."

Lily sipped her chocolate and watched him with an amused look on her face.

"Hey, how is it being a father?"

"Yeah, we're good. We'll be back before January first." There was no way he was telling Trev that he regretted not jumping on the plane Dalton had sent for the others yesterday. Instead, he'd wanted to give Lily and especially RJ time to adjust to having him around. He was a goddamned idiot.

"Can you book me two flights and an all-paid trip for a couple of days to the Bahamas or somewhere?"

"You are going on a honeymoon?" He could hear the clicking of a keyboard working in the background. Good, hopefully that meant Nemesis Inc.'s TOC was up and running again.

"No. It's not for us."

Lily's eyes narrowed, then understanding dawned. Her smile of approval almost made coming to this fucking mall on Christmas Fucking Eve worth it. Almost.

"Yeah, make it an open reservation, in the name of Matthew and Caroline Steel. We want to thank them for their hospitality."

"Who's paying?" Trev asked.

"Just take it off one of my cards." He had so much money stashed away that he'd never use it all, unless he bought a house for Lily, RJ, and him.

"Done," Trev told him a couple of minutes later. "I'll email it to you."

"Email it to Lily, I don't have email on this phone."

"Yeah, you do, dumbass, I set it up for you," Trev reminded him. "Don't touch anything; just ask your wife to open it for you."

"Asshole."

"But you love me anyway." Trev made kissing noises into the phone before cracking up with laughter. "Merry Christmas, bro."

"Thanks. Same to you, kid." He hit *end* on the call. "All done, Wolf and his woman have a trip to the Bahamas waiting for them when they're ready to take it."

"That's an awesome gift."

He reached for her hand and kissed her knuckles. "That's us, the Mitchells. We're the awesome gift givers."

"But I'm not a Mitchell anymore."

Everything screeched to a stop in his head. Fuck, he'd forgotten she'd changed her name.

"You have two choices." He chose his words carefully. He'd rather not piss her off today, thank you very much. "We can either get your name changed back…"

"Or?"

"Or you can marry me again."

"Did you just ask me to marry you?"

What the heck did she have to be all mad with him for? This right here was why he kept his mouth shut. When he opened it, stupid shit fell out. Stuff he thought was perfectly reasonable, but she didn't.

"I did."

"Are you insane?"

"Possibly." Two shrinks and more doctors than he'd bothered counting before the Navy had told him he was too fucked in the head to serve. Did that make him insane? "Probably."

"We are already married, and you haven't told me you love me in nearly five freaking years." She slammed her mug into the saucer and pushed back her chair. "I'm going to get that dessert."

He watched her stomping toward the counter… he hadn't told her he loved her? Impossible. He'd never stopped loving her. Even through the torture, even when they showed him pictures of Lily and told him she'd betrayed him. Somewhere deep down inside he might have buried his love for her, for his own protection, but he'd never stopped loving her.

"Son, if I was in your boots," an older gentleman leaned toward him from the next table, "I'd get off your backside, gather those bags, and go after your wife."

"You'd better have an epic present for her," said the woman sitting next to the man, "because if you don't, you're going to spend Christmas night in the doghouse and rightly so."

Fuck, a present... for Lily. Shit.

"Thank you," He nodded to both and did what they suggested—grabbed the bags and trotted after his wife.

She scowled at him when she saw him standing behind her at the counter. "I'm mad at you."

"I know." He didn't miss that she checked to see if he'd brought the bags with him. He'd dropped a fortune in the toy store. But Lily, how the fuck had he been so stupid as to forget a gift for her?

He scanned the mall, studying every store name he could make out.

Kitchenware…

Hell no, I'm stupid, not double-stupid.

Bookstore.

Lingerie shop.

Clothing.

More kitchen stuff.

Fuck.

When he spotted the cashier talking to Lily, handing over a box, he pulled out his wallet and handed it over her head.

She slapped at his hand. "Stop that, I have it."

"Darlin'." He ignored the cashier's admiring look. Clearly, she needed her eyes tested and didn't see the scars yet. "I'm paying. You get to eat it tomorrow."

"Do you have to be such a jerk?" She took the box from the cashier. "Let's go."

"Keep the change, ma'am." He nodded to the cashier and grabbed Lily by the upper arm before she took off in the opposite direction to where he wanted to go. "This way."

"I thought we had everything?"

"We haven't got yours yet."

"If it's a frying pan, I'm going to use it on your head."

Scratch that idea. Fuck.

He led her into the only other store on that end of the mall and offered a silent prayer that it didn't backfire on his ass.

"Why are we here?"

"To get your Christmas present." He watched her warily as she scanned the store, her eyes huge in her head.

"Are you serious?"

She isn't losing her shit, phew.

"Yes, I'm always serious."

"Which one?"

"Go wild darlin'. Pick as many as you can carry."

"What?"

"As many books as you want." He could see the spark of interest in her eyes. "Any kind, any price. Pick what you love. If they don't have it, we'll order it."

"You are buying me books for Christmas."

Shit.

Retreat.

Retreat. STAT.

It's too late to retreat.

"Yes."

She flung herself against him and planted a kiss smack straight on his mouth and was gone again in a flash.

"Best present ever."

Phew.

If he hadn't been in public and didn't have half a dozen women staring at him, he'd have wiped the sweat off his brow with the back of his hand. He trailed after Lily, curious to see what she'd pick. There was no way he'd dare question a single title. Not one. He'd just gotten himself *out* of trouble.

Lily placed the dessert she'd bought on an end table next to a comfy looking chair.

"Rexar sit down, this could be a while."

She could take as long as she damn well pleased. He'd buy every damn book in the store if it made her happy. Hell, he'd buy her the fucking store if she wanted it.

"Eeek! this one is signed by the author."

Her squeal of happiness settled deep into his heart. "Who's that, darlin'?"

"Riley Edwards signed it, look." She opened the front of a novel and stuck it under his nose. He had to squint to see the title, never mind the autograph across it. "And it's *Fractured*. Holy cow."

"If it's broken, put it back and get another one."

"The title is *Fractured*, not that it's broken." She looked at him like he was today's class idiot, but dropped the book into his lap, "Keep that safe. I'm going to look for more."

For the next hour and a half, he watched her as she perused shelves, read the back of some books, and flipped through others. He picked up the ten books on his lap and scowled at the covers. Someone needed to pay those dudes some extra cash to buy more clothes. A nice shirt or two wouldn't go astray.

"I think that's it." Lily stood in front of him. "I've got Riley, Olivia Michaels, Caitlyn O'Leary, Susan Stoker, and Kris Michaels." She frowned at his full lap. "It's too much, isn't it? I'll put some back."

He stacked the books in his arms and stood up. "Darlin', sit your ass in this chair right here and I'll go and take care of this." If she thought he wasn't buying every single book she wanted after watching her loving on all of them, she was the one who'd lost her mind. He carefully carried them to the counter and placed them in front of the lady behind the cash register.

"Can I pay for these please?"

"Sir, please tell me there are more of you at home and that you can introduce me."

"Excuse me?" He eyed her in shock. Was she coming on to him?

"If more men knew how to do Christmas presents like you do," she nodded to the books, "then it would be a whole lot better than tableware or a kitchen appliance."

"I was kinda hoping to avoid being whacked over the head with a frying pan this year."

"Good choice." The woman scanned the books. "Can I get you anything else, sir?"

He looked at the display behind her. "Can you pick me a bunch of those bookmarks, please? The books my wife picked should tell you what kind she likes. Just can some of them have shirts on?"

The woman snickered, then placed her hands on her knees and doubled over in laughter. "No shirts, got it."

"*With* shirts. Please, with shirts."

She grabbed a handful and placed them into the bag. "There you go."

He handed over his card and tapped in the pin to pay for them. "Thank you. Merry Christmas."

"Happy holidays, sir."

"Darlin', are you ready to go rescue Wolf and Caroline from the one-hundred million whys that come out of our son's mouth on a daily basis?"

"Yes." She took the bag of books he offered her and hugged it to her chest. "Thank you."

"You're welcome." He dropped a kiss on her head. "C'mon, let's get outta here before everyone decides they're leaving too, and we don't get back until the day after tomorrow."

"We aren't missing Christmas. Move your ass, hotshot."

Like any smart man, he replied in the only acceptable answer.

"Yes, ma'am."

CHAPTER TWENTY-NINE

"Where did we park the truck?" The whole parking lot was full to overflowing. Cars circled waiting to pounce as soon as a place became vacant. Her feet hurt, her back ached. She'd had way too much exercise last night for shopping today. But it had been totally worth it.

He bought me books.

Who does that?

Rexar does.

"Fucked if I know," Rexar grumbled. "Which door did we come in?"

"East side, I think."

"Why don't you wait here, and I'll find the truck and circle around and pick you up."

It was so sweet of him to offer, but she distinctly remembered an incident at the airport in Zurich where there was almost a requirement for bail money, and she didn't have the energy for that today.

"I'm okay," she reassured him. "Let's just get out of here. It's only going to get worse before all the stores close for the night."

"Okay, if you're sure."

"I am." If she'd thought town was bad the last time she'd come here, when she'd first met the girls, now she knew different. "We are never doing this on Christmas Eve again. Ever."

"Agree."

She stumbled when someone hit the back of her heels with a cart, but didn't have time to focus on the pain as Rexar turned and snarled at the careless woman.

"I'm okay."

"No, she doesn't get to be a dick just because she's in a hurry." He tugged her in front of him and pressed up against her back, protecting her heels from any more over-exuberant cart pushers. "We are all in a hurry today."

"Easy, hotshot, your caveman is showing."

"Damn straight it is, darlin', damn straight."

He guided her toward the exit they needed. Protecting her all the way. The next time someone called him a badass she was going to laugh herself silly. They didn't see him now.

"The next time the boss hires trucks, imma going to ask him for one in hot pink. It would make it a darn sight easier to find in this fucked-up mess."

"Tell him to throw in some glitter too, and maybe one of those things." She pointed at another car's antenna.

"Darlin', that's a dildo hanging on the antenna." He put pressure on her left hip to move her to the right, out of the way of a reversing vehicle. "Who the hell puts that on their car? Shit like that belongs behind closed doors."

"Maybe they want to deter people from robbing it?"

"I wouldn't…"

She wouldn't either, not if someone paid her a million bucks. Well maybe…nope… not even for that.

Finally, she spotted the rental plates on a black truck. "Is this us?"

He hit the key fob and the lights flashed.

"Thank God. My toes don't want to wear my shoes anymore."

He opened the rear door and stored the shopping bags. "Do you want the dessert in with you, or back here?"

"I've seen you drive," she reminded him, "I'll keep it on my knees."

"I'm not *that* bad."

"Hotshot, you muttered, 'floor it, motherfucker' three times on the way over here on yellows at the lights."

"You heard that, huh?" He lifted her into the seat and slipped off her shoes, tossing them into the back. "Swing around so I can buckle you in."

"I've been driving for years," she reminded him, "I can buckle a belt."

"You're pretty good at unbuckling belts, too." He winked at her and twirled his finger.

"Smartass." She faced forward and once she was settled, he leaned in and secured the belt. "Thank you."

"You're welcome, darlin'." He closed her into the truck and rounded the hood to climb in next to her. "There's three cars waiting for me to pull out." He gestured to the left. "This right here is why I combat-park with my nose pointed out; reversing out of here would be fucking shit."

She nodded in agreement, crossing one leg over her knee to massage the kink out of her toes.

"Ready?"

"Yeah."

"Then let's go."

He'd just put the truck in gear when the dumbass who was first in line for their parking spot decided they weren't moving fast enough and laid on the horn. Rexar glared at him, then switched off the engine again and leaned back in his seat. He turned his head to grin at her.

"Do you have any idea on how to waste a good five minutes?"

"I might?" She tilted her head toward him. "Do you?"

"Oh yeah."

Who sucked all the air out of the truck? Why was it suddenly so hard to breathe?

"You wanna make out like teenagers?" He kept his eyes on her but offered the dick with the loud horn the middle finger.

A giggle escaped her mouth before she could stop it, and she unclipped her seat belt.

"You have awesome ideas. You know that, right?"

"Do I now?"

Did he know how much she loved when he just hovered his lips over hers, ramping up the anticipation between them.

"Yes."

"Good." He brushed his lips over hers. "As soon as everyone is sleeping and we've played Santa, what do you say we go find ourselves somewhere private?"

Her girlie bits all but screamed in delight and clenched all by themselves. She nodded as a shiver raced down her spine at the promise in his voice. "It's a date."

"Ha," he barked out a laugh. "A date, I like that." He kissed her once more, hot and deep. "That's to hold us over until then."

When he finally let her up for air, the impatient driver had moved on.

"Let's get out of here." He helped her with her seatbelt and once more started the engine, waving at the young man in the pick-up truck waiting for them to pull out.

"People are insane." She braced her hand on the 'oh shit' bar when he hit the brakes for the fourth time between the parking spot and the exit, this time to avoid a shopper who just strolled out between two cars without even looking to make sure it was safe.

"Never, again." He turned to her. "Promise me we never do this on Christmas Eve again."

"I swear I'm going back to ordering from catalogues and sending everything to a PO box in October."

"Thank fuck." He eased the truck forward and waited for a space to pull into traffic and escape the parking lot. "Finally."

"Do you know which turn-off for Caroline's?"

"No. Don't you?"

"No, I only lived here for about six months. I lived on the opposite side of town and only came over this way for the mall."

"Shit. Grab my phone and call them."

"Do you have the number in there?"

He lifted his butt off the seat and pulled out his phone. "Wolf's one of the last called numbers."

She swiped open on the phone. "You need to put a password on this."

"I have nothing on it." He grinned at her, "Trev, our coms tech at home in Montana, doesn't let me have anything techy that I might break."

"At least someone up there has braincells. Because someone let you outta the gate unsupervised." She tabbed through to the calls window and frowned at the list. "Who is Kid?"

"Trev."

"And Woo-woo?"

"That's Wolf."

"Hotshot, why do you have Wolf in your phone as Woo-woo?"

"What does the wolf say?"

"I'm sure I played this game with RJ when he was about two. Woof?"

"Not like a dog. Wolves don't bark." He slowed for a red and hit the gas again as it turned green just as they reached it.

"So the wolf says woo-woo?"

"No, the wolf says woooooo-woooooo." I just couldn't be bothered to type in all those o's."

"Someone come get me. Save me from his crazy." She hit the name Woo-woo and held the phone to her ear. It rang and rang.

"Nobody's answering. Did they say they were going anywhere today?"

"No answer?"

"It's still ringing." She hit *speaker* and the sound filled the cab of the truck. "Do you people not believe in voicemail?"

"I don't have it unless Trev set it up." He grinned at her. But she could tell it was forced, "Call Fiona. You have her number from last night, right?"

"Yes." She dug into her purse for her own phone and pulled up the number. She hit *call* and once again put it on speaker.

"Hello?"

"Fiona, it's Lily."

"Hi, Lily."

"Have you heard from Wolf and Caroline? They are looking after RJ while we're doing Santa shopping, but when we called Wolf's phone to find out the turn-off to get back there, nobody answered."

"That's weird. Wolf always answers unless it's a private number," Fiona replied. "Do you want me to ask Hunter to call him?"

"Yes, please."

"Hey, Fiona, it's Rexar. What's the turn-off for the house?"

"Fourth and Elm."

"Got it. That's coming up in about a mile. Thanks."

"You're welcome," Fiona replied, then yelled, "Hunter, can you call Matthew? Rexar and Lily can't get a hold of them and they have RJ."

"Sure."

"I'm calling Caroline too," Fiona told them.

"Something's wrong, Rexar, I feel it."

"Me, too."

"They aren't answering for us either," Fiona said. "We'll meet you at the house, we're five minutes from there. I'll call Tex on the way."

"Thank you." She pressed *end* on the call. Her stomach churned and roiled. "They've taken him."

"Who?"

"The people who chased me out of Zurich, and then started chasing us again when you escaped."

"They probably went to the park to feed the ducks."

She appreciated that he was trying to reassure her, but when she could hear the worry in his voice it didn't help very much.

"Hit speed dial one for me." The truck took the turn off Fourth and Elm so fast it felt like they were almost on two wheels. "I want Trev on the line too, just in case we need him."

"Okay." She did as he asked and waited for the call to connect.

"Did you change your mind on booking that honeymoon already?" Trev said by way of a greeting.

"Hello?"

"Um, shit. Sorry, ma'am... why do you have this phone?"

"Hang on a second, Trev," Rexar called. He swung the truck into the drive and yanked up the parking brake. Both jumped out without turning off the engine, or even closing the doors behind them.

* * *

One hour earlier

"Miss Caro, cans I play wif the kitty?"

Caroline tapped the off button on the vacuum cleaner with her foot and caught RJ before he tripped over the cable. "Careful."

"Oops." RJ grinned up at her. "But the kitty?"

"Where did you find a kitty? We don't have a kitty."

He caught her by the hand and tugged her to the patio door.

"Sees, it there."

He was right, there was a kitten sitting on the fence.

"Oh, it's a tiny little baby."

She allowed him to tug her out the door and across the garden. If the kitten had been on the other fence, she might have thought it belonged to their neighbor, but on the back of the property there were no houses as development hadn't started there yet.

"You gets him down?"

She reached her hand up, rubbing her fingers together to coax it toward her.

"Here, kitty."

But he stayed just out of reach. She stood on her tippy toes, trying to see where the kitten was half hidden in the branches of the tree overhanging the fence.

"Oh, are you tangled up in something, sweetie? One minute; we'll figure out a way to get you free." Of course, this would happen as soon as Matthew went to the hardware store for something to attach the Christmas lights to the gutters.

"He's tied up with something, RJ."

"Is scared?"

"He's just a baby and must be missing his momma," Caroline explained. "Let me go get the ladder from the front of the house. I can use it to climb up and get him free. You stay right here, okay? Do not come out of the garden."

"Okay."

She ran inside the house for the key to the padlock on the back gate. They were probably being overly cautious about being responsible for someone else's child. But neither she nor Matthew had wanted to take a chance on RJ somehow getting out of the gate and onto the road.

"Rexar and Lily had better be wanting to add a kitten to their family, because with the hours we work we aren't keeping it here."

She opened the padlock and opened the gate and walked straight into the muzzle of a handgun.

"RJ, hide!" She screamed the warning as she was knocked to the ground and felt a stinging in her neck.

"Assholes, he's just a little boy."

"He's my ticket to a new life." The man sneered in her face. "Did you think you could run forever, Lily?"

He jerked his chin toward the gate. "Grab the kid."

"Yes, boss." She counted three pairs of boots passing by her face.

"I'm not Lily…." Her words were slurring as the drug kicked in. "I'm Caroline, and my husband will make you pay."

"Oh, I'm counting on Rexar wanting to make me pay." The man chuckled. "He's not the only one who can rise from the grave."

Whoever this was obviously thought she was Lily, but they'd have to be seriously blind to think her Matthew was Rexar Mitchell.

"Hide, RJ, hide." She tried to scream the words again, but they came out as a whisper, and everything went dark.

CHAPTER THIRTY

Rexar's stomach churned as he bolted for the front door. He slammed against it when it didn't open under his hand.

"Back gate, try the back gate." He spun on his heels, then steadied Lily as he tripped over her.

A black truck pulled into the driveway as they ran to the corner of the house.

"That's Wolf." Relief slammed into him. They'd overreacted. "Fuck, thank fuck."

"What's going on?" Wolf stepped out of the truck. "Did something happen?"

"Sorry, dude." He had to work harder than he wanted to for his voice to be steady. "We couldn't get an answer from your phone. I panicked." Lily's hand petting his lower back was the touchstone keeping him from sliding straight into the flashback he could feel knocking on the edge of his subconsciousness.

"Did Ice not answer?" Matthew led them to the front door and put his key in the lock just as Cookie and Fiona's car screeched to a stop across the front of the drive. They got out and jogged to the front door.

"Cookie and Fee?" Wolf asked, opening the door.

"We called them to get the turn-off for coming back here." Rexar felt like an idiot now. Yet something kept picking at him. An unease he wasn't able to push aside.

"Ice?" Wolf called into the house as they went in. He tossed a small bag from a hardware store on the counter, next to where a phone was plugged into a charger. "My phone was dead. I forgot to grab it when I ran to the store for wire for the gutters."

"Back door's open," Cookie called. "They must be in the garden."

"Stop." Everything in him screamed to pay attention. "Something's wrong."

"I feel it, too." Wolf muttered. He went to the cupboard over the fridge and pulled down the box they'd locked their personal weapons in when they had a child in the house. "Cookie, you carrying?"

"Always."

"Rex?"

"Is there any other way to be?" He reached under his shirt for the Glock he kept holstered there. "Search the house."

"Hey, hey. Answer me, damn it."

Shit, he'd forgotten about Trev. He made a give me motion for his phone and put it to his ear when Lily handed it to him.

"Trev, we're not sure what's going on. Grab the boss."

"He's already in the cage gearing up with Alpha and Bravo. As soon as you give the go-ahead, they'll be wheels up and can be there in three hours max."

Relief snuck in under his skin. He'd take the shit the guys would throw him for overreacting for the rest of his life if Wolf's woman and his son were just playing in the basement. But he knew they weren't... he just knew it. What he'd been waiting for—the nightmares from his past—had decided today was a good day to die.

And die they would, because now he had someone—two someones—to live for... there was no way in hell he was giving them up without a fight.

"Fee, call Tex," Wolf ordered. "We will clear the house."

"Lily, you need a weapon?" If this had been Italy or Zurich, he knew she'd have been carrying a lady Glock strapped to her thigh and a switchblade tucked into her bra, but it wasn't and she had a child to consider.

"In my purse."

"Get it," he ordered. "Protect Fiona. Wolf, it's your pad, you lead." He snapped into mission mode. His brain needed to be there to function. Fucking up wasn't an option anymore, "I'm on your shoulder, and Cookie on my six. Understood?"

"Yup."

"Let's roll." Just as they would have in Iraq or Afghanistan, they fell into position and began to methodically clear the property.

* * *

CC_CopyCat: Favorite drink?

Tex: Coffee – it makes the world go around.

CC_CopyCat: Sometimes it makes the world stop too.

Tex: And that's why they say, stop and smell the coffee.

CC_CopyCat: Ha, you're funny.

She thought he was funny? Who else thought that?

CC_CopyCat: Favorite food?

Tex: Lasagna, but made the Italian way, not the American. What's yours?

CC_CopyCat: Mexican, especially if it's from one of those food trucks run by an old Abuela.

Tex: Truth. Those Abuelas know how to cook.

CC_CopyCat: okay, hard question next... are you sitting down?

Tex: I am, my leg aches today.

Shit, what did he tell her that for? She—and he was still assuming she was a she—didn't need to hear him whining.

CC_CopyCat: can you take something for it?

Tex: I will later tonight.

Tex: ask your question.

CC_CopyCat: It's important so make sure you think about your answer. Okay?

He chuckled. Her comment tickled his funny bone. What was it about this person... she fascinated him.

Tex: Go on...

CC_CopyCat: What's your favorite color?

Tex: That's your question?

CC_CopyCat: It's important, someone's favorite color tells you more about them than anything.

Tex: What does blue say about me then?

Tex: hold that thought. Phone. Tell me yours while I get this.

CC_CopyCat: pink and okay.

He hit *answer* on the call.

"Hey, Fee. How are you doing?" He spun around in his chair, facing away from the computer screen. Even though he knew Fiona couldn't see it through the phone, he wasn't quite ready to share this connection he was building with his friends just yet. He wanted to hoard her all for himself... for now.

"I think we might have a problem."

"Talk to me." He spun back around and typed a message as fast as he could.

Tex: I gotta go.

CC_CopyCat: it was the pink wasn't it? I knew I shouldn't have mentioned it. Be safe.

Rex: HAHA. Later.

He clicked out of the screens.

"Fee, spitting it straight out is a good way to start. Don't try to choose your words."

"I'm not sure what's going on." He could hear murmuring in the background, as if she was talking to someone else. "I'm going to put my friend on the phone."

"Okay."

"Hello, my name is Lily. I'm T-Rex's wife."

Fuck, it had been a long time since he'd heard that name. Even Rexar hadn't used it when he'd called him.

"Hello, Lily, it's good to hear from you." Was the fact Fiona was asking him to talk to Lily a good or a bad thing?

"My son and Wolf's wife weren't at their house when we got back from Christmas shopping at the mall." Lily's voice changed as if she had gone into debriefing mode. He could work with that. "T-Rex feels like it's all wrong. Me, too. He's clearing the house right now."

"Where's Wolf?"

"He got back from the hardware store about two minutes after we did. Cookie is here, too, because we called him."

"Okay, those are the players..."

"You're a tech guy, right?" She cut him off. "The one who found me?"

"Yes."

"If I give you a code, can you track it?"

"I can." He flipped through the screens. "Who am I tracking?"

"My son." She rattled off a mix of numbers and letters. "RJ has a GPS tracker in his shoe. I put it there."

"Nobody else knows about it?"

"No."

"Smart." He opened up the program and put in the tag number for the tracker. "What's the pin code?"

"Fifty-four R, twenty-seven E, sixty-nine X."

"Got it." Tex watched the line across his screen as the dots moved from red to green. "It's calibrating. Two minutes."

"Thank you." Lily sighed. "Because my other option was to call Aria, and she'd lose her shit and murder my husband for losing our son."

"Your friend sounds protective."

"She is."

The screen in front of him flickered, and then thankfully a dot blinked a couple of times, then started moving across the screen,

"Have him."

"Thank you, sweet baby Jesus."

"It's Tex. Jesus is a whole different dude."

"Smartass." She murmured. "Cover your ears, I'm gonna yell."

"Okay." He pulled the phone away from his ear and winced when he heard her shout loudly for her husband. If she'd done that without the warning, he'd have had a headache for a month. "Jesus."

"That's not me, either." She threw his words back at him, "Here's T-Rex."

"Tex?"

"I've got eyes on your boy." Tex launched straight into the intel. "He's heading east toward Blossom Valley, moving fast, so best guess is he's in a vehicle."

He felt for Rexar when he heard the harsh intake of breath. "And Wolf's wife?"

"No confirmation, just your boy's tracker."

"Who the fuck tracked my son?"

"Your wife."

"What?"

"Dude, we don't have time for that shit. Gear up, get your asses on the road," Tex ordered. "I'm going to work some magic and see if I can figure out the who and the where."

"Look into former Col. Lang, and a Bill Braxton." Rexar said. "Don't ask me why."

Tex typed the names into the program on his second laptop and scanned the files.

"Both are dead."

"I'll call Drax. He has contacts with a former Delta Force Team that now works private out of Texas," Rexar said.

"Panthers. I know their tech guy. I'll give him a call."

"Thanks," Rexar said. "Call me when you find something. Trev will be in touch, too. My boss will be wheels up in about ten minutes."

"Roger."

And just like that, multiple branches of former and current military spec ops teams were mobilized. Wolf and his people. Rexar and Nemesis. Panthers. And if he had to hazard a guess, Red Squadron's asses would be in the air on a transatlantic flight the second he called Drax in Italy. Each team, each man, dropping everything to help protect and find two of their own. 'Protect the innocent' was a motto every team lived by.

"Do you even know what kind of hornet's nest you kicked over, dumbass?" He spoke into the empty room. Whoever it was, they were about to find out what happened when you fucked with the family of a man named after a dinosaur.

He stood up and grabbed some more coffee, "Let's go to work, Keegan."

CHAPTER THIRTY-ONE

"Wolf, have you got a map?" Rexar paced back and forth—eight freaking steps across the kitchen and eight back—like a caged lion waiting on feeding time.

"Get me online," Lily cut him off, "I don't care what format, but I need access to Google Earth."

"Why…"

She didn't even give him time to finish what he'd been about to ask. "Because we can track them based off the information Tex gives us on GPS."

"I'll grab some gear." Cookie kissed the top of Fiona's head. "I'll drop you off with Alabama and grab Abe."

"Okay."

"Will Caroline's laptop work?"

"Yes." Lily snatched it from Wolf's hands, flipped it open, and placed it on the kitchen table. "Password?"

He leaned in past her and typed it in. She pulled it toward her and searched the applications.

"I'm going to log her out of Google and use my accounts to download Google Earth. I have a pro account and we may need it for intel." Her fingers flew over the keyboard. She had to find him. Had to. It was not possible to find one half of her heart and lose the other again.

"He said they were headed in the direction of Blossom Valley." She could feel both Rexar and Wolf leaning over her shoulder, watching the screen as it zoomed in on the location. Using the mouse, she drew a straight line from Blossom Valley to San Diego.

"They had to go east. That puts them on 94 South and probably merging onto 1-25 somewhere."

"Dead fish lake is out that way a bit," Rexar said. "We could stage out of there."

"It's not called that," Wolf muttered, "but it should be. I'll call command as soon as we know for sure."

"Damn straight."

Lily zoomed out a bit, searching for anything which might stand out.

"Where are you going, asshole?" She drummed her fingers on the tabletop. "Call Tex and put him on speaker."

"Did you get him?" Tex asked immediately. "Tell me it's just his shoe in that car?"

"Nope. Do you have sat footage?" That wasn't a sob in her voice. Breaking down wasn't freaking happening. Thankfully, she had Tex and didn't need to call Aria to track RJ. If this had happened and she hadn't known her husband was still alive, she wouldn't have been able to stop herself from falling apart.

"Pretty much," Tex said.

"They're heading to Blossom Valley. Why, I don't know. The only thing I see out that way are canyons and some private developments."

"There's a private airport farther up, near Ramona," Tex muttered.

Her analyst's brain started putting pieces together. "T-Rex, you get Nemesis and tell him to land his plane there."

"We don't—"

Suddenly the connection she hadn't been able to find before made all kinds of horrible sense in her mind.

It can't be that simple, can it?

KISS—Keep it simple, stupid.

Yes, it could be that simple and it made a fucked-up kind of sense. She snapped her fingers just like she would have years ago in Italy, telling him to pay attention

"We have to wait to see if they turn off 1-25 and on which road. If Nemesis heads to Ramona, he can swoop in from one side and cut them off. If this asshole plans on flying out of the country with our kid and Caroline, that's where he'll fly from."

"How do you know?"

"I just do."

"Gimme a name," Tex ordered over the phone. "Now."

"Damn it." Of course he picked up on that. Only an intel nerd would have. A glance over her shoulder showed confusion on the faces of both men in the room with her. She huffed out a long slow breath, and her fingers hovered over the keyboard.

"JD Fuller... aka Fullybully... aka..."

"Fat Tony?" Tex muttered. "How? What's the connection?"

"He'd infiltrated a group who were buying weapons from a Col. Lang." Lily had to work to keep her voice even. "Shit went down at COP Wild-Wolf, in Nuristan Province, and the weapons deal fell through."

"I remember that." Wolf paused at the door to the basement.

"Lang is dead; isn't that what you said, Tex?" Rexar asked.

"Yeah, reason is classified. How is Fat Tony connected?"

"He's Lang's brother-in-law." Lily didn't need a file to read off intel. She'd connected dots and made connections for years. She flipped screens to an internet search and pulled up her email and file storage.

"Here's a newspaper story that didn't run. It was pulled by the publisher." She attached the file to an email. "Tell me where to send it."

She typed in the email Tex rattled off and hit send.

"Can you enlarge that image?" Rexar asked. "He looks familiar."

"Sure." She clicked the mouse on the corner of the photo and dragged it larger on the screen. If she was correct, her husband was either going to snap into a flashback or lose his shit.

"Fuck."

Dead silence followed the curse.

"What's happening?" Tex asked.

She didn't dare look at Rexar. He needed to face this nightmare on his own. She could not help him and it freaking sucked.

"He wasn't telling me you sold me." Rexar's voice was void of any emotion, sending a slither of ice down her spine. "As he burned, stabbed, and tortured me, it wasn't about me, was it?"

She shook her head slowly. "No. If Fullybully was showing you my picture, it was because he wanted you to tell him where I was."

"Why?"

"Because I was the one who blew his cover in Italy."

"How?"

She swallowed hard, twice. Opened and closed her mouth and tried again, yet still the words didn't come.

"How?" He grabbed her by the shoulders, pulled her out of the chair, and shook her, hard. "How, Lily?"

"He's my uncle. I told my bosses he was in bed with the

Mob, and I linked him back to a potential nuke the Iranians were trying to buy."

"Fuck. The sale I was sent undercover to?"

"Yes."

"They just turned off the I-25 onto Wildcat Canyon Road," Tex informed them, "Asses in gear, get moving. I put the other players in place."

"Roger."

Rexar dropped her back into her seat and she immediately bounced up onto her feet again.

"I'm coming. RJ is my son, too."

He snatched the M16 that Wolf tossed his way out of the air, followed by the Kevlar, which he caught with one hand. He pointed the weapon at the wall and dry fired to make sure it wasn't loaded.

"Then you travel with them." She'd never heard his voice so cold when it was directed toward her, "Because I can't even look at you right now."

This wasn't her fault. She hadn't seen her uncle since she was a child and had been sent into the foster system. As soon as she'd recognized him on the intel coming in from Afghanistan and Iran, she'd informed her leadership. They'd told her they'd take care of it... their taking care of it had given her and Rexar the downtime to travel to Zurich. Yet still, his rejection ripped open old wounds, ones which had barely started to heal over the last week. She swallowed down every emotion, every thought. The past wasn't important right this second. Finding RJ was.

"Let's move." Wolf growled the order. "Mitchell, you're with me."

She grabbed the computer and the USB charger from the counter. "Okay."

"Other Mitchell." Wolf pointed to where Cookie had

come to a stop in front of the house. "You travel with Cookie."

She didn't care if they strapped her onto the roof rack as long as she was going with them.

"Someone bring the fucking phone." Tex's voice yelling from the countertop sent her dashing back to grab it.

"I've got you."

She jumped into the back of Cookie's car and slammed the door after her. The tires screeched. Cookie wasn't waiting around to make sure she was strapped in. He slammed his car into reverse to allow Wolf out of the drive.

"Good," Tex said. "The guys will have comms, but I don't think there's enough for you. Leave this on speaker and you'll hear the intel as they do."

"Thank you," She whispered softly.

"He still didn't read the damn file," Tex growled. "If he read the damn file, he'd have seen everything but that picture which I didn't have, and be over it already. Stubborn-ass SEALS will be the death of me."

As long as they weren't the death of her child she could deal with Rexar and make him understand.

* * *

"I'VE GOT a car stopped at the entrance to a property on Wildcat Canyon." Tex's voice over the comms sounded reassuring to Rexar.

"Is it them?"

"Yes."

"You're sure?"

"Yes. It looks like the asshole is making Ice change a tire."

"Fucking gents right there," Wolf muttered. "Assholes."

"Is there any sign of my son?" Rexar needed to know he was okay. If he was breathing, they could figure out the rest.

"Is there snow on the ground?" The higher elevations might have it, but he knew Jack-shit about Wildcat Canyon at freaking Christmas time.

"No, thank fuck." Tex said. "I'll tell you where to stop, then you can stage up."

"Copy that." He fucking hated working without a plan. Missions and rescues should be planned to the nth degree, but then there'd never been a mission or a rescue where the HVT was his own son. His twin once, when the dumbass has gotten himself in a mess in Iraq. Mozart in South Sudan, hell even Dalton not once or twice, but three times. But never his own son. He'd go straight back to fucking Evin Prison and tell them to do whatever they wanted to him, as long as his son was safe.

"All stations, TOC." Tex had clearly snapped back into mission mode. "All halt."

"Go ahead, TOC," Mozart responded.

The team decided Rexar and Wolf were too close to both Caroline and RJ to lead. He understood the reasoning behind it. But it chapped his ass to not be the one calling the shots.

"Your tangos are half a klick ahead. Ice is still working on the tire."

"Roger."

"Thank fuck your misses doesn't know how to change a tire," he whispered softly to Wolf.

"She does." Wolf whipped the truck into the side of the road. "She's buying time for Tex to find her and me to get to her."

"Mini T-Rex is throwing a shit fit over something."

"Fuck."

"Go ahead, Mrs. T. I got you," Rexar heard Tex talking in the background. "Yeah, I'm looking at that, too. Thoughts on which outcropping?" There was a pause before he spoke again. "That's where I'd go. Good job."

"Cookie, Benny, Mozart, Abe, Dude," Tex ordered, "you are infiltration. Wolf, T-Rex, I want you on the outcropping on the left."

"What the fuck, TOC? I'm not..."

"We *need* a sniper, T-Rex," Tex snarled over the comm, cutting him off. "Any of y'all can do it, but you are the expert here."

Shit. He listened to the rest of the plan being laid out. Hell, he agreed with it. It was how he'd do it himself. But he wasn't T-Rex anymore. He was Rexar. He held his hands out in front of him, and watched them tremor at even the suggestion of going behind a long gun.

"An M16 isn't going to cut it, I don't have a—"

"In the trunk." Wolf jerked his thumb over his shoulder. "I have a McMillan TAC-338."

"What the fuck for?"

"It's my Christmas present to myself." Wolf shrugged. "You get to play tire kicker and run it around the block a couple of times."

There goes that argument.

"Ammo?"

"Six boxes of .338."

"That will do it."

He and Wolf had split from the rest of the team earlier. To ensure he didn't compromise the rescue, Wolf would act as spotter for him. Wolf led the way in silence, stopping periodically to check the Google Earth map on his phone. He sent scheduled texts to Tex to inform him of their progress. Following nonexistent trails and tracks freaking sucked, but as they approached the hidden position on the outcropping over where Caroline, RJ, and their kidnappers were still working on the car, he knew it would be worth it.

As long as he didn't fuck this up.

His hands still wouldn't stop freaking shaking, even as he

went through the process of setting up the rifle. He could have spent an hour building a nest. But they didn't have a fucking hour.

Wolf already lay against the rock with a set of binos in his hand. "Target acquired."

Rexar settled himself behind the weapon and turned his rifle scope in the direction Wolf provided and waited for their tango to enter his crosshairs.

From their position, they watched the scene playing out in front of them. The team approached the tangos around the bend in the road on foot.

"This fucking sucks," he muttered.

"I agree."

He held his breath when they saw Caroline's head shoot up at the first sound of Mozart's voice, yelling for the assholes to drop their weapons. When she rolled under the car, taking herself out of the line of fire, it made it so much easier for the team to subdue the man who'd been guarding her. Shooting him in the kneecaps counted as subduing... right?

Wolf had to be feeling a hell of a lot of relief when Mozart's voice over comms confirmed he had Ice.

Rexar scanned the area, searching for his son's tiny frame.

"Come on, son, where are you?" He didn't dare take his eyes from the scope. "Do you see him?"

"Got him," Wolf said. "Quadrant C, section C."

He adjusted his weapon to the area Wolf had indicated.

"Fuck."

There was nothing like seeing your son with a knife to his throat from down a scope without being able to do anything about it. Absolutely nothing like the whirlwind of emotions, with fear as the lead horse in the race to fuck with your brain.

He ignored all the chatter over the comms, waiting for the one word which would tell him he was in play.

"Wind?" he asked softly, slowing his breathing, adjusting his scope, fine-tuning his view as he listened to the directions Wolf gave him.

"One minute right."

"I cannot fuck this up. "

"You won't, T-Rex. You've got this."

He appreciated the vote of confidence from Wolf, but it did little to convince himself that he was still that man. He wanted so badly to flex his fingers on the weapon but he didn't dare move.

If you miss, you kill RJ.

If I don't, he's dead anyway.

Don't do it. You aren't T-Rex anymore.

Do it. Take the shot.

Everything in him was at war. The father with the warrior. The SEAL with the prisoner of war. The success of this shot came down to who won the battle. The Daddy who wanted to spend his first Christmas ever with his wife and child, or the SEAL, battle-hardened on too many trouble hotspots across the globe to count.

He studied his son's face, committing it to memory. And blew out a slow breath, waiting for Fat Fucking Tony to shift or move, and give him the best chance possible of saving his son.

"On target."

"Fire when ready." Wolf kept his eyes on the scene almost half a mile away down the mountainside from them.

Please.

Please no I can't if I hit him...

There will never be a better opportunity.

Take the damn shot.

Now or never.

Take it.

Take it.

Fuuucck.

I'm so sorry, baby.

I love you.

Daddy loves you.

Rexar exhaled and gently squeezed the trigger, and his long rifle fired.

The large-caliber bullet ripped through Fat Tony's chest from right to left and his body crumpled to the ground.

Rexar's son disappeared from view, and a woman's scream—his wife's scream—echoed up the canyon.

"Target down," Wolf called.

Rexar knew Wolf was confirming it was safe for the team to move forward. He didn't want to see, even if he'd been able to see. He fell back on his butt and pulled his knees up under his chin, wrapping his arms around them. There was no fucking way he could watch the team on the ground as they raced toward RJ. His breath sawed in and out of his lungs; it fucking hurt to breathe. His eyes burned with tears, but he couldn't find it within himself to wipe them away. Yet, he needed to know…

"Did I kill him?"

"Yup," Wolf confirmed.

"No!"

The word ripped from his chest. It probably should have been a scream, but it croaked out as the vision of a small white coffin moved across the back of his eyelids.

"No."

"Shit." Hands pulled at his shoulders. "Fat Tony," Wolf yelled in his face. "You killed Fat Tony, not RJ."

"My boy."

"Is fine. Lily has him. I swear. I swear it."

He ripped himself out of Wolf's arms, spun to one side,

and puked his guts up, just like he had the first time he'd made a kill shot. This time the burning was tinged with a relief so deep he didn't know how far it went.

Fat Tony would join the reel of faces which haunted his dreams, and probably would for the rest of his life. There were some lives he'd taken that he regretted—this one he wouldn't regret killing, not now, not ever.

Wolf thankfully left him to gather his metaphorical shit together. Then he laid a hand on Rexar's shoulder.

"Let's go, T-Rex. Our families are waiting."

Going down the hillside took less time than working their way up. This time they didn't need to keep under cover and didn't have to work their way around to keep out of view of the people below. Through someone's comms, Rexar could now make out RJ's voice as he hiccupped through telling Lily what happened, but until he had his hands on him...

"Last jump." Wolf's voice warned him about the drop onto the road. Their boots kicked up dust as they ran at full speed toward the bend, around which they would finally lay eyes on their families.

As they approached the bend, Wolf put on a burst of speed and pulled away from him.

Rexar slowed his steps.

Three more steps and he would see how much damage he'd done with a .338.

Two more steps, and RJ would see it was his Daddy who'd given him nightmares for years to come.

One more step and he'd learn the woman who'd owned his heart hated him for destroying their child.

When the scene he'd watched through his scope came into view, he couldn't take another step. He dropped to his knees and back onto his calves, his gear scattered on the ground around him. He dropped his eyes to the dirt road. If he didn't look, it wasn't happening.

"Rexar!"

Lily's voice screamed his name, but still, he couldn't bring himself to look. He could hear footsteps running toward him. Maybe someone would kill him, too, and this nightmare would all be over. He didn't brace himself; he wouldn't fight. When someone hit him full-force, he allowed them to knock him flat on his ass.

"Rex..." Lily's voice sobbed in his ear.

"I....sor..."

"Daddy." Another weight landed on his chest. "Daddy, you saves me again."

"We got you, baby." Lily lay next to him in the middle of the dirt road, trying her best to wrap herself around both him and RJ.

His heart exploded with relief when what was happening finally made sense. He managed to move to sitting and pulled both of them into his lap.

"I love you; I love you both." Behind him he could hear sirens and vehicles approaching. But he refused to move. *They can fucking wait.* He sniffed hard and wiped his eyes with the collar of his shirt.

"I love you, Lily Mitchell. Promise me you don't hate me."

"Idiot, I love you, too."

"Me loves you, Daddy."

He kissed the top of his son's head. "I love you, son."

EPILOGUE

Mushologue
6 months later – Nemesis Inc. Headquarters, Montana

Six months?

How the hell could six months both fly by and yet seem like a million lifetimes?

Lily folded the last of RJ's t-shirts and put them into the drawer. Today was a big one for her little family. Today would be their first day here in the house Rexar and the guys had built for them on the ranch where her husband felt most at home.

As if she'd conjured him up just by thinking about him, she heard a door slam and Rexar calling out for her.

"Darlin'?"

"In RJ's room."

"Hey you." He appeared through the door and swooped in to give her a kiss as had become his habit lately. He cupped his hand over the tiny bump of her belly.

"How's our girl doing?"

"We don't know yet if it is a girl." She snuggled into his

chest. No matter how many times she reminded him that they hadn't had an ultrasound yet, he insisted he knew this baby would be a girl.

"It's a girl. Momma said so."

"Your momma and her old wives' tales." She could just stay like this forever. "Just because my wedding ring went in a circle when you hung it over my belly, instead of swinging side to side, doesn't mean she's a girl."

"Ha, you said she's a girl." His chin rubbed over her head. "Promise me you won't move all the big stuff while I'm in town picking up our mail."

"I'll wait for you, hotshot, I promise."

"Love you." He squeezed her into a hug again, then released her. "Want me to pick up RJ from town?"

"No, it's okay. Willow is bringing him back." She rubbed her hand down his back. "Kiss me again, then go do your boy stuff."

"Boy stuff, my ass." But he did as she asked and kissed her until she forgot how to breathe. "I'll see you when you get back. Safe."

"Safe, hotshot." They'd gotten in the habit of saying 'safe' when either one of them left the house. It had started out as 'be safe' but over the months they'd shortened it to safe. And she loved it. It was their little sidenote reminder to each other that the other person loved them.

She walked with him to the bedroom door and watched him leave. Watching Rexar walk anywhere from this viewpoint was never ever going to get old. Ever.

"Yummy. I still wouldn't throw him out of bed for eating cookies."

"Did you say something, darlin'?"

Of course, he heard that. If she was asking him to empty his freaking pockets before putting clothes in the washer, would he hear her? Nope, probably not in this lifetime. That little gem just went in one ear and out the other.

"Nope, just talking to myself."

She went back to setting up RJ's room. Next, she'd work on hers and Rexar's room. Not that they used it much for sleeping in. but it was theirs and she had a whole closet. He'd wanted to help; in fact he had been helping over the last three days since the contractors had left. But today she'd made him promise that he'd leave her to putter around and take their house and turn it into a home.

The next time she looked at the clock, it was almost four and her belly growled multiple times. If she went to Alpha house, she could grab the supplies and groceries Kayce was storing in the kitchen for her. A grilled cheese would be pretty freaking awesome right about now, too. She wandered into the open-plan kitchen and living room and turned in a circle. This could not possibly be theirs. All theirs. Someday it might sink in... but probably not for the next ten years or so.

"Knock, knock. Anyone home?"

"In the kitchen, Aria." Rexar was still pissed with Aria and had been even more so when he'd found out that Aria was his son's godmother. That showdown had been epic. Rexar had sulked for days because he hadn't been allowed to lose his shit about it. She'd made him promise he wouldn't. If that was done in bed... well nobody else needed to know it.

Besides, if it wasn't for Aria, she wouldn't have had a tracker for RJ's shoe and none of them would be here today.

"Do not ever tell your husband that I love your house." Aria said as she came in. "Mind if I grab some water? It's hot out today."

"There's sparkling in the fridge or grab a glass and help yourself." She narrowed her eyes at her friend, "It's the middle of June and it's hot out, how far did you run?"

"Only eight miles." Aria shut the fridge and twisted off the top of the bottle.

"Eight miles... you're crazy."

"Well, it is the Crazy Mountains; it gets all of us at some point."

"I'm just going to Alpha house for a grilled cheese, want to join me?"

Sure, and Kayce will yell at me for stinking up his kitchen with BO." Aria grinned at her, "Let's go do it. Did you walk down?"

"No, I drove, why?"

"Because the jerk's truck is in the drive and not your SUV."

"What?"

"Yeah."

She went to the window and tugged the drapes aside, confirming that Rexar had left her his beluga whale of a truck and taken her SUV to town.

"And you came in here to wind him up?"

"I've been in Syria for three months; I have catching up to do."

"You two are impossible." She pinned Aria with a stare. "You are going to have to figure it out at some point."

"He was a jerk and assumed you tried to have him killed and he wanted to take RJ from you. As RJ's godmother, isn't it my place to remind him he was a stupid asshole?"

She shook her head. "Fine. Come on, his keys will be in the truck. We can take it to Alpha House."

"Can I fuck with his radio stations?"

"No, no you can't."

"Spoilsport."

She didn't bother to lock the house. If someone managed to get through the fence lines and all the way down from the main road to here, then they had probably earned whatever it was they'd wanted to steal.

Climbing into the massive truck, freaking sucked. "They really don't make these things for short people do they?"

"Nope."

She adjusted the seat twice so she could press the clutch all the way before starting the engine. An orange light on the dash caught her eye.

"You know what? I changed my mind. Fuck with his radio stations."

"Why?"

"Because my wonderful husband left me his truck with the fucking empty tank light on." She put her finger on the fuel gage. "Look, it's on E."

"Motherfucker."

"I'm going to fuck with him." She put the truck in drive and headed toward the space in the yard where the fuel tanks were kept. "Get me my phone from my purse."

"Whatcha gonna do?"

"I'm sending him a message asking him if it's gas or diesel." She tapped the message out as she spoke. "I'm going to fuck with him so hard."

"Ha!" Aria spewed a mouthful of water onto the dash. "This right here is why we are friends. I fucking love that you aren't falling all over him and give him snark and shit."

The phone beeped in her hand.

Hotshot: Diesel.

She tapped out a response and tilted the phone to show Aria, making her friend cough and hit her chest a couple of times when the water went down the wrong pipe.

"He'll lose his shit."

"Serves him right."

Lily: too late, I just filled it up with gas.

As soon as the message showed as sent, she pressed another button on the phone and stuffed it back in her purse.

"Freaking awesome." Aria chortled the entire time Lily was filling the truck. "How long are you leaving it on do not disturb?"

"Until he gets home."

"You, my friend, are creative when it comes to revenge. I need to start taking notes."

"Watch and learn, sister. Someday you're going to need all this intel for your own operator, so watch and learn."

"Hell no, I'm not going to touch someone in our line of work with a ten-foot pole." This was an old argument between them. "I know better. Been there, done that, and have the scars on my heart to prove it. A nice accountant, or maybe a rancher or something will do just fine."

"And you'll be bored in a month." She pointed the nose of the truck toward Alpha house, standing in her seat to see over the hood so she didn't hit the gatepost again. Someday Aria would figure out that Rexar just wouldn't have been able to let her die with her spotter on that rooftop, and someday Rexar might stop hating her for keeping them apart. But that day probably wasn't going to happen anytime soon so she refused to worry about it.

"Nope. Not happening," Aria said.

Just you wait and see, sister. Life has a way of blindsiding you with what you never knew you needed. But she didn't say that out loud. Aria would figure it out when the time came, and she'd be right there to remind her of this conversation like any good best friend should.

"Now, I've just got to figure out how to stay out of his way for a few hours." She parked the truck and climbed out.

"Lock it. Take the keys with you," Aria advised. "I'll hide you in my apartment until you decide he's suffered enough."

"Deal. But I can't stay too long because it's our first night at the house."

"We can have dinner. I'll have wine, you have soda, then I'll drive you home."

"You just want to fuck with him as much as I do. No to the dinner, but I will have soda and cookies if you have them?"

"I'm not passing it up, that's for sure. And yes, I have cookies."

She might be mad with Rexar for now, but she knew it would blow over in a little bit. Pissing each other off was a part of life. Neither would stay mad for long… they had their rule after all.

* * *

"You're mean, wife," Rexar drawled the second he heard her footsteps hit the front porch. "I thought you'd really filled my truck with gas."

"You could have filled it instead of leaving it on empty."

"I forgot. I'm sorry." He snagged her hand and tugged her toward him, but instead of pulling her into his lap as he normally would have, he stood and pushed her into the chair. "Wait here."

"Okay."

He could see she was confused. Hopefully the reason he'd been in town would make up for it. He snagged the items from the counter.

"Where's RJ?"

"He's staying with Willow and Cormack tonight. They have a new kitten and…"

"And when you're five, a new kitten is more exciting than a house you've been in and out of every day for weeks."

"Right." He fluffed out the blanket and placed the cushions where he wanted them.

"What are you doing?"

He reached around the door and pulled out the basket. "I thought we could have a picnic under the stars and just breathe." He opened the basket and pulled out a plate. "I had a friend who knew someone who was flying in from Italy, so I had him pick up this." Fuck, he hoped she liked it as much as he remembered.

"Is this…?" Her eyes widened as she read the label on the box. "No way…" She popped open the lid and inhaled. "Oh my God, that smells so good."

Thank fuck.

"You remembered."

"Of course, I remember." Next out of the basket was a tiny model Vespa which didn't even fill his palm. He placed it in front of the picnic blanket and reached for his phone for the music. Getting Drax to call the hotel to get a copy of every freaking song they'd played five years ago sucked. But the second he'd heard it, he'd been right back on the hotel rooftop, feasting on tiramisu with Lily, so the trauma of that phone call had been worth it.

"Dance with me, darlin'." He took her hand and helped her to her feet, tucking her against him as the first strains of the Italian music played softly through his phone. "I'll always remember, Darlin'." He nuzzled his chin against the top of her head. "In Italy, it began with a Vespa, a closet, a picnic, and a dance under the stars to this music." He'd never been good with words. If he fucked this up, he was going to kick his own ass. "Tonight, we start our lives in our forever home, with the same music, a slightly smaller Vespa, and a way bigger closet. The same dessert, stars seen from a different viewpoint, and a love that's bigger than ever."

She hiccupped against his chest. Shit, had he screwed up? He leaned back to peer down at her tear-filled eyes.

"I love you, Lily Mitchell. What do you say we do this for the rest of our lives?"

"I love you too, Rexar. Yes, a million times yes."

He hugged her close and together they swayed to the music, tonight an echo of the past, how far they'd come and a promise of how far they had to go. Life was officially worth living again and he was going to enjoy every second from here on out.

Will their surprise wedding be their downfall, or will it bring them a love that lasts a lifetime?

Navy SEAL Dalton Knight only wanted a night of drinking with his team brothers. The last thing he expected was to meet the other half of his soul.

Lina Maxwell knew she should have stayed at home. Drinking and dancing is so not her jam. When her drink is spiked, a knight in shining Kevlar insists he marries her to protect her from the demons who haunt her nightmares. Will their surprise wedding be their downfall, or will it bring them a love that lasts a lifetime?

#1 DALTON

The war on terror tore them apart. Will a terrorist bring them back together?

Former Navy SEAL, Dalton *Nemesis* Knight thought he had it all. A Navy career he loved. His SEAL Team brothers, and her... his Lina. The war on terror proved him wrong. It cost him everything, including his wife. With his trust broken, he'd had to find a new way forward and a new system he could believe in. Eventually, he picked the shattered pieces of his broken heart up off the floor and built Nemesis Inc. from the ground up. Now he makes the rules, he signs the checks, and his heart is off the table for good. Nobody is ever going to get close enough to destroy him again.

For years, Lina Maxwell has watched him from the shadows. Cheering his successes and mourning his losses. He's always been hers; she's always been his. Neither anger nor distance can change that. The time has come to gather her courage and fix the wrongs of the past. In leaving him, she protected him the only way she could, Lina needs Nemesis to see that she did not betray him, that she still loves him with everything that she is. Her bosses and her mission will not allow her to make contact. Her whole life is an illusion. She no longer has an identity, no longer has a name. As far as anyone, including her husband, is concerned, she never existed at all.

Just when Lina is ready to ignore her orders and step silently out of the dark, a terrorist wages war on Eastern Europe. With Nemesis running headfirst into danger, she will use every contact and source in her network to protect him. Will showing him she's still alive destroy not only their memories but any chance they might have had of a future?

Will this mission be the bandage to fix two broken hearts, or will it finally destroy them both?

#2 CORMACK

His happy sunshine girl didn't deserve to be pulled into his world of fire and brimstone. All he could do was hope like hell he found her in time.

As a Black Ops Contractor for Nemesis Inc. Cormack *Jeep* Ford, has seen the worst humans can inflict on their fellow man—in some of the shittiest hellholes on earth. With a twenty-year military career under his belt, he's not one bit sorry when Nemesis Inc. relocates from Kabul to Montana. Maybe now his boots are firmly on US soil, he can peruse a happy ever after with woman who calls to his soul.

To Willow Black it feels like she's waited a lifetime for her soldier to come home. Who'd have thought a connection made over emails and letters would lead her to the man who makes her heart and body sing. With Cormack moving back to the US full time, she can't wait to see if the connection between them can withstand the test of time spent in the same freaking time zone. Just when she's starting to believe he may be her happy ever after, a terrorist destroys everything she trusts in— dragging her into the terrifying reality of the world's underbelly.

A man forged in fire and brimstone—a woman made for sunshine and roses—and a terrorist determined to make them pay. Can Cormack convince Willow her life's not over? Can she convince him to let her go? Or will their hearts have the final say?

#3 LOGAN

They say opposites attract, but can two such different people really find an everlasting love?

Losing his parents in the south tower of the World Trade Center on 9/11 changed the trajectory of Logan Sensei Winters' life. Once an up-and-coming MMA fighter, the rancher's kid from the Midwest crossed over the line of right and wrong in a haze of grief-fueled fury. A second twist of fate changed his world again. Nemesis Inc. gave him a soft place to land and taught him how to direct the rage living in his soul toward targets who deserve it—tangos and terrorists across the globe became his focus… until fate threw him yet another twist and cast his meticulously organized life into chaos.

Eedana Crawford is tired of the rules. She's over the 'show the world a happy family in their Sunday best' façade her family demands. There is no way on earth she's giving up the freedom she's worked so hard to earn—spending the rest of her days in her art studio, teaching classes and painting pretty pictures—following her dreams. When a request for a commissioned piece turns those dreams into a nightmare, the freedom she loves becomes impossible to keep. But trusting Mr. Tall, Dark, and Deadly who appears when she needs him would be a bad, bad idea. Right?

Eedana is his to protect—even if she doesn't know it or agree with it. But Logan will make sure she survives The Organization's attempt at a power grab. There is no way in hell he's losing another person he cares passionately about. Not on his watch.

She is his to protect. End. Of. Discussion.

Coming Soon in Nemesis Inc:

Rory

Aria

ABOUT THE AUTHOR

Bella Stone is the MF Pen name for Annabella Stone, all books published under this name will be MF. While there may be character crossover to my Annabella stories, the storylines etc. will be different to the story arcs in Panthers, Tags of Honor, etc.

Newsletter/Free book: https://BookHip.com/CTQKFRD
Facebook: https://www.facebook.com/authorbellastone
Website: https://www.annabellastone.com/bella-stone

Annabella Stone and Bella Stone are the alter egos of a wife and mom, who was lucky enough to find happy ever after with her own personal hero.

Annabella loves to write Military Romance and Romantic Suspense where warriors love harder when bullets fly. She believes in love at first sight and wants everyone to have the happy ever they deserve. Even if they have to dodge bullets and fight with everything that they are to get it.

Born and raised in Ireland, Annabella has a Grá for a good story and the breakfast blaa, but funnily enough, prefers Jack Daniels to Irish whiskey. Having lived across 7 countries and 3 continents over the last thirty years, she loves to explore new places and cultures. In her world, coffee is king, and she is 100% sure it deserves it's own food group.

Annabella is owned by a pack of malamutes, whom she loves to both work and show. If you can't find her at the computer writing, chances are she and her woofers have escaped to enjoy at day at a dog show, or they are on a mountain trail with the dryland rig or the sled, depending on the time of year.

Annabella's motto is "Live life like a malamute who found the gate open, but take the time to enjoy the sights while you're running."

Binge Books: https://bingebooks.com/author/bella-stone

facebook.com/authorbellastone

instagram.com/bellastoneauthor

bookbub.com/authors/bella-stone

amazon.com/Bella-Stone/e/B09FBQKBZG

There are many more books in this fan fiction world than listed here, for an up-to-date list go to www.AcesPress.com

You can also visit our Amazon page at: http://www.amazon.com/author/operationalpha

Special Forces: Operation Alpha World
Christie Adams: Charity's Heart
Linzi Baxter: Dangerous Rescue
Misha Blake: Flash
Anna Blakely: Rescuing Gracelynn
Julia Bright: Saving Lorelei
Cara Carnes: Protecting Mari
Kendra Mei Chailyn: Beast
Melissa Kay Clarke: Rescuing Annabeth
Samantha A. Cole: Handling Haven
Lorelei Confer: Protecting Sara
KaLyn Cooper: Spring Unveiled
Janie Crouch: Storm
Jordan Dane: Redemption for Avery
Tarina Deaton: Found in the Lost
Riley Edwards: Protecting Olivia
Dorothy Ewels: Knight's Queen
Lila Ferrari: Protecting Joy
Nicole Flockton: Protecting Maria
Hope Ford: Rescuing Karina
Amy Gamet: Guarded by the SEAL
Desiree Holt: Protecting Maddie
Danielle Haas: Crossroads of Betrayal
Jesse Jacobson: Protecting Honor
Rayne Lewis: Justice for Mary
Ireland Lorelei: The Detective
Kristin Lynn: Worth the Risk

Callie Love & Ann Omasta: Hawaii Hottie
JM Madden: Rescuing Olivia
A.M. Mahler: Griffin
Ellie Masters: Sybil's Protector
Trish McCallan: Hero Under Fire
Naomi McKay: Twist
Rachel McNeely: The SEAL's Surprise Baby
KD Michaels: Saving Laura
Olivia Michaels: Protecting Harper
Annie Miller: Securing Willow
MJ Nightingale: Protecting Beauty
Melinda Owens: Betraying Katie
Victoria Paige: Reclaiming Izabel
Danielle Pays: Defending Sarina
Lainey Reese: Protecting New York
KeKe Renée: Protecting Bria
TL Reeve and Michele Ryan: Extracting Mateo
Ariana Rose: Chasing Paige
Deanna L. Rowley: Saving Veronica
Angela Rush: Charlotte
Rose Smith: Saving Satin
Tyler Anne Snell: Cowboy Heat
Lynne St. James: SEAL's Spitfire
E.M. Shue: Discovering Tyler
Bella Stone: Rexar
Jen Talty: Burning Desire
Reina Torres, Rescuing Hi'ilani
LJ Vickery: Circus Comes to Town
R. C. Wynne: Shadows Renewed

Delta Team Three Series
Lori Ryan: Nori's Delta
Becca Jameson: Destiny's Delta
Lynne St James, Gwen's Delta

Elle James: Ivy's Delta
Riley Edwards: Hope's Delta

Police and Fire: Operation Alpha World
Freya Barker: Burning for Autumn
B.P. Beth: Scott
Jane Blythe: Salvaging Marigold
Julia Bright, Justice for Amber
Hadley Finn: Exton
Emily Gray: Shelter for Allegra
Danielle M. Haas: Crossroads of Betrayal
Deanndra Hall: Shelter for Sharla
Jenna Harte: Dead But Not Forgotten
Amber Kuhlman: Protecting Paisley
Reina Torres: Justice for Sloane
Aubree Valentine, Justice for Danielle
Maddie Wade: Finding English

Tarpley VFD Series
Silver James, Fighting for Elena
Deanndra Hall, Fighting for Carly
Haven Rose, Fighting for Calliope
MJ Nightingale, Fighting for Jemma
TL Reeve, Fighting for Brittney
Nicole Flockton, Fighting for Nadia

As you know, this book included at least one character from Susan Stoker's books. To check out more, see below.

SEAL Team Hawaii Series
Finding Elodie
Finding Lexie
Finding Kenna
Finding Monica
Finding Carly
Finding Ashlyn
Finding Jodelle (July 2023)

Eagle Point Search & Rescue
Searching for Lilly
Searching for Elsie
Searching for Bristol
Searching for Caryn
Searching for Finley (Sept 2023)
Searching for Heather (Jan 2024)
Searching for Khloe (TBA)

The Refuge Series
Deserving Alaska
Deserving Henley
Deserving Reese
Deserving Cora (Nov 2023)
Deserving Lara (Feb 2024)
Deserving Maisy (TBA)
Deserving Ryleigh (TBA)

Delta Team Two Series
Shielding Gillian
Shielding Kinley

Shielding Aspen
Shielding Jayme (novella)
Shielding Riley
Shielding Devyn
Shielding Ember
Shielding Sierra

SEAL of Protection: Legacy Series
Securing Caite (FREE!)
Securing Brenae (novella)
Securing Sidney
Securing Piper
Securing Zoey
Securing Avery
Securing Kalee
Securing Jane

Delta Force Heroes Series
Rescuing Rayne (FREE!)
Rescuing Aimee (novella)
Rescuing Emily
Rescuing Harley
Marrying Emily (novella)
Rescuing Kassie
Rescuing Bryn
Rescuing Casey
Rescuing Sadie (novella)
Rescuing Wendy
Rescuing Mary
Rescuing Macie (novella)
Rescuing Annie

Badge of Honor: Texas Heroes Series
Justice for Mackenzie (FREE!)

Justice for Mickie
Justice for Corrie
Justice for Laine (novella)
Shelter for Elizabeth
Justice for Boone
Shelter for Adeline
Shelter for Sophie
Justice for Erin
Justice for Milena
Shelter for Blythe
Justice for Hope
Shelter for Quinn
Shelter for Koren
Shelter for Penelope

SEAL of Protection Series

Protecting Caroline (FREE!)
Protecting Alabama
Protecting Fiona
Marrying Caroline (novella)
Protecting Summer
Protecting Cheyenne
Protecting Jessyka
Protecting Julie (novella)
Protecting Melody
Protecting the Future
Protecting Kiera (novella)
Protecting Alabama's Kids (novella)
Protecting Dakota

New York Times, *USA Today* and *Wall Street Journal* Bestselling Author Susan Stoker has a heart as big as the state of Tennessee where she lives, but this all American girl has also spent the last fourteen years living in Missouri, California,

Colorado, Indiana, and Texas. She's married to a retired Army man who now gets to follow *her* around the country.

www.stokeraces.com
www.AcesPress.com
susan@stokeraces.com

Made in the USA
Coppell, TX
03 March 2024

29676568R10193